FATAL IN THE DUNES

TEDD SMITH

FUNDRAISING in the HAMPTONS CAN BE MURDER

ISBN: 978-1-7354486-0-2 (paperback)
ISBN: 978-1-7354486-1-9 (eBook)

Cover design and Typesetting by Stewart A. Williams

Printed in the United States of America

for MP, NC, DA
my three angels

ONE

"Arriving at destination," announces the robo-female voice of the GPS, very pleased with herself.

Brandi Napoli looks through the windshield at the house. She turns off the engine and gets out of the car, locking it. Reaching into the purse slung over her shoulder, she retrieves a small keyring. She walks up to the front door and inserts one of the keys on the ring into the lock and lets herself in, closing the door behind her. She is standing in the entrance foyer. A staircase rises on her right. Through an archway at the base of the staircase is a large, handsome formal dining room. On the other side is an even larger living room. There, double-hung windows extend from just below the ceiling almost down to the floor. She turns and walks straight back to the kitchen. On the left, she passes the euphemistically named powder room, its door ajar. Good, she needs to use it. She deposits her purse on the kitchen island

and heads for the toilet. After two minutes, she emerges to check out the kitchen.

It too is generously proportioned with a long center island that houses a deep stainless-steel sink and a six-burner stove top.

"This is nice," she says aloud. Looking around at the oven unit and the refrigerator, she adds with a frown, "It'll need new appliances."

The kitchen opens into a great room with a fieldstone fireplace. She walks into the great room. She looks up. "Get rid of the ceiling and take it right up to the rafters," she says to herself. To the left are triple sets of French doors opening out onto a deck overlooking the beach. Brandi walks up to the doors and looks out at the ocean. The late afternoon sun glints brightly off the water. Brandi looks down and sees a steel rod running through grommets along the base of the doors, firmly padlocked in place at one end. *Good idea*, she thinks, especially for houses in the Hamptons that sit vacant for months during the winter or for ones like this that are on the market.

Brandi walks back into the kitchen and looks around. "Where's the goddamn listing sheet?" she says. It's usually on the counter somewhere. Then she remembers that she picked it up from the real estate office earlier in the day along with the keys.

"On the front seat of your car, Brandi," she scolds herself.

With a grunt of exasperation, she goes to her bag and retrieves her car keys. She heads out through the foyer for the front door. She turns the handle but the door doesn't open. It's locked! If there had been a turnkey, it has been removed. There is only a bare keyhole. "What the fuck!"

Brandi heads back into the kitchen to get the door key from her purse. She checks the top side pocket where she had put it. It's not there. She rummages deep into her purse. After a minute of furious searching, she turns her purse over on the island. She paws through the myriad objects strewn across the counter: notebook, pens, lipstick, compact, glass case—but no keyring. And no cell phone either! She stops and becomes very quiet. She listens. Only silence rewards her.

"Okay, funny, funny. What's the big joke? I don't get it. If I were you I'd get out of here while you can. Breaking and entering is a serious matter and I will press charges. So just skedaddle and leave the door open when you go."

Again, the house offers only silence. She feels a nervous flutter in her stomach. On the opposite counter is a set of knives in a wooden holder. She silently slides over to the counter and extracts one. She remembers the living room windows—large and near the ground. She can get out that way! Holding the knife down and behind her, Brandi slowly inches toward the foyer. As she enters the foyer, there is a noise from the living room. She stifles a gasp. She flattens herself against the staircase opposite the entrance to the living room. Did she imagine it? She feels the blood throbbing in her neck as she tries to calm herself. She listens intently. Yes, there it is again! Some kind of movement! She looks around desperately for another means of escape.

A noose drops over her head and is immediately pulled tight. Brandi drops the knife with a clatter on the marble floor. She grabs at the noose with both hands, trying to free herself. She flails, throwing her arms behind her trying to grab her attacker but the stair railing is between them. Slowly, her feet lift off the floor as her assailant mounts a step. She kicks wildly, sending her Swarovski-encrusted flip flops flying. She tries to scream but she can't get a breath. The word "fucker" dies in her gullet as she starts to lose consciousness. Dimly, in the archway leading to the living room, a shadow figure stands watching. Then Brandi's lights go out.

TWO

The man unlatches the slider to the deck. He walks through the opening and closes it behind him. He breathes in the sea air. It is blessedly cool at this hour. He takes a swig of coffee from the mug in his hand. He squints into the bright sunlight coming off the water. He removes a pair of sunglasses from the breast pocket of his shirt and puts them on. He walks forward to the edge of the deck and places his mug on the rail. A neighbor jogging toward him at the water's edge waves. The man waves back. He looks down to retrieve his mug and notices a brown bramble protruding up from the beach grass on the other side of the rail. The bramble has something glittering attached to it which catches the sun. He bends in for a closer inspection. The bramble is wearing a ring! A large diamond ring! And bangle bracelets! It's not a bramble, it's a hand. A woman's hand! The man turns and runs to the slider and goes back into the house, leaving his coffee on the rail.

■

Three police officers from the Southampton police department respond to the man's call within minutes. The man is quite shaken by his early morning discovery. One officer waits with him on the deck for Suffolk County homicide to arrive. The other two provide crowd control for curiosity seekers who have gathered on the beach. It takes almost an hour for the county detectives to come from Riverhead. Detective Mark DeMarco, alongside his partner Detective Angela Rooney, rings the front door bell. A woman who speaks halting English answers the door. The detectives show her their badges. She admits them and leads them to the deck, opening the slider for them. As they step out onto the deck, they can hear the man saying to the police officer in a loud voice, "This is Southampton for chrissakes not Gilgo!" DeMarco shoots his partner an amused look. She just seems confused. They approach the man and the officer. Yellow crime scene tape encircles the beach grass below. DeMarco and Rooney identify themselves and shake hands with the police officer.

DeMarco turns to the man, "You're the one who found her, you called it in?"

"Yes."

"Is it anyone you know?"

"I didn't look. If it's someone I know, I don't want to know."

The police officer hands DeMarco a driver's license. "Her purse was in the grass near the body. Brandi Napoli. Lived here in Water Mill."

"Have you seen any strangers around or heard anything suspicious recently?" DeMarco asks the man.

"No."

DeMarco looks at the license in his hand. "So, she was killed here or elsewhere and her body was dumped in the grass, along with her

ID." He turns to Rooney. "Shall we have a look?"

The two detectives descend the steps to the beach. The body is lying where it was found. Under the body is a large blue tarp.

"Tarp indicates a body dump," Rooney says. "She was brought here."

DeMarco leans in for a closer look. "What the —! Look at her tongue!"

Rooney bends in to look. "Forked."

"What's the message? Liar?"

"Devil?"

"Both? What else do we have?" DeMarco asks.

"White female in her fifties. Took good care of herself. Nice manicure. Expensively dressed."

"So, not sexually assaulted?"

"She could have been re-dressed." Rooney continues with her assessment. "The neck wound is the apparent cause of death."

"Ear to ear. I'd add ligature marks on her wrists indicate she was bound." He looks down to her feet. "With zip ties just like her ankles."

"But the tongue," Rooney says. Then she adds incredulously, "Pinking shears?"

"Pinking shears?"

"They're used by tailors and seamstresses. They cut a zigzag pattern. It keeps fabric from fraying. My aunt had her own tailoring business when I was growing up and I used to help her on weekends. I'd have to say that is definitely what caused those tongue wounds."

"Let's see what the ME has to say."

Rooney calls up to the police officer on the deck. "Do you have her purse?"

He hurries down to the beach with the bag. He hands it to Rooney who starts to root through it.

"What are you looking for?" DeMarco asks.

Rooney pulls out a set of car keys. "Maybe she parked around here," she says, hitting the red alarm button on the key fob. From somewhere a car horn beeps repeatedly. It sounds like it's coming from the house next door. Rooney gives DeMarco a surprised and pleased look.

They trudge through the sand, following the blaring of the car horn which gets louder as they approach the other house. They follow it around the side of the house and come upon Brandi's car parked in the driveway. Rooney presses the alarm button again, silencing it. They walk to the front door and Rooney rings the bell. They wait a few moments. She rings again. No one comes to the door.

∎

Getting back into their car, Rooney asks, "What's Gilgo?"

"Gilgo Beach. You never heard of that case?" DeMarco asks, surprised.

"Oh, wait a minute. Is that where all those bodies turned up a few years ago?"

"It started almost three years ago. I used to surf there when I was a teenager."

"Prostitutes, mostly?"

"You got it."

"They ever make an arrest?"

"Still an open case."

Police don't like open cases even ones that aren't their own. It makes the killer or killers larger than life. It's why horror movies that don't show the monster are the scariest. Human imagination imbues them with gigantism. They stand just out of sight at the edges of existence, masked and at liberty. Taunting, taunting, always taunting. The two detectives drive in silence.

At forty-seven years of age, Mark has been with the Suffolk County homicide detective squad for eleven years. He began his career with the New York City police department where he served in the patrol unit for three years. He resigned from the NYPD and moved to the Suffolk County town of Wading River with his wife and young daughter, where they currently still live. He was hired by the Suffolk County police department where he was in patrol for nine years. In 2002 he joined the detective division where he serves today. He grew up on the upper West Side of Manhattan where both of his parents were professors at Columbia University. He is of Italian American descent on his father's side and Jewish on his mother's. He is six feet tall and solidly built with dark eyes and curly brown hair. His parents' heritages tended to cancel out most of the stereotypes associated with each of those ethnic groups, although he admits to the occasional bout of unreasonable guilt. To help deal with the often gruesome murder scenes he encounters on his job, he loves getting out on Long Island Sound on his thirty-two-foot motorboat whenever he can.

Angela is new to the detective squad and Long Island. She joined the SCPD a little over a year ago having moved to Manorville, Long Island from upstate Syracuse after her divorce. She had served on the local police force there in the detective unit for thirteen years. She is thirty-seven years old and single. Her dark auburn hair and fair, freckled skin bespeak her Scottish-English background. Her father, who is deceased, worked for over thirty years for the local telephone company. Her mother and two older brothers all live in the Syracuse area. Her mother's sister and Angela's favorite aunt, lives as she always has, two doors down from the Rooneys. Angela misses being near her close-knit family but she likes her job with the homicide squad. She doesn't have a boat to deal with her job-related stress; she plays on an amateur women's basketball team. *Go Court Stars*!

■

A short, fit-looking man in his sixties answers the door in Water Mill. He is wearing suit slacks and a dress shirt open at the neck with a tie pulled down. "That was fast," he says. "I just got off the phone with the precinct. Did you find my wife? Is she okay?"

∎

In the living room, Mr. Napoli sits with his head in his hands. De-Marco and Rooney stand in the center of the room, at a respectful distance. DeMarco speaks. "I know this is a very difficult time but we would like to ask you a few questions, if we may."

Mr. Napoli takes a deep breath. "Okay."

"We found your wife's car in the driveway of a house in Southampton. We rang the bell but got no answer. Do you know whose house that is or why your wife would have gone there?"

"Brandi is a…was, a real estate agent. She bought properties, up-graded them and sold them."

"When did you discover she was missing?"

"I got home this morning from a business trip. She wasn't here. I spoke to her yesterday and she wanted me to go with her this morn-ing to look at some plantings." Mr. Napoli pauses. He tears up. After a moment, he composes himself. He explains. "She was having rose-bushes put in by the pool. I thought maybe she had changed her mind and gone in to the city instead. I called the number at our apartment but got the answering machine. I spoke with the management office and they said she hadn't been in. I called a few of her friends but no one had seen her. That's when I called the police."

"Do you know of anyone who would have any reason to want to hurt your wife?"

"No."

"Any recent arguments she had with anyone? Difficult business dealings?"

Mr. Napoli thinks for a moment. Then he gets up and crosses to the coffee table. He picks up a thin booklet. "Brandi co-chaired a charity event last month." He hands the booklet to DeMarco.

DeMarco looks at the front cover. In bright pastel colors, there is a graphic in the foreground of a pair of flip flops next to a stemmed martini glass. In the background are suggestions of sand dunes. Above the graphic reads:

National Cancer Foundation
Presents

Inaugural Hamptons Summer Bash

Below the graphic:

FESTIVE IN THE DUNES

Saturday, July 13, 2013

Southampton Pool and Beach Club
1215 Spud Lane
Southampton, NY

DeMarco flips open the cover and on the left-hand page at the top reads:

Co-Chairs

Brandi Napoli
Gupta Ritter

Below are smiling headshots of each of the women alongside one another.

"Gupta is someone that Brandi knew casually through a mutual friend," Mr. Napoli says. "Brandi recruited her to serve with her as a co-chair. It started out cordially enough but it soon became—how shall I say, contentious. My wife was a very success-driven woman. She relentlessly pushed herself and everyone around her. She had no patience for those who could not keep up."

"They fought?"

"They had words, to my knowledge. Once, very publicly. It got quite unpleasant. I told her to back off. It's a small community out here. Oh, she agreed with that. But she just couldn't help herself."

"You think this woman could have killed your wife?"

"I don't know her that well. But you asked if there was anyone she had quarreled with."

"Is she local?"

"She lives in Amagansett. I'll get you her address."

■

In Amagansett, a woman who is obviously a domestic answers the door. The detectives show their shields. DeMarco says, "Detective De-Marco, this is Detective Rooney. We're with the Suffolk County detective squad. Is Mrs. Ritter at home?"

■

Gupta's hand flies to her mouth as she sinks into a sofa in her living room. "Oh my God! That's awful!" After a moment, "This is such a shock. I'm sorry, please sit down. Can I get you something to drink? Coffee, water, iced tea?"

"No, thank you," DeMarco says.

"I'm fine," Rooney adds.

They take seats opposite Gupta. DeMarco leads the questioning.

"When was the last time you saw Mrs. Napoli?"

"At that event. Last month."

"*Festive in the Dunes*?"

"It wasn't," is Gupta's terse reply.

"We understand from speaking with Mr. Napoli that there was some friction between you and Mrs. Napoli?"

Thinking about it helps Gupta recover from her initial shock. "The way she treated me was unforgivable."

DeMarco gives Rooney a look. "Enough to want to kill her?"

"Enough to threaten to sue the NCF!"

"National Cancer Foundation? Why?"

"They were complicit in the whole thing. They let her do whatever she wanted. The most outrageous behavior!"

"We understand that there was at least one public scene between you."

"It was at the Princess Diner. If you don't mind, I don't want to go into the details. It was just wrong. You can ask Margo Schumacher about it."

"And who is that?" Rooney asks.

"She's with the NCF. She was there."

"Where would we find her?"

"She lives in Westhampton Beach. I have her address around somewhere."

"Don't bother," Rooney assures her. "We'll look it up."

Silence follows. Then DeMarco asks, "May I ask where you were yesterday?"

"Home."

"All day?"

"Yes."

"Alone?"

"My husband was here."

"Is there anyone else who can confirm that?"

Gupta sees where he is going. "It was the maid's day off. Look, Detective, I despised that woman. I wouldn't dial 9-1-1 if she were being mugged right in front of me. But I did not kill her."

DeMarco and Rooney stand. "We may need to speak with you again," DeMarco says.

Gupta reaches over and removes a card from a silver case on the end table next to her. She holds it out to DeMarco. "Please call first," she says. "I'm not always home all day."

■

The inner door opens in answer to their ring. Dimly, through the sun's reflection off the screen of the outer door, the detectives can make out the head of a large dog. "May I help you?" intones a throaty voice. At first, it seems like the dog is speaking. Then, peering through the screen, they are able to make out the form of a diminutive woman. After looking at their IDs, Margo Schumacher opens the door and leads them back to a combination kitchen and great room. At the back of the room double French doors lead out to a deck overlooking the beach. "Would you like some water?"

"Yes please," Rooney says.

"Me, too," DeMarco adds.

Margo turns and opens a refrigerator. She removes two bottles of water and hands one to each of the detectives. "Sit down," she says indicating a couch. She walks to a large, winged chair opposite and seats herself. Immediately, an Irish Setter appears and lies down at her feet. She and the Setter stare at the detectives. "You said that this is about *Festive in the Dunes*?" Margo says.

Looking at this tiny woman seated in a huge chair with a beautiful but cross-eyed dog at her feet, the phrase *legend in her own mind* flashes through DeMarco's head. "We understand you had something to do with that event?"

"I had everything to do with it! I'm the senior vice president for development at the National Cancer Foundation," she replies haughtily.

"Was it a success?"

"Absolutely. I achieved two hundred percent of net goal. In this business, Officer, that's what you call success!"

"Detective."

"What? Oh...yes, sorry."

"But it was not without some unpleasantness?" Rooney probes.

Margo gives her a dark scowl. "You mean between Brandi and Gupta." It's not a question. "That was completely mismanaged! It should never have been allowed to get to that point," she says hotly. "But not to worry. I'm handling this now and I'll have those two back together playing nice for NCF very soon." A puzzled look crosses Margo's face. "Why does any of this concern the police?"

"Because you're not going to be getting them back together. At least not Mrs. Napoli. Her body was discovered this morning on Southampton beach. She was murdered."

Margo sits staring dumbly for a moment. Then her eyes pop open in horror as if she is suddenly being propelled headfirst into a vortex. "No!" she screams and leaps to her feet.

The Irish Setter follows suit. DeMarco and Rooney watch amazed as the dog runs to one of the French doors, opens it with a paw and bolts from the house. They exchange a look. He's obviously done this before. Margo pays no attention.

"No! No!" Margo paces back and forth, her face a cauldron of not grief but raging fury. "Do you know who did it?" she directs at DeMarco.

"Not yet—"

"Well, I do," she cuts him off. "Max Short!"

"Who's Max Short?"

"He worked on the event. He hated Brandi. Too big for his britches. He didn't know his place. Thought he could talk to her like he was her equal. I knew something bad was going to come from him. I could see it in his eyes. It was probably the sheets and pinking shears that sent him over the edge."

DeMarco and Rooney exchange a long look. "Pinking shears?" Rooney asks.

"We'd gotten some sheets donated that we planned to cut into top cloths for the tables. Brandi had them at her house for most of the time. She was supposed to organize a party of her friends to cut them up. But she never got around to it so she sent them to Max to do. When something like that happens you just do it and forget about it. But not him."

"Is he still with NCF?"

"God, no. There was no way to go forward with him. We got rid of him."

"We may want to speak with him," DeMarco says to Rooney.

"You may want to arrest him!" Margo snaps. "He lives somewhere in Westchester. Go find him and arrest him!"

DeMarco and Rooney share a glance.

Margo has moved on. Her body goes slack. She stands looking like a lost little girl. "What am I going to do now? Without Brandi I have no event. I have to start all over."

DeMarco and Rooney stand. "We may need to contact you again," DeMarco says.

Margo's eyes blaze fiercely. "Yes, do keep me in the loop, Detective. I want to be on the other side of the glass when they plunge the needle in."

Rooney squints at Margo. "New York no longer has the death penalty."

"Maybe it's time to bring it back." She shakes her finger at the detectives. "Go arrest him! He's your killer. Max Short!"

THREE

Margo looks down at the résumé in front of her. "Why don't you tell us a little about yourself, Mr. Short?"

Max looks across to the two women who have just introduced themselves: Margo Schumacher, senior vice president of development, National Cancer Foundation and, seated beside her, Gladys Ortiz, the foundation's Suffolk County regional vice president. The women look back at him. What they see is a fifty-nine-year-old man dressed in a well-tailored navy blue suit with a conservative blue and maroon patterned tie over a crisp white shirt. He is about six feet tall with black Irish coloring—almost black hair, white at the temples, with black eyes and olive skin. He also has a neatly trimmed beard which is cotton-wool white. Once his hair started thinning about ten years ago, he took to shaving the top of his head. Despite the chrome

17

dome and white hair, many people take him for younger than he is.

Max leans slightly forward, a trace of a smile on his lips. "I'm a development professional with expertise in raising money for not-for-profit organizations with a specialty in major, big-ticket events. In that capacity, I have engaged corporate and individual volunteer leadership. My experience includes securing corporate sponsorships, major gifts and grants, donor development and recognition, and recruiting new board members. I am a hands-on manager with interpersonal skills. I relate well to staff and create environments that embrace and cultivate volunteers at all levels. At my last position, I raised over fifteen million dollars."

Max stops there. Every career coach he has ever worked with taught him that. Don't say too much. Don't let the air out of the room. He had learned interviewing is a studied art. Much the way he had learned the same thing about auditioning for a role when he was an aspiring actor years ago. The skill sets you need as an actor to build a character are completely different from those you need to get the part. You need to understand those differences and you need to trust them. Didn't Shakespeare say that we are all actors in this life—or words to that effect? Now he looks directly back at the women and realizes with satisfaction and a great deal of relief that he has hit pay dirt. They're definitely interested.

Margo launches into what Max always thinks of as the public relations speech. What a wonderful organization we are, how wonderful the people are, how wonderful the benefits are—whatever is needed to make the job sound—well, wonderful. Another good sign. As she prattles on, Max doesn't exactly tune her out but turns the volume way down so he can think clearly. He's not out of the woods yet.

"And on the top floor of this building is Tranquil Cove. Are you familiar with it?" Margo asks.

"No," Max replies. Usually a bad answer. It shows you haven't done your homework. But in this instance, he can tell she's dying to tell him all about it.

"It's a temporary residence for patients undergoing cancer surgeries and treatments at New York City hospitals. It is completely free to them and a caregiver, usually a spouse or other family member. I'm the lead fundraiser for it."

"What a wonderful service," Max says.

"The specific job that we are interviewing for today is to launch a new event on the East End of Long Island. Naturally, this event would be scheduled for some time during the summer season." Margo glances back down at Max's résumé. "I see that you have run a Hamptons event in the past. Tell us what your strategy would be if you were to run one for us."

That was two jobs ago when he worked for the respiratory/digestive disease charity. Not by choice but by happenstance, Max has spent his entire career working for health-related organizations. In retrospect, he often thinks of his work history as one long "Disease of the Week" made-for-television movie.

Max immediately has a response on the tip of his tongue for Margo but he resists the urge to charge ahead. Obviously, this is an important question for them and it is better if they don't think he's handing them a pat answer. Max lets his eyes drift upward and slightly off to the side. Then, slowly, he lowers his eyes, letting his head follow suit and looks directly at both women.

"A Hamptons event is a New York City event held there during the summer season. Most fundraising, particularly events fundraising, is a people-to-people business. People give to other people not to organizations."

"But surely during your career you must have had the experience of dealing with people who give to organizations that they strongly believe in," Margo says in a slightly incredulous way.

"Certainly. But those are the people who are already there for you. I'm talking about reaching beyond. To those ever-expanding concentric circles that you need to engage in order to ensure success. Especially with a new event—you want to bring in fresh blood."

The two women stare back at him saying nothing but looking somewhat uncomfortable. *Dear God,* Max thinks. He forgot how prissy people in this business can be. He needs to turn this back on them and get a positive response.

"In order for me to successfully run a Hamptons event for you, I am going to need access to your New York City donors and key stakeholders. People who live and work in the city and have places in the Hamptons or know people who do. Is that going to be possible?"

"Of course," Margo replies quickly. "I should explain at this point that Gladys, as the head of the Suffolk County office, would be your immediate supervisor. The National Cancer Foundation is organized geographically. The Hamptons, being in Suffolk County, falls under her purview."

Max well knows how this works but decides not to comment.

"However, while reporting to her," Margo continues, "as senior vice president of development for the foundation working out of the Manhattan office, I would have significant involvement with the event. I would be your conduit to our New York City volunteers."

"Sounds good," Max says.

"And I'm sure, with all of your years of experience in this arena, there will be volunteers with whom you have worked that you will be able to bring to bear."

Oh, here we go, Max thinks. The old 'how many ready-made donors are you bringing with you?' question. A former boss of his was always looking to hire someone with a golden list of donors to tap. He was a lazy slob. Not unlike so many people working in not-for-profit. Max is not going to be vague on this issue. He has no intention of being put in a position where he is expected to pull rabbits out of a hat.

"I have worked successfully with many donors over the years. Whenever I left a particular job, those donors did not come with me. That's not how it works. And anyone who tells you differently, I would suggest, is pulling your leg."

Margo sits up erect in her chair. "But you must agree that fundraisers exist who do have donors who they can prevail upon," she says with a pout. Max has the distinct feeling she has herself in mind.

"Yes," Max allows noncommittally. *Now shut up, Max, and don't say another word on this topic.*

Margo changes tack. "Why did you leave your last position?"

This is coming late in the game, Max thinks. But maybe that's a good thing. They were so impressed, they forgot to ask.

"I worked for the Westchester County office and ran their big gala in White Plains. Last year they decided to combine that event with their New York City gala. There were still a few smaller events I could have continued to work on but not at the same pay grade. It was a mutual parting."

This was, mostly, true. In any event, if they checked with his former employer, their response was confined to "lack of work" which amounted to the same thing.

"What have you been doing since you left?" Margo can clearly see from the dates on his résumé that he hasn't worked in seven months.

"A good friend of mine died earlier in the year. I was his designated caregiver and had power of attorney for all of his affairs during his extended illness. I am also the executor of his estate and am now working with an attorney to probate his will and get his apartment ready to put on the market."

Max had practiced this answer with his career counselor. While the counselor said he usually did not recommend that clients reference personal business, he felt that this response was honest and, given that it involved working with bankers and lawyers and real estate agents, it wasn't "soft." Still, after seven months, Max is worried about how long he is going to be able to use it. Frankly, given his age, he is getting desperate. This position sounds like a perfect fit for him and he really, really hopes that he will get it.

"We'll be in touch," is all Margo says. Gladys just smiles.

FOUR

Detective Mark DeMarco is seated at his desk talking on the telephone. Seated across from him at her desk is Detective Angela Rooney. "Uh-uh…okay," he says circling his thumb and index finger giving her an "okay." "Alright. Listen, thank you for putting this on the front burner. Right." He hangs up. "That was ME Bellows. Good call on the pinking shears. He's matched that to the mutilation of the tongue."

Rooney smiles, pleased.

"Keep it up. If we solve this one quickly, lunch at Popeye's is on me."

"Alright."

"But he says that couldn't have been the murder weapon. The neck wound was made with a sharp, straight blade. At least two inches

23

thick. He added that the victim was garroted first to collapse the carotid arteries to knock her out. He said, given that, the killer probably has some medical knowledge."

The intercom on Rooney's phone buzzes. She picks it up. "Rooney. Right away." She replaces the receiver. "Perkins wants to see us in her office."

∎

Lieutenant Nancy Perkins sits behind her desk. She is a willowy African American woman in her early forties. DeMarco and Rooney sit in chairs before her.

"Pinking shears!" Perkins says. "That's a new one." She continues, "Her husband is on his way in to identify the body. When you spoke with him yesterday, did you mention the mutilation?"

"No," DeMarco replies.

"Good. That's the way I want it kept. Nothing about the pinking shears. That's all to be kept off the record as exclusionary evidence. Having that get out is not going to help us solve this case and I don't want her killer getting his jollies from lurid media stories." After a moment, "Was this done post-mortem?"

"Bellows is not sure but he thinks so. There was puffy redness around the lips indicating her mouth was taped to prevent her from screaming and then ripped off after her throat was slashed. He believes that is when the tongue would have been cut. He mentioned another thing. After washing away the blood from the neck wound, he found ligature marks. He surmises she was garroted first to knock her out. He added that most rope you can buy today is synthetic. It leaves a very distinct patterned impression. These were more like rope burns from a thick, natural fiber."

"How about sexual assault?"

"Negative. You just said killer. Do you think it's a lone murderer?"

"What's your take?" replies Perkins.

"The victim seemed to be fit. She likely would have put up a fight. She had to be subdued. Bellows said that the ligature marks on her wrists were definitely caused by zip ties like the ones on her ankles."

"Which were then removed. Why?"

"We think so that her body would be found quickly. She was discovered because one of her hands was protruding from the beach grass where it was dumped. Which brings us to the fact that the body had to be carried from the basement of the house next door, where the killing took place, up to the beach."

"So killer or killers," Perkins says.

"And how do you know it's a man?" Rooney asks.

"Well, the violent nature of the crime…" Perkins voice trails off.

"Women can be pretty vicious, too," Rooney replies.

Perkins weighs this.

"I'm glad you said that and not me," DeMarco interjects shooting Rooney a smile.

"Granted, woman on woman homicide is usually more along the lines of cyanide in cheesecake," Perkins concedes. "Possible suspects?"

"Two so far," DeMarco says reviewing his notes. "Gupta Ritter. Lives in Amagansett. Last month she co-chaired a charity event along with the deceased for the National Cancer Foundation. Event was held at the Pool and Beach Club in Southampton. According to reports, including from the deceased's husband as well as from Mrs. Ritter herself, theirs was not a happy, uh…co-chairing. There was even a very public quarrel that occurred at the Princess Diner in Southampton. We contacted the owners who confirmed it. She claims she and her husband were home all day on Friday. There is no one to corroborate that."

"Number two?"

"Max Short. We haven't spoken with him yet. But we did speak with a Margo Schumacher from Westhampton Beach who works for the foundation and she told us that he worked on *Festive in the Dunes*, the event that the two women co-chaired. She claimed that Max 'hated'—her word—Brandi Napoli. Told us we had to arrest him."

Perkins lets out a sigh. "There are too many cop shows on TV. Does he still work at the foundation?"

"No. But she did tell us something very interesting. One of the main reasons that Mr. Short bore ill-will for Mrs. Napoli was that they had received donated sheets that they were going to cut up into some kind of decoration for the tables. Mrs. Napoli had volunteered to take care of it. But she never got around to it and had all the sheets delivered to Mr. Short at his office. He cut the sheets the way she wanted them—with a pair of pinking shears she included."

There is silence in the small office. Lieutenant Perkins sits back in her chair, wrapping her arms around in front, appearing to hug herself. The detectives know this gesture. It means that their boss is interested.

"Where does he live?"

"New Rochelle."

Perkins thinks about this. "For now I think we should just keep an eye on him and Mrs. Ritter."

"DMV is running Max Short's plates to see if there is any video of his car going across the Whitestone or Throgs Neck bridges on or around last Friday. We'd also like to search his office and computer at NCF."

"If they'll sign a consent to search, go for it. And let's get in touch with our friends in New Rochelle and have them send an officer over to visit Mr. Short on some pretext. See if they can get a feel for him. If he is involved in this murder, it might shake him up. Make him do something stupid."

FIVE

Patricia Short walks in the front door. Patricia is an attractive woman of average height in her fifties. She has the fair complexion and dirty blond hair and blue eyes she inherited from her Polish father. She deposits her purse at the foot of the staircase leading to the second floor and proceeds straight back to the kitchen. Max stands at the kitchen counter.

"Hi, babe," she says to his back.

Max turns to her. "Hi."

She walks up to him and kisses him on the lips. She looks around him and sees two split lobster tails in a broiling pan on the counter. "What's the occasion?"

Max turns back and sprinkles Old Bay seasoning over the tails. "Does there have to be an occasion?"

"No."

"I saw them at the seafood counter and they spoke to me."

"What did they say?"

"Take us home, Mr. Director of Social Events for the National Cancer Foundation."

There is a pause as what he said dawns on Patricia. "You got the job?"

Max turns to her. "Yep."

"Congratulations!" They hug and kiss again. "That was fast."

"I guess they saw what they wanted."

"When do you start?"

"A week from Monday."

■

Max met his wife, Patricia Antol, when they were students at Catholic University in Washington, D.C. Five years older than Patricia, Max was in his second year in the Graduate School of Drama finishing up his Master of Fine Arts degree in acting. Patricia was an undergraduate freshman studying marketing. After graduating in 1977, Max took a job working at the John F. Kennedy Center for the Performing Arts. A fellow alumnus worked there in a telephone room for a newly launched service called InstaCharge.

In the days before Ticketron and Ticketmaster ruled the universe, all legitimate theaters used "hard wood." These were traditionally printed tickets that were ordered for every seat for every performance of every show produced by a theater. When they arrived at the theater, tickets that had been ordered through subscription were pulled and set aside. The remainder of the tickets went to the box office where they were sorted and racked by performance date and location for sale at the window. There was no other way to buy tickets.

InstaCharge changed that. Now people could call the InstaCharge number which connected them to a phone room at the Kennedy Center where some two dozen operators covered the phones at any given time. The operators had seating charts for every performance currently for sale. The Kennedy Center had three theaters: the Eisenhower Theater, the Opera House and the Concert Hall. In order to avoid duplicate sales, there was only one seating chart for each performance. When an operator had a client on the line requesting tickets, the operator would have to put them on hold and call out for the seating chart for that performance to be passed to them. Available seats were clearly indicated. The operators had sales forms that they would fill out with information regarding the performance, date and seat location(s) along with the individual's name, address, telephone number and credit card information. Once the sale was confirmed, the operator crossed through those seat locations on the seating chart, indicating they were no longer available. At the end of the business day, the sales receipts were collected and delivered to the appropriate box office, one for each of the three theaters. There the orders were filled from a separate rack of tickets called "dead wood," meaning that they were not available for sale at the window but only through InstaCharge. The tickets were then placed in an envelope with the individual's name, date and performance written on it and racked in yet a third section marked "will call." It was a primitive system but it worked.

Max arrived for an interview to work in the phone room although he would never spend a moment working a telephone there. The manager of InstaCharge desperately needed an assistant. The problem with the system was that, although InstaCharge had its own allotment of tickets held at the box office, it was impossible to predict how well tickets for a particular performance would go: InstaCharge versus box office and box office versus InstaCharge. When InstaCharge's supply of tickets for a performance was running low, additional locations were requested from the box office. When this happened, tickets for that performance were pulled from "hard wood" in the box office and reracked in the appropriate "dead wood" section. Then, those locations were given to InstaCharge so the seating chart for that performance could be updated. When the box office needed more locations to sell for a particular performance, the reverse had to be done. With an especially hot ticket, InstaCharge often had to suspend phone orders until the seating charts were updated. Times this by the number of performances currently on sale and complicated by having to deal with three separate box offices, it was a situation that needed to be handled by one very organized person. In speaking with Max, the InstaCharge manager perceived that he might be just the person and offered him the newly created position as his assistant.

Max liked his new job well enough but he was anxious to pursue a career as a professional actor. He knew that staying in D.C. was not going to help further those aspirations. The shows that played the Kennedy Center came mostly from somewhere else on their way to New York. Even the few shows that the center itself produced were cast out of New York. The same was basically true of the other professional theaters in D.C. like Arena Stage and Folger's Shakespeare Theater. Still, he and his new boss sat in what was, essentially, the general manager's outer office and everyone of importance came through it. After working there only two weeks he had already struck up a cordial relationship with a representative from New York's Public Theater in town to arrange for a D.C. production of *A Chorus Line*. He and Patricia planned to marry when she graduated in three years and, in the meantime, Max was going to make as many contacts in the business as he could. He knew from friends' experiences that New York can be a cold, unfriendly place and he wanted to be as prepared as possible when he went there. Besides, after being in school for all of his life, he was enjoying being out in the working world making some money and living with Patricia in their small apartment near Catholic University's campus.

Yes, sitting outside the general manager's office brought with it some opportunities. One was soon going to change his life for the immediate future and, in a subtle but inexorable way, pull him into a life current that would ultimately wash him up on the National Cancer Foundation shoreline.

When the Kennedy Center was founded, the chairman, Roger L. Stevens, presided over a massive white marble building situated on the banks of the Potomac River in the section of D.C. known as Foggy Bottom. Directly next to the even more massive Watergate complex, locals often referred to it as "the box the Watergate came in." In the early years, in addition to the three theaters and one small film theater, there was a lot of unused space. Most notably, on the roof terrace level there was a room called the atrium. It was no true atrium. Its ceiling rose to a height of only about fifteen feet and instead of any kind of skylight, there was a recessed section of the ceiling illuminated by fluorescent lighting. Down the center of the room, there were three large, square, permanent banquettes ringed with red-tufted seating surrounding a single ficus tree. Being not only a Broadway producer but the consummate real estate developer who bought and sold the Empire State Building soon after his fortieth birthday, Stevens was not going to let this space along with a few others sit idle. There were air conditioning and light and heating bills to pay. Very reasonable rental rates were established for the various spaces and made available for private parties. At the time, the D.C. area desperately needed alternatives to its handful of hotels. And so, the Office of Special Events was born and Stevens put one Henrietta "Hetty" Stem in charge of running it.

Hetty was in her early thirties with a bob of dark hair and ample cleavage. And she was a firecracker. As with that explosive device, most people were afraid to get too close but were attracted to her snap, crackle and pop nonetheless. Most people that is, with the definite exception of the center's general manager, Alan Lessing.

The center opened as soon as possible once the theaters and their backstage areas were operational. What took longer was the completion of the executive offices. In those days, many employees were still sitting on cinder blocks in front of makeshift desks. However, it provided the perfect opportunity for an ambitious person to mark their turf. And Hetty and Alan were nothing if not ambitious.

Alan was Stevens' fair-haired boy and he was ceded the lion's share of authority and control at the center. Stevens' time was consumed by raising money and bringing world-class plays to the Eisenhower Theater. The center's executive director, Martin Feinstein's passion was opera and symphony orchestras. Everything else—lumped under the broad umbrella of "theater operations"—fell to Alan. The stagehands reported to him, the box office managers reported to him, the house managers reported to him, the National Park Service and Park Police reported to him, the parking garage concession reported to him, Canteen Corporation, which ran the center's restaurants, reported to him. Only Hetty Stem didn't report to him. Her domain existed outside the reach of theater operations as it consisted of all public and private spaces. It was considerable. Much too considerable for Alan's pleasure. He detested her for it.

Alan ran theater operations along with assistance from his wife, Rita. They had come up together working in regional theaters in the Midwest. Everyone knew if you wanted something from Alan, you needed to go through Rita first. Rita liked Hetty for her bawdy sense of humor. Rita had a sense of humor herself but it ran more to the perverse. She knew how much Alan hated walking in to his office and finding Hetty siting there kibitzing with her, so Rita let Hetty know that she was welcome anytime. When Alan came in and saw Hetty there, he would walk to his desk in silence. In no hurry, Hetty would conclude her conversation with Rita and get up. She would turn to Alan and toss him a remark that only she laughed at, heartily. She would turn back to Rita, say her goodbye and walk out, not with her tail between her legs. It was during these almost daily occasions that Hetty became friendly with the new guy, Max, sitting in the outer office. After he had been there a few months, Hetty's assistant got another job and promptly left. Hetty approached Max and asked him if he would like to come over and be her assistant. He had already grown bored with the sameness of the InstaCharge job and accepted. Thus was Max's entrance into the world of special events marked.

Barely six months later, just as Max was beginning to get the hang of working on events, Hetty announced that she was forming a partnership with another woman and starting her own events firm. Max was left in a very strange position. The Office of Special Events only existed because Roger Stevens wanted it to. So technically, Max worked for Stevens. But Stevens had no interest in overseeing the office. His only interest was that rental income continued. Max tried to foster a new, positive relationship with Alan, but after their one and only meeting, it was quite clear that he viewed Max as another Hetty. Although the position did not pay well, he was not anxious to have to start looking for another job. Once Patricia graduated, they planned to leave D.C. anyhow and move to New York. So, without any official sanctioning, promotion or salary increase, Max ordered new office stationery listing himself as "Director of Special Events" and continued to run the office single-handedly.

In 1980, Patricia graduated from college. The following winter,

Max and Patricia were married in Patricia's hometown in New Jersey. By that spring, they had moved to New York to pursue their careers: Max in acting and Patricia in marketing. They found a remarkably affordable one-bedroom apartment on the upper West Side. They loved the city and their new lifestyle. It was so different from D.C. Max would have enjoyed it more if he had had greater career success. He did the usual showcase productions of established and classical plays but it was almost impossible to get any industry professionals to come. He joined the Screen Actors Guild and got some extra work but it was too sporadic to be lucrative. He took acting lessons and enrolled in workshops and was very diligent about making it. But the opportunities were scarce. His part-time job as a bank teller was not doing enough to help pay their bills.

He continued to audition for parts that he thought he was right for, but in 1986 he drifted back into event work with a job that he got through a friend at a consulting agency. Although his previous experience with events had helped him get the job, he soon came to realize that there was a world of difference in what he was doing now. At the Kennedy Center, he had been a booking agent. His work at the consulting firm was true fundraising. He was working with major not-for-profit organizations running black-tie dinners with goals starting at the $350,000 level. He was dealing with the presidents and CEOs of Fortune 500 companies who participated in these events as chairs and honorees. Even though he considered it his "day job," he was realizing with great surprise that he was acquiring a marketable skill.

By any measure, Patricia was outstripping him. She had found work almost immediately at a small public relations firm on the East Side—so far over it was almost in the river. She started editing copy but was soon given greater responsibilities. When she decided there was no further she could go in that shop, she switched to a large firm in midtown. Slowly but steadily, Patricia ascended the corporate ladder with increasingly important positions at ever-more prestigious firms. In 1998, she was offered the position of senior vice president for marketing with the New York Yankees, where she has remained.

After a few years at the consulting firm, Max took his acquired experience and went on to work at a number of healthcare not-for-profits. He has raised money for lung disease, hemophilia and birth defects. His most recent and longest-held position was with a heart disease group where he worked for seven years. Wherever he went his job was handling large, big-ticket events. That was his specialty. However, he was mystified when interviewing at non-healthcare agencies that they seemed to dismiss him because their business was not in his wheelhouse. Max always maintained that he could raise money for any cause. He truly believed that. Most nonprofits make a big deal about their missions and wanting to hire individuals who have a passion for them. He had, in fact, worked places where many of his co-workers did have personal connections to the cause. Max had never had a direct connection to any of them and never pretended he did. He had been successful because he could deliver the bucks and, when you stripped away the politically correct bullshit, that's all that charities really wanted.

In 1993, the Shorts left the city and moved to a two-bedroom co-op apartment in New Rochelle, the Westchester County suburb about twenty miles north of the city. It was time for them to try to have a child and the prospect of raising a kid in the city was too expensive and problematic. They tried for a couple of years to get pregnant—everything to that end except fertility drugs. They had read too many stories about multiple births. They wanted children not headlines. In the end, they decided to adopt. In 1996, Jeremy and Gabby entered their lives. They were brother and sister. Jeremy is fair with sandy-colored hair and blue eyes. Gabby has dark hair, olive skin and black eyes. In that way, Max and Patricia were assumed by most people who didn't know otherwise to be their birth parents. With the sudden expansion of their family, the Shorts moved to the house where they currently live, also in New Rochelle.

■

Lobster shells are all that remain of dinner. Patricia looks over the rim of her glass of wine across the table at Max. "Isn't that where Tranquil Cove is?"

"Yes," he says. "It's on the top floor of the headquarters in Manhattan where I interviewed."

Five years ago, Patricia was diagnosed with breast cancer. They caught it early and, thanks to excellent doctors and the advances that have been made with treating that disease over the past forty years, she is cancer-free. It occurs to Max that this will be the first job he has ever held where he will have a personal connection to the mission of the organization. It gives him a good feeling. This job will be different. He'll have some skin in the game. It can only make him a better fundraiser. He has been angry and fearful and depressed since leaving his last job. He even imagined that he would never work again. Working for the National Cancer Foundation is a good omen. It bodes very well. He feels the fire inside him begin to sputter to life once more. Not fearful anymore. This job could take him into retirement on his own terms. Not that he is thinking about retiring. He's had friends who talked retirement when they were in their twenties. Not him. He likes being productive. He's planning to work until he's seventy. Why not? It's better than just sitting around staring at the tube. He can resume making deposits into a retirement account. After six months or so, he and Patricia can apply to refinance their mortgage at the current cheaper rates. One last hurrah! Patricia can stop worrying.

He isn't just going to succeed at this job—he is going to knock it out of the park!

"But I won't be working in Manhattan," he says.

"Where?"

"Since the Hamptons is in Suffolk County, it will be at that office."

"Where is it?"

"A town called Islandia."

SIX

"You'll be working in Manhattan."

"I will?" Max is confused.

"One day a week. At least to start," Gladys continues. Gladys sits behind her desk in her office. Max is seated in a chair facing her desk. He figures she is in her late thirties, maybe forty.

"You made your case at the interview that you needed access to New York City volunteers and you were heard. The event belongs to this office. I am your supervisor and you will report to me."

It was quite clear to Max at the interview that this proposed Hamptons event is more important to Margo than it is to Gladys. Maybe important is not the right word. He definitely feels he needs to probe the relationship between these two women, and between them and the event.

"What role will Margo play in this?" he asks.

Gladys looks vaguely pained. "Margo is an interested party. She will be closely monitoring the event's progress. You will coordinate with her. Certainly on the day that you will be working in Manhattan."

"But I will be submitting my progress reports to you?"

"Yes," Gladys says slowly. But it doesn't sound like yes. After a moment she continues. "You are helping us break new ground. I have worked here for eight years and during that time or forever, really… there has never been anyone who has worked out of two offices. It is a completely new experience for all of us at NCF. In a way, we're all going to have to see how it works best. What works best for the event is best for the foundation—that's what's important."

Max has the feeling that she is regurgitating directives that had been recently given to her.

"I find it very exciting," she says, suddenly brightening.

Or scary, Max thinks. "What day will I be working out of the city?"

"Thursday. To start. That can be adjusted as needed. Also, we can increase your city days if we decide. Especially as we get closer to the event. But any changes to your schedule, you have to clear with me."

Max assents to this with silence.

"I want to reiterate that we cannot provide you with full-time help. All the staff here are committed to other projects. We may be able to get you some support from one of our summer camp interns next year. They come on board in May. You'll see some of this year's group around now."

"Understood," Max says.

"I've arranged for you to meet with Carolyn Petrie," Gladys says. "She's our director of corporate relations. She has some wonderful contacts she can share with you. Corporations with a keen interest in the right kind of sponsorships. I'm sure that wouldn't bother you?"

"Bring it!"

■

Carolyn is a tall, rangy woman in her late thirties with short, curly brown hair and a round, cherubic face which, though out of place on her frame, is thoroughly welcoming. Gladys makes the introductions and then departs.

"Have *the* seat," Carolyn says wryly, indicating the only chair in her cramped office except for the one behind her desk which she re-takes. Max sits opposite her.

"I don't know what Gladys told you," Carolyn begins, "but I am most likely not going to be able to help you a whit. However, I will try anything short of extortion to assist you in any way I can."

"I prefer that to people telling me they are going to give me the moon only to find out what they meant was a view of their quickly departing ass."

Carolyn laughs. "I can tell you've been around the block a few times." After a moment, "I'm working with a few prospects right now—banks, a car dealership. They might have some interest in an event but, obviously, I can't mention it until it's on the books. Do you have any idea when this might be?"

"I'm thinking a year from August," Max replies. "I want to give myself as much time as possible."

"August might be good. There's a lot less going on out there then. With the last one being in July, I don't think that helped. Kind of got lost in the shuffle."

"Last one?" Max asks with surprise.

"Two years ago."

"I was told this was a new start-up event."

"Oh…" Carolyn says, her brow knitting. "Well, maybe it is. In a way."

"What does that mean?"

Carolyn looks down. She extends her arms across her desk and picks up a crystal paperweight with a flat side for a base. She cups it in both hands. She rolls it back and forth between her palms. Max waits for her answer.

"I'm surprised Gladys didn't mention it…Or, maybe not." Carolyn puts the paperweight down and sits back in her chair. "It wasn't very successful."

"How much money did it make?"

Carolyn glances up at the open door to her office. In a whisper she says, "It lost sixty-eight thousand dollars."

"What!" Max exclaims.

Carolyn grimaces and waves both hands at him to lower his voice.

"Sixty-eight thousand dollars!" he whispers back.

Carolyn gives him a wide-eyed nod of confirmation.

"How?"

Carolyn shrugs, both palms extended up.

"I can't believe they didn't tell me this," Max says.

"Not exactly bragging rights."

Silence in the small office. After a few moments Max speaks. "This may be a silver lining. There should be a file on that event. Even though it failed it must contain donor history. I'm not starting at absolute zero."

"You should talk to Dana Daniels."

"Who's that?"

"The woman who ran the event."

"She's still here!" Max says, incredulous.

Carolyn gives him a knowing grin. "Oh, yeah, baby."

"Losing sixty-eight thousand—most places would have fired her before the dessert dishes were cleared."

"Not Dana."

"Who's she fucking?"

"That's not it. At least, I don't think so. Dana's special. She's a breast cancer survivor. You can skate pretty far on that at this place."

■

Max finds Dana seated in her cubicle.

"Hi, Dana," he says, extending his hand. "I'm Max Short."

Dana is a petite woman in her forties with shoulder-length brown hair. She looks like a cheerleader type whose cheer has mostly abandoned her.

She shakes his hand. "Nice to meet you. You're going to be working on the Hamptons event, right?"

"Yep. What are you working on, now?"

"I've got a *Jump Rope for Hope* coming up on Friday."

"What's that?"

"It's a program we do in the schools. Kids get people to pledge money based on how many times they can jump rope. And then in July, I'm fielding a team for our *Step Off Breast Cancer Awareness Walk*. It's my job to make sure the bikers show up."

"Like motorcycle bikers?" Max asks.

"It gets peoples juices flowing. You'll see. That event's all hands on deck for everyone in the office."

"Cool. If you have time, I really would like to pick your brain about the last Hamptons event."

Dana looks at him for a long moment then says, "Sure. What do you want to know?"

"I was hoping to look at donor files. People who participated."

"Okay…uh…" She pulls open the lower drawer of her desk. There are numerous hanging folders there. She begins to sort through them.

While she does this, Max looks over to her desk. On it is a framed picture of two teen-aged boys. *Must be her sons*, Max assumes. He doesn't see a picture of a possible husband. Maybe he split after the diagnosis. A lot of men do.

"I've changed cubicles since then. Maybe it got misplaced," Dana says, straightening up. "But it's all right here in my head. Why don't we go into the boardroom if it's free? More privacy."

They walk down the hall in the direction of the front desk. The door to the boardroom on their left is shut. They can see through the glass panel flanking the door that the light is off and it is empty. They enter and sit in chairs next to each other.

"As I'm sure you know, starting a new event is hard. It's doubly hard in the Hamptons. Not only is it so far away but it's so difficult to find a way in. Very closed-off community," Dana tells Max who does not need to be told. He has had his own Hamptons experience.

"And the expense," Dana goes on. "I don't know about you but as a single mom, it was very hard for me to afford those shoes and that bag."

Max is confused. "I'm sorry?"

"The designer shoes and bag. I had to run all over the place to find a deal somewhere. I finally got them at Filene's."

Max's expression clearly tells her he doesn't have a clue.

"For the parties," she explains. "So I could fit in at those parties out there to meet the right people. They have to know who you are or you don't exist."

No wonder your event failed, Max thinks. I don't need designer shoes and a bag to do this job. I need to find people with designer shoes and bags. This woman not only doesn't have donor files for him, she has nothing of any use to share.

■

"I saw you talking to Dana in the boardroom." Gladys is standing at Max's cubicle.

"I was trying to get some information on the last Hamptons event."

This will be interesting, Max thinks. *I wonder what she is going to say.*

"I would have directed you to talk to Dana if I thought it would be of any help."

"I was hoping to get a file on the event. Even though it tanked, there were people who gave money." On the word "tanked" Max detects an almost imperceptible jerk of Gladys's head as if she's been slapped. "Does that information exist?"

"Gee, I don't know. I'll have a look in my office. There might be something there." Then, as if to demonstrate to Max the futility of his query, "All the wrong people, Max. That was the problem—all the wrong people."

∎

"Gee, I don't know?" Max is sitting across the dinner table from Patricia that evening. "This, from fearless leader?" he exclaims.

"Gladys?"

"Yes! This event happened in her chapter on her watch and she doesn't know if any records exist?"

"Like that other woman said to you, not exactly bragging rights."

"I should have been told at the time of the interview that there had been a previous event regardless of its outcome," Max fumes.

"Would it have made a difference in your taking the job?" Patricia asks.

Max's ire abates somewhat. "No. But it's the principle of the thing. What else is she not telling me?"

"This is good," Patricia says indicating her plate.

"Thanks."

Ever since the early days of their marriage, Max has been the cook—on weeknights anyhow. While Max was auditioning as an actor and taking classes and appearing in showcase productions in dismal off-off-Broadway theaters, Patricia was busy plying her trade and moving up in the marketing field. A process that saw her not getting home until 8:00 p.m. or, sometimes, much later. Even after Max started at the fundraising firm, he was always the first one home. That is, except on nights when he was working an event. Logically, he took up the role. Max had always liked to cook, so it was not an onerous task. And after they had kids, it became even more imperative that he be the first one home to pick them up from school and feed and bathe them and help with their homework. He stipulated at the start of any new job that he had a non-negotiable quitting time of 5:00 p.m., unless previously arranged.

"I use a pinch of curry in the sauce," Max says, then continues his line of thought. "Did she think I wasn't going to find out?"

"Doesn't make sense."

"I just don't want to be sent out on any fool's errands. Some bosses like to keep the new guy in the dark about certain things. This has never worked in the past, they reason, but this guy might be able to make some magic happen. It doesn't work and all it does is piss people off—mostly me!"

"I would get friendly with as many people as you can. People love office gossip. It's usually a font of information. That woman—"

"Carolyn."

"I would get on good terms with her. She's already told you about the first Hamptons event," Patricia says taking a sip of her wine.

SEVEN

Max sits in the cubicle that has been assigned to him and from which he works every Thursday. Finally, after four months of chasing down blind alleys and running into dead ends, he has some hope that this evening will yield results that will allow him to move forward with the Hamptons gala.

■

He has made numerous site visits to potential venues for the event. He has settled on two: the Maidstone Club in East Hampton and the Pool and Beach Club in Southampton. As one of the top golf clubs in the country, the Maidstone Club has more cachet, even if it's somewhat stuffy. The Pool and Beach Club is more pedestrian—a dining room and adjoining bar area that serves lunch to members on a regular basis. Its advantage is that it has a large deck right on the beach.

Unfortunately, Max can't hold space or even talk dates with either. Until he has volunteers—a committee that will commit to supporting the event and making it successful—he has nothing.

Fortunately, he has been able to work with Ricardo "Ricky" Colon, the longtime director of social events and his counterpart in the Manhattan office. Calling him his counterpart is a bit of a stretch. Ricky oversees three gala dinners throughout the year, along with a spring women's luncheon which is the largest and most successful social event in the division. Aside from the proposed Hamptons gala, the Suffolk office's events are all grassroots affairs of the breast cancer walk and jump rope in the schools ilk. On top of that, Ricky manages the Manhattan Special Events Committee. This committee is composed of the foundation's top women stakeholders.

After much frustration, Max decided to try employing a strategy that he has used in the past with some positive results. It's called a recruitment committee meeting or search committee. The idea is simple. Assemble a group of individuals for a one-time-only meeting to identify potential volunteer event leadership. In this case, Max is looking for high-net-worth people who live in Manhattan and maintain summer places in the Hamptons. It is stressed to the invitees that they are not being asked to join an event committee. You want people in the room who have numerous other similar involvements and therefore, reach. But by the same token, the chance of recruiting them to a committee is close to nil. The point is to identify new candidates. The whole process is conducted right then and there. Usually, once he has laid out the ground rules, Max receives blank stares from around the table or protestations of 'I don't know anyone like that.' However, inevitably one person starts and, almost like magic, others jump in. Max has always put this phenomenon down to the competitive spirit. The people you invited to this gathering are no slouches. They are very successful people. They do not like being seen by a group of their peers as not up to the task.

Ricky is a grumpy man in his forties but he has turned out to be surprisingly helpful. He had sat down with Max and gone over the list of members of the Special Events Committee and indicated those who fit the profile. Not only that, but he wrote personalized notes of invitation, signed by him, which he had hand-delivered.

Helpful but not particularly cordial. Max gets it. From the first day he set foot in the Manhattan office, Ricky has been cold to him. Ricky's perpetually hooded eyes are a dead giveaway that he is not about to let some newcomer easily poach on his turf. So Max treads very lightly.

Max credits Ricky's assistance to Margo. Or, more precisely, in spite of Margo. Max didn't actually have to see it to imagine Margo hungrily sniffing around Ricky's Special Events Committee. Margo has only been with the foundation a little over a year and, in her position, she must be tasked with raising *beaucoup* bucks. The Special Events Committee is a potential gold mine for her. But Ricky is not about to let her get anywhere near his "ladies"—the ones he has recruited and cultivated over the years. Certainly not! As senior vice president of development for the foundation, Margo is Ricky's superior but he is not on her team and he does not report to her. And there is no danger any of his committee ladies would have anything to do with Margo if Ricky didn't want it. They all love Ricky and are unanimously loyal. These society babes would follow him unflinchingly into a Kmart if he told them that was something they needed to do for the foundation.

Max figures, between himself and Margo, Ricky considers him to be the lesser of two evils. Though they may be equals on the organizational chart, Ricky doesn't see Max as a serious threat. For one thing, Max works for the Suffolk County office. He is only in Manhattan one day a week. And, in terms of seniority, Max has none. Margo, on the other hand, is probably a perpetual burr under Ricky's saddle. That notion is confirmed when Ricky hands over the invitation list for the meeting, which includes addresses and phone numbers.

"Don't show this to Margo," he says.

∎

Max looks down at the list of acceptances for tonight's meeting:

Gwen Longacre
Mitzi Steineman
Brandi Napoli
Dolores delMar
Karin Bigalow

Five, Max thinks. Could be better. Could be much worse. After all this time, he feels that he is finally getting a toehold.

He knows Gladys and Margo have been antsy. Gladys often manifests this by watching him from a distance. He'll be at the copy machine and look up. Gladys will be standing just looking at him. He knows she is probably thinking, *What is this guy doing to earn his keep?* At least once a day she'll ask him how things are going. Does he have everything he needs? She tries to make it sound like she's just being helpful but her eyeballs are screaming, "What the hell are you doing?" One morning she came up to his cubicle when he was making file folder tabs while eating a yogurt.

"We're not paying you to just sit around and eat yogurt, you know." She said it with a laugh, trying to make it sound like a joke. Max knew it was not.

Margo was more direct.

"I think you need to be out on the East End knocking on doors. Going into shops and restaurants—business establishments. Get to meet people, get them to know you. Talk up the event, hand out your card, get their card. You can't just sit behind your desk and expect them to come to you."

In other words, cold calling. Maybe not on the phone but cold calling nevertheless. Great! Max has never cold called in his life and he is not about to start now. Statistically it offers the least chance for success of any method. It is a huge waste of time and extremely demoralizing. Besides, isn't it in defiance of Margo's big caution that they not appear to be a "carpetbagger organization?" In this Max completely agrees. His previous experience doing a Hamptons event had taught him that. Every charity in the greater New York area is either doing or trying to do or dreaming of doing an event on Long Island's gilded East End. That's why the houses are surrounded by such high hedges. Hamptonites don't like being bothered by outsiders—or even their neighbors. Wouldn't having him wandering around like a lost vagabond reinforce the notion that NCF is just such a "carpetbagger organization" seeking to infiltrate the inner sanctum and snatch the golden goose? In any event, local businesses are not going to help him launch an event. They might be good contacts for donating auction items but that would come later. And then, that is best done by committee members who patronize those businesses. The type of individuals he is hoping will be at his meeting this evening.

■

Max's phone starts ringing midafternoon.

"Mr. Short? This is Dolores delMar. I'm sorry to have to call you on such little notice but our daughter came home from school sick and I'm afraid I will not be able to attend this evening's meeting."

"Well, of course I understand."

"There's no one else here to care for her and I simply can't leave her alone."

"Certainly," Max says. "May I stay in touch as we move forward? Give you updates on our progress?"

"Uh…Oh, yes, that would be marvelous. You do that." And she hangs up.

Next is Mitzi Steineman.

"Hello, Max? Mitzi Steineman. First off, I have to tell you, I love your name. That's my favorite brother's name as well. I'm calling to apologize for being such a ditz but I completely misunderstood Ricky's invitation. I thought this was a Special Events Committee meeting. Like a *special* Special Events Committee meeting, not our monthly one. I just reread the invitation. Sorry to have to beg off. I know you'll forgive me."

As he replaces the receiver Max wonders if her brother's name is Max or Short.

Karin Bigalow doesn't even apologize.

"Calling to let you know I won't be there this evening. Out of the question. Good luck." Click.

Just two left on the list, Max thinks as he draws a line through Karin's name. *I hope they don't become no-shows.*

Both Gladys and Margo are coming to the meeting. Gladys is making the trip in from the Island solely for the purpose. Max had figured that if this meeting ended up being a bust, it probably marked the end of his brief career at NCF. Hours earlier he had felt very hopeful. It had seemed that he had put the right elements in place and things were now going to happen. Looking back down at the list, he is not so sure.

■

A few hours later, going on 6:00 p.m., Max sits in the conference room at the other end of the floor from his workstation. With him are Gladys and Margo. No one speaks. The tension in the air is palpable. They don't look at each other and all try to avoid getting caught looking at the telephone in the middle of the conference table. Max has informed them that three out of the five expected attendees have canceled. They are awaiting the arrivals of Gwen Longacre and Brandi Napoli. Margo claims that she has met Gwen but doesn't know Brandi. Gladys knows neither. After a few minutes, Margo stands and reaches across to the five bottles of water in the center of the table. She picks up two and puts them in front of the two vacant chairs. She then takes one for herself. She looks down at the thick cookies on a paper plate in the center of the table.

"Those look good. What kind are they?"

"Chocolate chunk with macadamia nuts."

"Oh, Max, you know these women hardly eat at all! You might have picked something more diet-conscious." Margo takes her water and resumes her seat.

The phone next to the cookies rings. All three heads snap in its direction as if fresh meat had just been tossed into a piranha tank. Max stands and picks up the receiver. "Yes?" After a moment, "And we're expecting one more...That's right." Max replaces the receiver. "Brandi Napoli is on her way up."

"Well, go out to the elevator and escort her in," Margo says.

Max turns for the open door to the conference room and as he exits he practically bumps into Brandi.

"Oh! I'm sorry...I was...I was just going to get you," Max stammers.

"I know my way around here," Brandi says. She extends her hand, "I'm Brandi Napoli." Max shakes her hand.

Margo is right at Max's elbow. She extends her hand to Brandi. "Margo Schumacher, senior vice president for development for the foundation." She and Brandi shake hands. "May we hang your coat?"

"I'll just hang on to it."

"I must say, you're right on time," Margo says walking back toward her chair.

"I had no trouble getting a cab."

"Can be dicey at this hour."

Gladys stands and offers her hand. "Gladys Ortiz. I'm the regional vice president of the Suffolk County office."

Brandi shakes her hand. "Nice to meet you."

"Sit here, Brandi," Margo says patting the back of the chair between her and Gladys.

Max sits in his chair across the table from the three women.

Brandi turns to Gladys. "So you don't work in this office?"

"No, my office is in Islandia."

"I don't think I know where that is."

"It's just a little past Hauppauge."

Brandi cocks her head. "Sorry, all I know is the East End. Do you live in Islandia?"

"No. Commack. It's not too far from the office."

"I'm in Westhampton Beach," Margo chimes in.

"So, we're practically neighbors," Brandi says.

Max checks his watch as the women engage in small talk. It's almost ten past. Max decides he'll wait for an opportunity to cut in and start the meeting. After a few minutes, the chitchat subsides.

"We're expecting one more attendee," Max interjects, "But in the interest of staying on schedule, I suggest we get started and bring her up to speed when she gets here."

The three women fall silent and turn their attention to him.

"By way of introduction, I am the director of social events for the Suffolk County office. I have been with the foundation for about four months. Among my duties, I have been tasked with mounting a brand-new Hamptons event slated for some time next summer. At this point, we are envisioning a seated gala dinner-dance. We have done research on potential venues for the event and we are currently looking at two: the Maidstone Club in East Hampton and the Pool and Beach Club in Southampton. We have not committed to any date at this time and are open to suggestions for both dates and other venues. However, the purpose of this evening's gathering is to help identify possible leadership for the event. To be specific, this would be the recruitment of an event chair. The duties of event chair are to pledge a lead-off gift of twenty-five thousand which would include two tables of ten to the dinner and to assist in donor solicitation. The goal for the event is one hundred thousand net. The only rule for tonight's meeting is for anyone who you suggest for a chair, you must also make the ask or arrange for the ask to be made by a person who in some way has access to the individual." With that being said, he continues, "If there are no questions, let us begin with suggestions."

Even to his own ears, Max sounds very confident. In reality, his strong urge is to curl himself into a tight ball and hurl himself through the nearest window. *My God, this is unbearably awkward*, he thinks. One participant! He's never done this with one participant! His earlier confidence envisioned people feeding off each other rising to a crescendo of an embarrassment of riches of candidates emerging with such rapidity that he would not be able to keep up writing down their names. Now the sole participant sits silently in her chair.

Neither Margo nor Gladys is looking at Brandi. Margo is even slouched in her chair at an odd angle tilted away from Brandi with a blank look on her face. Max is afraid she might have had a stroke. Max envies both of them because, seated as he is directly across from Brandi, he can't not look at her. So he does so from behind an imaginary inner set of translucent eyelids like an amphibian's. It is the only way he can keep from screaming, "Speak! Speak! Say something.

Anything. Just break this deadly nightmare, Brandi, and speak!"

Finally, Brandi speaks.

"I don't know if I can help you there," she begins.

Max feels his heart start to drop. *Don't say it,* he pleads wordlessly to himself.

"We've only relocated to New York from Jersey in the past year. And since we bought the place in Water Mill, I've spent most of my time there working with the contractors on renovations. I really haven't gotten much into the social whirl. I'm afraid I don't have anyone to suggest."

Max's heart hits rock bottom. *She said it.* Max senses inky black storm clouds swirling into the room and hanging above his head.

"But I'll chair the event," Brandi says.

There is a shocked silence. Max tries to respond, but for a moment his mouth can't form words. He looks at Margo and Gladys, two woodland creatures slowly stirring to life after a spell has been broken.

"You will?" Max begins.

"Put us down for the twenty-five-thousand-dollar sponsorship. You did say sponsorship, right?"

"Uh, right," he says.

"It'll come from my husband's company. I'm not sure how he'll want it listed but I'll send you an email."

In a flash, a brilliant sun breaks through the clouds over the conference table. In slo-mo Brandi reaches for a cookie, dazzling rays shooting from the rings on her fingers.

"This should be fun," she says, taking a bite of the cookie. "And these are good."

The meeting lasts a few minutes longer. Max doesn't remember exactly how long and has no idea what else is said. It doesn't matter.

Mission accomplished! Thinking back on it later, the only impression he has is that if it were a scene in a movie, it would be scored to "Happy Days Are Here Again."

BRANDI

Born and raised in Flushing, Queens by parents of mixed European backgrounds, Brandi Napoli is in her late fifties. She is married to Anthony Napoli, president & CEO of a large advertising conglomerate in NYC. Anthony is in his early sixties. They have been married for twenty-six years after having met on a blind date under the Tiffany glass ceiling at Maxwell's Plum in the 1980s. They have three grown children, one of whom is still in college. When Anthony was promoted to president & CEO last year, they moved to New York from Short Hills, New Jersey. Their Manhattan apartment is in the Trump Tower on Fifth Avenue. Sometime after relocating, they bought a home in Water Mill on Long Island's East End.

She has a real estate license but does not work for a real estate company. Her one-woman "business" is buying and remodeling houses to flip on the market. This is originally how they came to own their Hamptons home. She was remodeling it to sell but then decided she loved it so much, she convinced her husband to keep it. Her appearance is youthful, if somewhat dated. She mostly resembles an aging "summer blond" from the 1960s—bottle blond with a perpetual deep tan that she cultivates on Hamptons beaches and, very likely, at a tanning salon. It never fades no matter the season.

There is a type of woman who has never worked because she has not had to. She relies on her husband for money. But rather than being content with that, she yearns for an occupation of her own. Something that she does that gives her satisfaction and the admiration of others. However, she has no marketable skills. Some of these women, either deliberately or by chance, find themselves working on charity events. They revel in the stature. They mistakenly see this activity as a road for them to gainful employment. It rarely is. When that doesn't happen, they become resentful of the salaried staff who they work with because they feel that they should be paid as well. Often, they see their own contributions as greater than those of the "professionals." This causes them to undermine staff members to prove that they can do things better. There is another type who gets involved with charity events because they are in the financial position to be the events' queen bee. This type is not in competition with staff. They don't soil their hands with day-to-day details. They just swing their huge purse around to bludgeon anyone who challenges them. Though more the former, Brandi is a unique blend of both of these women. As a volunteer, she is a perfect storm.

She sits on the Manhattan Special Events Committee at NCF. They have monthly meetings at their headquarters in midtown. The chair of the committee is Manhattan socialite, Ceci Bombeck. Brandi idolizes her. On occasion, as during the holidays, Ceci will host a committee "meeting" at her spectacular West 57th Street apartment. In reality it is purely a social event to wow her fellow committee members. Brandi wouldn't miss one for the world. Once, while spending the holidays in Bermuda, Brandi flew into New York just for the day in order to attend. She has furnished her Trump Tower apartment to resemble Ceci's as much as possible, mimicking the chintz-covered furniture and small silver-framed photographs scattered everywhere. Ceci also chairs NCF's annual spring women's lunch at the Pierre Hotel. When Brandi gets the invitation to attend a meeting for a planned Hamptons event, she sees it as the opportunity she has been longing for to distinguish herself to Ceci and the other ladies. She jumps at the chance.

EIGHT

"Knock, knock."

Max looks up from his desk. Brandi is standing at his cubicle. With her is another woman.

"Max, I'd like you to meet my co-chair…I guess I should say, your new co-chair. This is Gupta Ritter."

Startled, Max stands and extends his hand. "Very pleased to meet you…"

Gupta shakes his hand. "Gupta," she provides for him again. "I know, it's a little unusual. It's my mother's family's name. My middle name, actually, but everyone's always called me Gupta."

"Pleased and surprised," Max responds. "Brandi didn't tell me why she wanted to meet me in the city today, did you?"

"Then it wouldn't have been a surprise."

"Have you told Margo?"

"No, but we don't have time to go up to see her now. We've got a lunch date across town. You tell her."

There is an awkward pause as no one knows what to say next.

"Yay!" Brandi finally says in a subdued mock shout waving her fists in the air.

"Yay!" Max mimics her. His impulse is to give her a hug but he suppresses it. Their relationship is still new and he doesn't want to presume too much. Plus, then he'd have to hug Gupta and that just feels wrong.

"Now we need to schedule a meeting to start making some decisions," Brandi says as she starts off.

"I'm on it," Max says.

"Bye," says Gupta following after Brandi.

As soon as they go, Max Googles Gupta. He finds out that she is in her mid-thirties, is Indian American and comes from Columbus, Ohio where her family owns a chain of grocery stores. She is married to her hedge fund manager husband, Bradley. They live on Park Avenue in Manhattan and in Amagansett. *Short but very sweet,* Max thinks. *The perfect profile for our needs.*

NINE

Max pulls off Montauk Highway into the small parking area to the left of the office. There are two other cars parked there but he doesn't know if either is Brandi's. However, it is just before their 1:00 p.m. appointment so he decides to go straight in. As is the case with many businesses in the Hamptons, the building looks like a beach bungalow that has been expanded and repurposed as a commercial space. Max walks up the three wooden steps to the covered front porch. He glances through the window in the door and sees a woman seated behind a counter inside. He opens the door and enters.

He goes to the counter. The woman looks up. "Can I help you?" she says.

"I'm Max Short from the National Cancer Foundation. I have an appointment with Eileen Boyer."

The woman gestures to a small round table and four chairs positioned off to one side by the front window. "Have a seat. I'll let her know you are here."

"We're expecting one other person to join us."

"I'll tell her," the woman says, picking up her telephone.

Max goes to the table and sits down. He had contacted *Dan's Papers* about being the media sponsor for the event right after Brandi had come on board. He had been directed to speak to Eileen. Since he didn't have a date or venue at the time, he had only been able to give her general information regarding their plans. She had sounded positive—well, she didn't say no. He had worked with media partners in the past. Most often they had been radio stations for events like walks. This is going to be different. *Dan's Papers* is *it* in terms of Hamptons event coverage. He is hoping that they are going to offer more than a calendar listing. But like everything and everybody out here, they play by their own rules. He is going to have to play by them, too.

"Max," the voice breaks in on his thoughts. Max turns to see a compact woman in her forties coming out from behind the counter. Max stands.

"Hi, I'm Eileen," she says. They shake hands. "I know we're expecting another person but I have a staff meeting coming up and I want to get started." She hands him her card. Max glances down and reads "Assistant to the Publisher" printed beneath her name.

They sit across from each other at the table. She plops down a thick folder. It looks to Max like a giant sandwich, reminding him he didn't have time to stop for lunch on his drive out from Islandia.

"So, have your plans jelled since the last time we talked?"

"Yes. As of just last week. The date is Saturday, July thirteenth at the Pool and Beach Club in Southampton."

Eileen opens her folder and removes a yellow legal pad from the top. She takes a pen and writes this down. "Name of the event?"

"I'll have to get back to you about that."

"Okay." .

"We figure we'll start cocktails at six-thirty followed by dinner at eight."

"That's a good time. In July, you'll have plenty of daylight before dinner service."

She sounds more like a caterer than a journalist, Max thinks. But he is glad of her participatory approach. It's a good sign.

"*Dan's Papers* is very much a part of this community," she continues. "When we're the media sponsor for an event, it's about more than just sending a photographer. You'll also be listed on our monthly and weekly calendars, of course. But what we pride ourselves in is providing context on the organization. Too many groups are trying to get in, raise money and get out."

And that's all she says. Then she sits back in her chair and fixes Max with a steady gaze. Max's mouth goes dry. He wasn't expecting this. *She's good at throwing you off balance,* he thinks. Now it's his turn. If he doesn't respond appropriately to her, this meeting is over. The gauntlet has been thrown down.

Max's mind races. He thinks about what to say. Then he hears Margo saying in his ear, "carpetbagger organization." That's what Eileen is talking about! Don't be a "carpetbagger organization." He had no idea that this would come up today.

Once Max focused on Margo's admonition regarding "carpetbagger organization," he had researched exactly what the NCF did that could be seen as having particular relevance to the Hamptons. Max looked at the programs. They provided free wigs to women undergoing chemotherapy. That wasn't particular to the Hamptons. They had a program to drive cancer patients to and from their doctor's appointments. That was not only not specific to the Hamptons but, as Max learned, not available to anyone living that far out.

The truth is the foundation provides precious few direct services anymore and is progressively moving away from doing them at all. The powers that be are concentrating on moving the organization to a complete gold-standard national entity that spends its time and treasure pumping out comparative statistics and consumer-based recommendations. In many ways it reminds him of the heart disease organization when he first started there. At the time, they had numerous programs that they ran in the schools and communities. But after a while, those were slowly phased out. He was even in an NCF meeting at one point when one of the big bosses talked about how they were using his former employer as a target model but lamented how difficult it was breaking some people's old habits. To Max, it sounded like a justification for terminating some people's jobs. He did find that NCF funded two small, basic research projects at two facilities on Long Island but they weren't on the South Fork.

And then it comes to him—Camp Quest!

Camp Quest is a summer camp operated by NCF in Montauk for two weeks every year in August. It is open to one hundred fifty cancer patients ages six to sixteen and their siblings. The camp is completely free to attendees. Located as it is at the very tip of the South Fork of Long Island's East End, it is undeniably part of the Hamptons. Although the population it serves is not necessarily from the Hamptons, for *Dan's Papers* requirements, it geographically qualifies as within the community.

"We run a program in Montauk that I think you might be interested in," Max offers. "It's called Camp Quest. It's a summer camp for kids diagnosed with cancer."

Eileen sits forward in her chair, picks up her pen and starts writing.

Max describes the program to her. She is clearly interested.

"Can we speak to any of the families who have participated?" Eileen asks.

"We'll have to talk to Aggie Potter. She's the woman who runs the program. I'll send you her contact information as soon as I get back to the office."

"Sorry I'm late."

Max and Eileen turn to see Brandi standing in the doorway. She walks in, closing the door behind her. Max stands.

"Eileen, this is Brandi Napoli. She's co-chairing the event."

Brandi holds out her hand. Eileen holds out her hand but does not get up. Brandi leans across the table to shake Eileen's hand. Brandi takes a seat at the table. Max retakes his chair.

"Right now, this is what I'm looking at," Eileen says, looking down at notes she has written on her legal pad. "We'll do a feature article on the camp sometime in the spring. We'll close with a mention of the upcoming event. I can't guarantee how much space we can allot. That'll depend on what else is planned for the issue. Tell Aggie to give me as much as she can, and I'll do my best." Eileen glances at her watch. "That should do it for now. I'll send you a letter of intent outlining our agreement," Eileen says to Max. "Sign it and send it back to me and we can get started." She looks at both Max and Brandi.

Very pleased with the meeting, Max flashes Brandi a smile. Brandi sits looking bewildered, her mouth open.

Eileen gets up, hugging her folder in her arms. Max and Brandi rise. Eileen shakes Max's hand. Then she shakes Brandi's hand. "Very nice meeting you," she says to Brandi.

"Yeah…you, too," Brandi says.

Outside in the parking lot, Brandi turns on Max. "What's this about a camp? What camp? And who the hell is Aggie?"

"Camp Quest is a summer camp that the foundation runs for kids with cancer in Montauk. Aggie Potter is the staff person in charge of the program."

"Please don't tell me they're doing an article about this camp instead of covering our event," Brandi says, archly.

"They're covering the event. But they need to see us as having roots in the community not just coming out here one evening to raise money. What we're getting is so much more than just event coverage."

"I didn't hear one word about the event," Brandi counters.

If you'd gotten here on time you would have, Max thinks. Looking at her, a reason occurs to him as to why she was late. She's mighty dolled up. Maybe she thought they were going to take her picture today. "Don't worry. This is going to be great."

"If you say so," Brandi says and heads for her car.

TEN

They had decided that committee meetings would be held every two weeks on Thursdays unless circumstances required otherwise. Max looks around the table at his new host committee.

■

Two weeks earlier on January 24th, Max had met with co-chairs Brandi and Gupta to solidify their commitment to those posts and expand on ancillary responsibilities. As with most events, nothing happens around the holidays. It was the soonest he was able to get a meeting on both women's calendars. He had prepared two documents: one for the co-chair position and one for host committee members. Max went over the primary responsibilities of being a co-chair:

Meet an event fundraising goal of a minimum of $25,000 through personal or corporate donation and/or securing support from other individuals or corporations.

Attend all event committee meetings.

Provide NCF with a personal solicitation list rated for targeted solicitation levels.

Allow the use of your name, company affiliation and photo to promote and publicize the event.

Attend event and participate in the program.

In addition to these, Max outlined the following secondary responsibilities:

Assist in the solicitation of 1-5 host committee members.

Assist in the procurement of at least one night-of-event live auction item valued at a minimum of $2,500. Also, consider procuring items for the silent auction (no minimum value). There will be 5-6 items in the live auction and 15-20 items in the silent auction.

As to the responsibilities of a host committee member, Max went over these provisions:

Meet an event fundraising goal of a minimum of ten tickets at $500 each or equivalent through personal or corporate donation and/ or securing support from other individuals or corporations.

Attend all event committee meetings.

Provide NCF with a personal solicitation list rated for targeted solicitation levels.

Allow the use of your name to promote and publicize the event.

Likewise the host committee had secondary responsibilities:

Assist in the solicitation of 1-2 additional host committee members.

Assist in the procurement of at least one night-of-event silent auction item. There will be 15-20 silent auction items.

Brandi was fine with all of the above. Gupta not so much.

"I don't think we should require the host committee to pledge to raise a minimum dollar amount. I don't mind making that kind of commitment myself, but I don't want to have to ask people who I know to do that."

Max is a big believer in using "job descriptions," as he calls them. You have to set the ground rules and let people know what is expected. You have to give them a goal to shoot for. His motto in these matters is, "You don't ask, you don't get." So many volunteers want to just ask people to do as much as they are comfortable with. In Max's experience, when that is done, most people are comfortable with buying a ticket, if that. Still, he knew he needed to step carefully.

"How do you think we could best modify it?" Max asked Gupta.

"Get rid of the ten ticket part. Just say, help sell tickets."

"Okay," Max said slowly. "I'll send you the revision."

Branching off of that conversation, they had next focused on the pricing structure and naming levels. After several minutes of conversation and uninspired suggestions, they decided that the $25,000 level would be called Gold Sponsors, a $10,000 gift would be billed as a Silver Sponsor. Individual tickets would go for $500 with full tables of ten discounted at $4,500.

At the same meeting, they decided on the name for the event, at which point Margo had joined, too. As with the process of naming giving levels, a number of suggestions were made. *Sundown on Cancer Gala* was put forth. Max thought it was too depressing. He suspected everyone else did as well, judging from the way they pondered it for too long with no one having the nerve to say that it stunk.

Others that bubbled up were *Wave of Hope Summer Party, High Tide of Hope, Hamptons Soiree, Midsummer Bash...*

Somebody made a suggestion with the word *dune* in it. Nobody picked up on the suggestion but everyone picked up on the word *dune*. It became *dune* this and *dune* that.

Margo said, "*Boogie on the Dunes.*" There was a pause as people considered this.

"That's good," Gupta said. "But I'm not sure about the word boogie."

"*Festive in the Dunes*," Max said.

There was silence.

Then Brandi said, "I like it."

"Me, too," said Gupta.

"It's decided then," Margo announced. Quickly, she added, "We can always change it later."

Thank you, Margo, Max thought as he wrote the name down on his pad. *You really know how to seal the deal.*

At the close of the meeting, Max reminded the women that the next meeting would be in two weeks on February 7th.

"Hopefully, by then, we'll have some host committee members joining us," he added.

"I'm thinking of three women I can ask," Gupta said.

Looking somewhat guilty, Brandi said, "I don't know. I'll have to think about it." She stood and put the host committee job description in her purse.

Despite her not responding positively, Max thought that was a hopeful sign. He did not find it very hopeful that Gupta left the job description on the table. Max would revise it for her, taking out the ten ticket proviso but he knew, at that moment, she was not going to mention that there were any requirements to joining the host committee.

FEBRUARY 7TH

The new faces looking back at him number three. True to her word, they are Gupta's recruits: Barbara Babette, Katie Scanlon and Cherry Akers. Max asks them to say something about themselves by way of introduction. They are all single women. All three live and work in the city. None has any connection to the Hamptons. True to her initial assertion that she didn't know anyone, Brandi has recruited none. Still, she had recruited Gupta and that had been above and beyond.

Max asks the three if they have personal solicitation lists for him.

They look back at him, mystified. This confirms for him his suspicion that Gupta told them absolutely NOTHING about what is expected of a committee member. It's already too late to correct the situation. He can't undermine Gupta. At least he knows what he's dealing with from the outset and won't waste too much time on these three. From this moment forward, Max associates Barbara, Katie and Cherry with a term that he borrows from his Kennedy Center days: "dead wood."

Max hands out copies of the latest financial report.

"As you can see, we are off to a good start. Ninety-one thousand, to date, paid and pledged."

The report is organized on a spreadsheet, each line representing a single donation. The donor's name and company affiliation, if any, are followed by the name of the contact responsible for getting the gift. Leading off are two $25,000 Gold Sponsors: Vulcan Partners, Anthony Napoli's agency and Stratton Global, Anthony's friend, Oscar Stratton's public relations firm. Both gifts are flagged in the contact field for *Napoli*. In fact, every entry except one is credited to Brandi. The exception is Gupta's own personal pledge of a $10,000 Silver Sponsorship. Brandi looks up from the report at Max and wrinkles up her face, confused.

Max closes the meeting by reminding everyone about the kickoff reception a week from Friday. "I've put your names on the guest list, so all you have to do is show up."

Brandi catches Max's eye and gives him a significant look. After everyone else has left, Brandi and Max are alone in the conference room.

"Ten thousand dollars! Are you kidding me?"

"That's just her personal gift," Max replies.

"It's supposed to be twenty-five thousand!"

"She said she's committed to the twenty-five. This is just from her."

"And what about others? What's she doing? There's no other money on this list with her name attached!" Brandi says smacking the paper with the back of her hand.

"We're all excited about the way you're leading the charge, Brandi. But people work differently. We didn't say it had to come in as one gift. Gupta still has time to make good on her pledge."

"She told me she was in for twenty-five. I don't know about you, but where I come from twenty-five thousand doesn't start with a one followed by four zeros."

ELEVEN

FRIDAY, FEBRUARY 15, 2013
6:08 p.m.
UPPER EAST SIDE
MANHATTAN, NY

Max stands in the lobby of the building. Behind him is a skirted registration table. Behind the table sit two young women from the public relations firm Margo hired from her own budget that is working with NCF on *Festive in the Dunes*. Behind them is a sea of goodie bags. Max greets guests as they enter. The invitation list was created by the PR firm and Max knows no one except for Gladys and Margo who are upstairs at the party. Of course, Brandi and Gupta are also there, with their husbands.

As guests are checked in, they are each handed a goodie bag and directed to the elevators and told to press the button for the penthouse. The PR firm has worked with a real estate development office to secure the penthouse apartment. The two-bedroom apartment, which has exclusive access to a full roof deck, is on the market for some million dollar number that Max was told but has forgotten. "Goodie bag" is something of a misnomer as there are no real goodies inside. Other than a piece of tissue paper and health bar, the bags contain NCF literature. The main purpose of the bags is they have a save the date card for *Festive in the Dunes*. The point of the bags, of the whole kickoff reception, is to announce *Festive in the Dunes* and get a save the date card in every attendee's hand. The PR firm had requested seventy-five cards. Max had hand-delivered one hundred fifty to their office in Manhattan, just to be safe. Looking at the bags, Max thinks it looks like more than seventy-five. *Maybe when they're stuffed and laid out like that, they look like more,* he thinks. Satisfied that check-in seems to be under control, Max heads for the elevators.

The elevator for the penthouse is clearly identified by a sign on a metal stanchion. It has been specially keyed for the evening to go directly between the street and the penthouse. Once the doors close, off it goes.

The elevator doors open into the foyer of the apartment. A coat rack with hangers is positioned off to one side. There are about two dozen coats there. *It's still early,* Max thinks.

■

At the small bar set up in front of the fireplace he orders a glass of red wine. Seeing Gladys in the dining room, he walks over to her.

"Max, I'd like you to meet my fiancée," Gladys says. Standing next to her is a darkly complexioned woman in her thirties with shoulder-length dark hair. She and Gladys look enough alike to be sisters. Max can't hide his surprise. He didn't know Gladys is gay!

"I didn't know you were…getting married," he hears himself saying with relief to Gladys. Quickly he adds, "Pleased to meet you," extending his hand to her fiancée.

"Ingrid Casales," she says, shaking his hand.

"August twenty-fourth. You're coming," Gladys says.

"Well…I certainly am," Max says.

"Would you ladies like to have a look at the roof terrace?" They turn to see a young man in a blue blazer with the real estate agency's pin on his lapel.

Gladys looks to Ingrid and then back at the young man. "Sure."

"Just go back out through the foyer. To the right of the elevator you will see an open door and stairs. And don't forget to grab your coats. It's chilly up there."

"Okay," Gladys says as she and Ingrid deposit their empty wine glasses on a small tray stand.

"How about you, sir?" the man says to Max.

"Maybe in a few minutes," Max says, nodding to Gladys and Ingrid as they go.

Max suddenly notices that the apartment has gotten quite full and is not nearly as spacious as it first appeared. *So this is what a few mil gets you in Manhattan.*

Through the open kitchen door, Max spots Gupta standing at the center island. He walks into the kitchen.

"Good evening," he says to Gupta.

Gupta leans in and gives him a peck on the cheek. Max is surprised. *This is the first time she's done that*, he thinks. Maybe it's the wine. Maybe it's the ambience. One thing he is sure of, once this door has been opened, there will be no going back. From this point forward, cheek bussing will be *de rigueur* not only with Gupta but Brandi as well. The host committee, too? *I'll cross that bridge when I get to it, thank you very much.*

"Honey, this is Max," Gupta says to the man she is standing with. "My husband, Bradley," she says to Max.

"So, this is Max. Mighty Max. Let me shake your hand," Bradley says. And he does. "You're the man who is going to lead us into the wilderness and spawn a brand-new event, like conjuring manna from heaven."

Max laughs. "Something like that."

"And in the Hamptons, no less. I have to warn you, it's a tough sandbox."

"I know. I've done this before."

"Well, then you should be fine. But seriously, I want you to know that we are in to help make this a big success." Bradley raises his wine glass.

Max clinks glasses with Bradley. "Thank you," Max says. "That's what I like to hear."

Max turns to include Gupta in the toast but she now seems very interested in her shoes.

A man's voice comes in from the living room. "Ladies and gentlemen, may I have your attention please?"

Gupta, Bradley and Max push into the dining room which has become quite crowded. Over a sea of heads, Max sees one of the partners from the PR firm standing in the far corner of the living room. He is holding a wireless microphone. The room has quieted but there is still some burbling.

The man comes back in a slightly louder voice, "I would like to welcome you to this evening's gathering and to introduce a co-chair of NCF's *Festive in the Dunes, Inaugural Hamptons Summer Bash*, Brandi Napoli."

Brandi steps up and takes the microphone from the man. There is light applause.

"Thank you and welcome, everyone. We really appreciate your coming out on this cold February evening. But our thoughts tonight are not on frigid New York City winter winds but on the balmy breezes we'll be having on July thirteenth in Southampton. That will be the occasion of the first-ever Hamptons event for the benefit of the National Cancer Foundation, *Festive in the Dunes*. I won't bore you with the details. It's all on the save the date cards in your goodie bags. But there are some people I would like to acknowledge for their participation in making tonight's kickoff reception possible. First, Ross Flanders Public Relations for organizing tonight's party. Second, Whitby Properties for providing this fabulous apartment for us to frolic in…It is fabulous, isn't it?"

There is applause.

"And last but not least, I want to thank *Avenue* magazine in advance for promoting our little shindig. Now don't feel you have to rush off. Have another glass of wine, an hors d'oeuvre, chat with old friends and meet some new ones. And most important, mark July thirteenth on your calendars when we will meet again in Southampton. Bye."

There is applause. Brandi hands the microphone back to the PR guy.

In the dining room, Max stands shocked. Given that this event was completely the work of the PR agency, Max had nothing to do with the speaking program. But what were they thinking? Brandi and Gupta should have been introduced together. Or, when Brandi was finished, she should have invited Gupta up to say a few words. *Christ, she didn't even mention her*!

Max looks at Gupta. She is giving her husband a hard look. Now it's Bradley who seems to have developed a keen interest in his shoes.

After Brandi's remarks, the room clears out substantially. Max is in the living room when Brandi comes up behind him, putting an arm through one of his.

"Let me buy you a drink, Max."

Brandi steers him to the bar.

"What's your pleasure?" the bartender asks Brandi.

Brandi defers to Max. "Red wine," he says.

"White for me," Brandi says.

The bartender pours their wines and hands them across the bar. Brandi and Max move away.

"So? How do you think it went?"

"Very well. We got a good-sized crowd," Max replies.

"I hope a lot of ticket buyers."

"I'm getting a copy of the invite list from tonight to add to our database."

"Good," Brandi says.

After a moment, "There is one thing I am curious about," Max says.

Brandi looks at him quizzically.

"I was kind of expecting that Gupta would get up and say something."

"Like what?"

"Well…as co-chair…welcome people. Whose idea was that? The PR firm?"

"What difference does it make?"

"Frankly, Brandi, I think it was a mistake."

"You're right about that. She's the one who made it."

"It's still early in the game. We have to give her a chance to do her job. It's not going to get us anywhere to just toss her out of the boat."

"I'm not tossing anyone out of any boat."

"I met her husband, Bradley. He seems like a nice guy."

"He is a nice guy," Brandi agrees.

"I think they're going to come through."

"What did he say?"

"We're in to help make this a big success."

"Who do you think he meant by 'we'?"

"He and Gupta."

Brandi closes her eyes, smirking and shaking her head. "No. He meant you and me. And he's right. We are going to make this a big success." She raises her glass.

Oh, shit. This is going to be one hell of a ride! Max clinks glasses with Brandi.

TWELVE

THURSDAY, FEBRUARY 21, 2013
6:04 p.m.
NCF OFFICE, CONFERENCE ROOM
MIDTOWN MANHATTAN, NY

Cherry Akers excitedly announces that she has a lead on getting donated bedsheets. There is a unanimous show of uncomprehending looks from around the table.

"The bidding on that should go through the roof," Brandi says sarcastically.

"Not for the auction," Cherry adds. "For the tables."

"I don't follow," Margo says.

"A good friend of mine from work is having a baby," Cherry explains. "We had a shower for her at our office last month. They set up round tables like they do for board meetings, with white table cloths." She turns to Max. "What color cloths are we getting from the caterer?"

"White," Max replies.

"Good!" Cherry says. "One of the woman's clients is a bedding company. She got them to donate flat sheets to be used as top cloths for the tables. They gave her one for each table. We got some pinking shears and one day on lunch break a bunch of us cut the sheets into squares to fit over the white cloths. It was a pink floral pattern—she's having a girl. They were so cute."

There is an appreciative murmur around the table.

"It's brilliant! I love it!" Margo shrieks.

"When will you know if you can get them?" Gupta asks.

"I've already spoken to the woman and she thinks it's a no-brainer. How many tables are we planning on having?" Cherry asks Max.

"The club holds twenty-two to twenty-four tables. We should plan for spoilage—I'd see if you can get at least twenty-five sheets."

"See if they have something beach-themed," Margo says.

"I'll ask," Cherry replies.

Max knows how these "brilliant" ideas that come out of committees go. Everyone's enthusiastic until it's time to actually make it happen. Then no one can be found. "Who's going to cut up the sheets?" he asks.

"Have them sent to me," Brandi jumps right in. "The Water Mill address. I'll invite some of my girlfriends over one Saturday. Get a couple bottles of wine. We'll nail it."

At the end of the meeting, people file out. Gupta remains in her seat engrossed on her phone. Brandi, too, is in her chair applying a fresh coat of lipstick. Satisfied with the results she sees in her compact, she closes it and stands.

"Good meeting, Max," she says. "Bye," she throws over her shoulder and goes.

Max deposits his meeting folder in his bag and stands. As he opens his mouth to say goodbye to Gupta, she cuts him off.

"Can we talk for a minute?"

"Sure," he says, sitting back down.

Gupta puts her phone down.

"She snapped that right out of Cherry's hands, didn't she?" Gupta says.

"Uh…I guess. I was just glad someone volunteered to cut up the sheets."

"Which she will, no doubt, take all the credit for. Make everyone believe it was her idea and isn't she clever?"

"Maybe we can suggest she invite the host committee out to her house to help."

"Those women are my friends. They're only doing this because I asked them. They don't live in the Hamptons and they are not going all the way out there to cut up bedsheets."

"Maybe Brandi would consider doing it at her apartment in the city."

"Can't you control her?" Gupta accuses, cutting through the crap.

Max steels himself for what's coming next. She is going to demand an explanation of why she had no part in welcoming guests to the kickoff party one week earlier. Max firmly believes that when he is running an event he takes full responsibility for anything that goes amiss. He never resorts to shifting the blame. He feels, even if it gets him off, in the end it diminishes him in others' eyes. However, the truth is he had no say in the program for that party. For any aspect of the party. Everything was handled by the PR firm from conception through execution. It wasn't that he had no contact with them but they are being paid by Margo. She is their master's voice. They don't need to listen to him or clear anything with him. A sinking feeling comes over Max. He looks across the table at Gupta. Her eyes seem to be sizing him up, wondering if he is strong enough to back her. Frankly, he isn't sure. It occurs to him that in this moment he could be losing control of his own event. He waits for her attack.

When she speaks, Gupta says, "You need to know that I am seriously considering bailing on this whole thing."

No! That would be a disaster! Not just because of the loss of the $25,000…well, Max the fundraiser reconsiders. Yes, because of that. But more. After all the time and energy put into getting to this point it would be seen as a major setback. Margo and Gladys would lose confidence in him. They would see this as his fault. Gupta's three host committee members would be history. Despite Cherry's bedsheets, Max still sees them as "dead wood" but at least they're names on an invitation. It could also affect Brandi. Yes, she's giving Gupta a hard time. But she recruited her all on her own because she doesn't want to be alone in this. Max has seen it happen before. If a volunteer feels that the entire weight of an event is on their shoulders, they become resentful. They feel that they are being taken advantage of. They pull away. Brandi could even drop out herself! This is serious.

"I think you, Brandi and I need to talk. Just the three of us. Before the next committee meeting. Some evening next week," Max says.

Gupta stares up at the ceiling. After a moment, "I'm free every day except Wednesday. It's my bowling night."

Notwithstanding the gravity of the situation, Max almost bursts out laughing. That was the last thing he expected from this woman. Who is on her team? Is it all society women like her? Could that possibly be? One thing years of working with rich and influential people had taught him is, never be surprised. She *is* originally from Ohio. Still, he wonders, could Park Avenue conceivably have lanes?

"Thursdays seems to work for you and Brandi. Shall we pencil it in and I'll confirm once I've checked with her?"

Gupta picks her phone up off the table to make the entry on her calendar.

THIRTEEN

Max checks his watch. Exactly 6:00 p.m. Both Brandi and Gupta are seated at the conference table waiting for him to begin. *This is a good omen. Both on time.*

"Thank you both for coming. I thought it would be beneficial for just us to get together and talk to each other a little bit about why we are involved with this event and what we hope to get out of it. I'll start. Why am I involved with this event? That's easy—it's my job. What do I hope to get out of the experience? I hope to have a successful event. By that I mean exceeding the dollar goal, which as you both know is one hundred thousand net. I also mean successful in terms of selling out the room to be able to message to a new audience for the foundation and, hopefully, make some new friends. I also count on our success propelling us forward so we will be able to establish *Festive in the Dunes* as an annual event. Crucial to that factor is that everyone involved, most especially both of you as co-chairs, comes away with a good feeling of having had a positive experience." Max looks at both of them for a moment to let his words sink in and create the right direction. "Anyone else?"

Both women sit staring at the gleaming surface of the conference table. Then Brandi looks up at Max.

"As you know I am on the Special Events Committee, here, in the Manhattan office. When I heard the foundation was planning to have a new event in the Hamptons, I thought it was a great opportunity for me to step up and get more involved. But now, let me ask you a question. I thought this was a Manhattan event and that Ceci and some of the other gals on that committee would get involved but that doesn't seem to be happening."

"Forgive me if I was not clearer in explaining the situation at the beginning," Max says. "I work for the Suffolk County office. NCF, like most national nonprofits, is organized regionally. With the Hamptons being in Suffolk County the gala is, by definition, a Suffolk County event."

"So that's why, uh—"

"Gladys."

"—is involved?"

"She's my boss."

"So why is Margo involved? Who does she work for?"

"Margo works for the Gotham Division which includes New York City, Long Island and New Jersey. It is my understanding that because so many organizations do events out there, she thought that we were missing an opportunity by not also having one."

Max glances at Gupta. She has not looked up but he senses she is as disinterested in this conversation as he. He needs to get Brandi back on track.

"So, Brandi, you say you joined the event to get more involved with the foundation?" Max restates for clarification.

"Yes. Because one of my girlfriends was diagnosed with breast cancer last year. I wanted to do everything I could. She lives in Vegas but I am hoping that she can come."

"I didn't know that," Max says. "Gupta, did you?"

Gupta looks up at Brandi. "No, I didn't. How is she doing?"

"So far so good. She's doing chemo now which is a bitch but her doctors are very positive."

"That's great," Gupta says.

Brandi smiles at her. She reaches out and places a hand over one of Gupta's and gives it a squeeze.

Alright! This is good. This is good. "Gupta? Would you like to share?"

"I spend most of my time in the city. Working, friends, social life. However, Bradley and I are expecting a baby later this year."

Brandi gives a doubtful look at Gupta's belly.

"Through a surrogate," Gupta continues. "When that happens, I am going to be out on the East End most of the time. When you asked me to co-chair," she says to Brandi, "I thought it was a good chance for me to get more involved in the community."

"And what would each of you like to get out of the experience?" Max asks.

Brandi shrugs her shoulders. "A great event."

"A great event," Gupta seconds her.

"That makes three of us," Max says.

There is a pause. Then Brandi says, "Look, I know I can be a little aggressive. That's my nature. When there's something to be done, I want to get right on it. My husband's always telling me that I need to be more aware of other people's sensibilities. I'll try."

Max is very pleased this has gone so well. It's time to leave them laughing.

"Are we done here?" he asks.

Brandi ignores him. "I know you were probably angry with me the other night at the party," she says to Gupta. "But I swear I had nothing to do with it. They just handed me the mike. No discussion. When you didn't come up to say something, I thought you didn't want to."

"Please, Brandi, forget about it. I have."

"Can I give you a piece of advice?"

Gupta nods.

"Be a little more…assertive. With fundraising, with everything. Talk to the guys at the PR firm. Tell them what you want. Don't be shy. They're working for us."

"Okay," Gupta says with little enthusiasm.

"What are you having?" Brandi asks.

"Boy," Gupta beams.

"That's so sweet."

Actually, Brandi, the PR guys are working for Margo, Max thinks ruefully. That was a nice, believable explanation Brandi just gave. But why would they want to ignore one of the co-chairs? Isn't that bad client management? Unless that's what the client wanted. But why would Margo want to cut Gupta out? Money? With all but $10,000 raised so far coming from Brandi, she is clearly the horse to back. But why get into that? It does us no good to play volunteers off each other. Not that Max isn't above using a little shame to prime the pump. He has always let everyone involved know where the money is coming from—who is producing and who is not. Fomenting an atmosphere of gladiatorial competition is what separates the fundraisers from the flops. But deliberately sidelining a volunteer, especially a co-chair, makes no sense. Knowing how Brandi felt about Gupta going into the kickoff party, Max isn't so sure he's buying Brandi's explanation. Gauging by Gupta's reaction, he isn't so sure she is either.

"Max," Brandi's voice cuts into his reverie.

Max looks up. Brandi has both arms extended, palms out, looking pointedly at the center of the table.

"What happened to the cookies?" she says.

FOURTEEN

THURSDAY, MARCH 7, 2013
6:12 p.m.
NCF OFFICE, CONFERENCE ROOM
MIDTOWN MANHATTAN, NY

AGENDA
Festive in the Dunes
Committee Meeting
3/7/13

- *Dan's Papers* to run story about Camp Quest and *Festive in the Dunes* at end of April.
- Financial update: $111,000 paid & pledged/112 expected attendance.
- Brandi to write letter to Shirley Eckstein at Corcoran regarding sponsorship and send to Max to be put on NCF stationery and mail out.
- Max to revise sponsorship solicitation letter for Brandi and Gupta to reflect a more global mission of NCF (beyond East

End) and add their contact information below their signatures.

- Max to send sponsorship letter to Howard Schultz, Starbucks, over Brandi's signature.
- Brandi to contact Brown, Harris, Stevens for sponsorship if Corcoran turns us down.
- Gupta to invite her friend Frieda to be on the host committee.
- Max to check current Johnson & Johnson involvement with NCF.
- Send sponsorship solicitation letters to King Kullen, Waldbaum's, Citarella.
- Max to check about getting Opus One to be wine sponsor.
- Margo to take Louise Rosen to brunch. She is with Douglas Elliman and a contact to the fashion industry. Margo to sound her out about participation in event—possible donation to auction.
- Brandi to have lunch with friends to try to enlist support for event (see her email dated 2/18)
- Draft letters for Margo re: host committee to go to: Joy Feldman, Vicky Grey and Colleen Bancroft (Skadden, Arps-NYC).
- Bistrians (farm family that got rich) owns East Hampton Point and East Hampton Golf Club—possible auction items.
- Margo to get name of man from Ernst & Young who she sat next to at 2012 NJ Bucket of Hope Luncheon at which their drug company client was being honored and who lives near her in Westhampton Beach.
- Other.
- Next meeting: Thursday, 3/21, 6:00 p.m., Manhattan.

Max has placed an agenda in front of everyone in addition to a copy of the latest financial report. So far, Brandi, Gupta and Margo have arrived, along with host committee members Barbara Babette and

Cherry Akers. Max glances at his watch and decides to begin. "Dead wood" who show up late don't matter. Max leads off with the news about the Camp Quest article that is slated to appear in *Dan's Papers* at the end of April. This item is greeted by general approval. Max believes in starting out on a positive note, so he follows this with the financial update.

"We've picked up ten thousand since the last report," Brandi notices. "Where did that come from? It just says NCF next to it."

Max is only too happy to respond. "Joan Lawrence sits on the Suffolk County board. She had expressed to me an early interest in the event. I sent her a solicitation letter asking for a Silver Sponsorship. It's from her and her husband Richard's family foundation."

"Good man," Brandi compliments Max.

Margo is looking down at her copy of the financial report. Her face is scrunched up as if she is smelling a big turd on it. She gives Max a hostile look.

"The Lawrences are deeply invested at the Gotham Division level. I've arranged for them to visit Tranquil Cove on numerous occasions. This is no surprise," Margo says to counter any credit coming Max's way.

I can't believe she is trying to steal credit for this! Max thinks. Or, as is often her way, leaving everyone with the impression that this is because of her. He had invited the Lawrences to the kickoff party and they had come. While he was talking to them Margo had walked up. She may possibly have known who they were but they, clearly, had no idea who she was. Confirmed by them greeting her with "Nice to meet you." *Whatever*!

Max launches into the rest of the agenda which is mostly focused on various items of sponsorship solicitation and volunteer recruitment. Once he has gotten through all of that, Max announces the penultimate item that usually precedes the next meeting date—the omnibus "other."

Cherry, who's been looking like she was about ready to burst for the past five minutes, pipes right up.

"The sheets are in!"

This is followed by a chorus of "oohs."

"They sent me their *Under the Sea Collection*." Cherry looks around the table at the others for their reaction. Margo gives her a wink.

"That's super," Barbara says.

"What color are they?" Brandi asks.

"Teal."

"Teal should look wonderful in that room," Gupta says. "Thank you so much for doing that."

Cherry glows.

"You've got my Water Mill address?" Brandi says.

"Of course. But, are you sure you want to take this, too? You've got so much else going on. I'm sure the host committee would be happy to handle this," Cherry says, looking to the only other member present.

Brandi pulls herself up straight in her chair, sucking in her cheeks. "I was happy to volunteer to do this. I thought it was acceptable to everyone. But, if not…"

"No, Brandi, you should do it. I've already put you down for it," Max cuts her off abruptly. Max doesn't know if Gupta suggested to Cherry that she make this offer but after having gotten Brandi and Gupta to agree to work together, he is not about to let another issue arise to have them at each other's throats again.

"Sure, I'll mail them tomorrow," Cherry says.

"Send the postal receipt to me," Max tells Cherry. "I'll reimburse you."

He says to all, "If there's nothing else, our next meeting is in two weeks, Thursday, three twenty-one."

FIFTEEN

At successive meetings, Max takes his committee through the evolving agendas. The main items are fairly constant: sponsorship solicitation, volunteer recruitment, financial updates, silent auction item updates and suggestions, liquor, beer and wine donations, vendor support of printing, audio-visual presentation, décor, etc. In all cases, the more that can be secured as donations or pro bono services, the better. As things are accomplished, those items retire. As new ideas are suggested and accepted, they appear.

One significant development that Max is able to announce at their meeting on 3/21/13 is the recruitment of a silent auction chair. She is Mary Taylor and is a member of the Suffolk County board. Gladys recruited her.

Back in January, Brandi had secured pro bono design and

reduced-priced printing services through her husband's advertising firm, Vulcan Partners. Then at the committee meeting on 4/4/13, she confirms that she has gotten audio-visual services, also through her husband's company. On 5/2/13, Brandi reports that she has booked the band, The Touch. Naturally, they aren't going to appear for free. Musicians never do. However, she used them for her daughter's birthday party last year and they are giving her a good price.

"Get the contract to me," Max says. "I'll have a purchase order made up."

Per usual, Brandi is letting no grass grow under her feet in getting things done. The manner in which she is doing them, though, has a downside. By presenting them as *faits accomplis* at meetings, she is marginalizing the rest of the group. Max can hardly say that he is unhappy that things are moving along. However, at the meeting on 3/21/13, the next one after Cherry had said that the sheets were in and Brandi told her to send them to her, something occurs that does make him uneasy. As was his custom, Max has made "other" the last item on the agenda right before the date of the next meeting. He is hoping that Brandi will use that slot to give an update on the status of the sheets/top cloths. When she does not, Max asks, "Did you get the sheets, Brandi?"

"Yes."

"Any progress on that?"

"No. I haven't talked to my friends yet."

After that, Max figures it best he hold her feet to the fire about this and ditches the subtlety of "other" in favor of an agenda item of "top cloth status." This first appears on the agenda at the 4/4/13 meeting. When they reach that part of the meeting and Brandi doesn't volunteer any information, Max asks directly.

Reading "top cloth status" off the agenda, Max looks at Brandi.

"Any updates?" he says.

"No."

4/18/13 meeting:

Max: "Any progress with the top cloths?"

Brandi ignores his question. She is involved in a deep sidebar conversation with Cherry that he can't easily break into.

5/2/13 meeting:

Max: "Have you had your cloth-cutting party yet?"

Brandi: "The friends I'm trying to reach have been away."

5/16/13 meeting:

Max: "And, finally, the ever-popular top cloth topic."

Brandi: "Not yet but I'll let you know," she says flashing Max a frozen smile.

Max can see that this is annoying her and decides that he will continue to put it on the agenda but won't ask. He'll wait for her to volunteer that information. Knowing her, he really has no choice.

▪

One evening, leaving his office in Islandia, Max decides to stop at a liquor store to pick up a bottle of wine for dinner before getting on the highway. As he walks into the store, he is stopped short by a large display opposite the front door. It is for a wine called *Beach Buggy*. It is not a brand he has ever heard of and it is certainly not a label that he is looking for. At first, he is not even sure why it arrested him so thoroughly. Then it hits him. *What a perfect brand for a beach party? Beach Buggy wine? Yes!* Max chooses a bottle of cabernet. He scans the label. It's from California. Unfortunately, it is not from the North Fork of Long Island. That is where the committee has been focusing on in getting wine donated. Still, they have distribution on the Island. And, so far, the volunteers have come up short with this piece. Max decides to get what information he can off the label, check them out on the Internet and get a request out to them for a donation. At the meeting on 5/30/13, Max informs the group of his discovery and that he has sent an online request for them to be the exclusive wine sponsor of the National Cancer Foundation's *Festive in the Dunes, Inaugural Hamptons Summer Bash.*

"It's purrfect," Margo purrs.

"I'm going to give it two weeks and then I'll follow up with a phone call," Max says.

SIXTEEN

TUESDAY, JUNE 11, 2013
2:47 p.m.
NAPOLI RESIDENCE
WATER MILL, NY

The next meeting on 6/11/13 is held at Brandi's house. Because of this, the meeting is called for 2:00 p.m. instead of 6:00 p.m. This gives those coming from further in time for the round trip. Also, because of a conflict Brandi has on Thursday, the meeting has been moved up to Tuesday. Brandi has put a pitcher of mimosas at a wrought iron and glass patio set out by the pool. In attendance, in addition to Brandi, are Gupta, Margo, Gladys and Max. Gladys and Max have driven out from their office in Islandia in separate cars. They have been meeting for over forty minutes when they get to the item on the agenda concerning the wine donation. Max says that he is calling *Beach Buggy Wines* in the morning to follow up.

"You're a little late," Brandi says.

"What do you mean?" Max says.

"I already called and got the wine donated."

Max is stunned. This was his idea, his initiative. He was on it. He has always given two weeks between submitting a request and following up. That's what he announced he was doing at the last meeting. If you did it too soon, you usually ended up getting nowhere because your ask hadn't reached the right person yet. He is glad that the wine has been secured but he feels sandbagged by Brandi. They talk and email all the time. If she thought waiting two weeks was too long, she could have told him so and asked him to get back sooner. She hadn't mentioned anything. He tries to put the best face on it that he can.

"Congratulations!" he says, clapping his hands. "Great news."

Brandi looks across the table at him with an unmistakable smirk.

"Give me the details and I'll arrange for delivery," Max says.

"Oh no, booby. I gave that to Cherry. She knows how to get things done."

Max does not respond. He looks around. Margo is checking her manicure. Gladys seems mesmerized by the bubbles that the aeration hose is causing in the pool. Only Gupta looks at him. Max thinks he sees a trace of *schadenfreude* in her eyes. *Shit! Now I'm going to have to call "dead wood" Cherry for the information to follow up. I'll be damned if I'm going to entrust that to her!*

"How many cases did you request?" Max asks.

"Six."

Max had calculated four bottles per table based on a setup of twenty-five tables. Using those numbers he figured they needed one hundred bottles. That meant a little over eight cases. He had planned on asking for nine.

"That's not enough wine for dinner," Gupta steals the words out of Max's mouth.

"I spoke to Andy. He said that six was right," Brandi says defensively.

There is a designated caterer for the club. Andy Fox is the partner handling their event. For the second time in as many minutes, Max feels the unease of discovering that Brandi has gone behind his back.

"And then there's the bar to consider," Gupta adds.

"I don't know about anyone else, but I'm hot. Let's continue this inside," Brandi says, getting up and heading for the French doors.

Once inside, they gather around the table in the kitchen. Brandi has successfully quashed any further discussion of the wine and Max feels that it is best to just let it drop for now.

"Okay. So we're up to master of ceremonies. Anyone have anything to report on that front?" Max asks.

There is a momentary silence, broken by Brandi.

"Where did this master of ceremonies crap come from? It's emcee."

Yet again, Max is caught flat-footed. "Master of Ceremonies" has been the line item on their meeting agendas from day one. What's gotten into Brandi? First getting ambushed by her over the wine donation and now this? Still, Max thinks about all the entries on the financial report flagged with her name and decides he is not going to let her drag him into this sand trap.

Max crosses through "Master of Ceremonies" on his agenda and writes "Emcee" above it.

"If you prefer emcee," he says making the correction, "no problem. After all that's what it stands for."

Max looks at Brandi and sees an expression of surprise on her face quickly followed by fury.

Holy shit. She didn't know that's what emcee stands for. He hadn't said it to be confrontational. On the contrary, he was trying his damnedest to be accommodating. But that was, evidently, not the way Brandi took it. For a long moment no one says anything during which the image of Brandi's reaction is seared into Max's consciousness as what he would come to think of as the "emcee face."

"Gupta, how about Matt Lauer? Did you ever get a chance to talk to him?" Max asks.

"Yes, I did. I'm sorry, Max, I forgot to tell you. He won't be around that weekend."

"Who else is on the list?" Brandi asks.

Max looks down at the wish list that he has been asked to prepare of celebrities who have homes in the Hamptons:

Paula Zahn, TV news anchor
Rosanna Scotto, TV news anchor
Joy Behar, comedienne, host, *The Voice*
Andy Cohen, host, *Watch What Happens Next with Andy Cohen*

Max reads from the list. "Paula Zahn, Rosanna Scotto, Joy Behar—"

"I want Joy Behar," Brandi asserts.

"Do you have a way to reach out to her?" Max asks.

"Isn't that your job?" Brandi shoots back.

"I'll find out the name of her management company and send them a letter," Max says, although he knows that it will be a waste of postage.

SEVENTEEN

Max arrives at his desk and immediately logs on to his computer. Once in, he Googles *Top Dogs*. From the list of websites displayed, he chooses one, *USA Network-Top Dogs*. It opens to reveal a slick, colorful page giving a brief synopsis of the television series. Below that is a list of the cast of characters. Leading off the list is "Dr. Sean Templeton" played by actor Nick Firestone.

On his drive into work, Max had heard an ad for the television program. He had never seen it and didn't know anything about it. But the ad had said that it is about a veterinarian and that it is set in NYC and the Hamptons. Max knew that did not necessarily mean that it is shot on the East End—Malibu could be a reasonable stand-in— but he decides that it is worth the effort to find out. Having an actor from a Hamptons-set television show being the master of—whoops, emcee—could be very cool.

The website indicates that the show is shot in NYC and the Hamptons. Therefore, Nick Firestone is probably local. Even if he resides on the West Coast, they could still be in production. Maybe. The website also says that the show is released through NBC Universal. Their offices are at 30 Rockefeller Plaza in the city. Max finds the main number for 30 Rock and calls.

Like a crusader holding his standard before him, Max uses the word "cancer" as often as possible. All throughout his career, wherever he has worked, Max has learned the value of using the organization's cause as a door opener. In the relatively short time he has been at NCF, he has come to benefit from the particular value of the word "cancer." Most people have had a personal experience with it either themselves or through someone near and dear. By making clear that the only reason for his call is to help in the fight against the dreaded disease, surely even the most cynical New Yorker will be moved to at least listen. After nearly thirty minutes of being passed around like a holiday fruitcake, he is finally rewarded by being directed to the in-house agent for *Top Dogs*.

The guy on the other end of the line couldn't have sounded more bored as he says, "Send me the letter."

Max gets it. He's asking for Nick Firestone to work their event for free. The guy's an agent. Ten percent of zero is zero. Be that as it may, Max has found the right person to put his request in front of Nick Firestone. Max is further encouraged when the agent tells him to email the letter to him and gives Max his address.

Max immediately sets to work drafting the letter. Gladys appears at his cubicle.

"What are you working on?" she asks.

Max doesn't want to say. The chances of this happening are remote so there's no point in talking about it. Max has always believed that information can be ammunition that other people can use against you. Max is not sure how Gladys might do that but he doesn't want to find out. The less she knows, the better.

"It's a sponsorship letter Gupta wants me to get out," he says.

"What has she done so far?"

"She's pledged ten thousand, personally, brought in another ten thousand dollar sponsorship and some individual tickets."

"Is that all part of her original commitment of twenty-five?"

"I'm not sure."

"So, she could be done."

"Could be," Max says.

"Where are we?"

"Almost one hundred forty-five, paid and pledged."

"Most of that being from Brandi?"

"Pretty much."

Gladys looks at him sourly. He braces himself for a pep talk. Glancing at his computer screen, "Get the letter out," is all she says and disappears.

And he does get the letter out—the one to NBC Universal. Max doesn't have great hope for its success. Experience has taught him that without having someone with pull making a personal plea, these celebrity asks go nowhere. On the off chance someone knows Nick Firestone, Max sends an email to everyone involved with the event explaining about *Top Dogs* and asks if anyone is in a position to follow up or knows someone who can. Similarly, Max isn't betting the farm that he'll get a response.

Which is why he is thunderstruck, not ten minutes later, when he gets a call from Oscar Stratton.

Oscar is one of the $25,000 Gold Sponsors of *Festive in the Dunes*.

Stratton reveals that he is related to Nick Firestone through his wife. Nick is a cousin. Max tells Oscar that he just emailed a letter to Nick's inside agent at NBC Universal asking for Nick to emcee the event. Max asks Oscar if he would be willing to follow up with Nick directly. "Happy to do it," Oscar replies. Max hangs up, elated. He may soon be able to cross this item off his list.

EIGHTEEN

Max pulls into the parking lot. The BlackBerry in the passenger seat buzzes. Max switches off the ignition, picks up the BlackBerry and looks at the screen. It's Brandi.

"Good morning," Max says.

"We can't meet here, today," Brandi informs him. "I forgot that I was having the floors done. Let's push the meeting up to noon and do it over lunch at the Princess Diner on twenty-seven."

Max retrieves his briefcase from the back seat and closes and locks the car. "I'll alert everyone. It might be a problem for Margo if she's coming from the city," Max says heading for the front door. Inside, he goes to Gladys's office and tells her about the change. She says it won't work for her because she has a meeting out of the office in a half an hour and won't be available. Max goes to his office and calls Gupta and Margo. Gupta is in and is fine with it. As it turns out, Margo is working from her home today in Westhampton Beach so no problem. Max is a little uneasy that Gladys won't be there.

■

He and Margo and Gladys had had a conference call the day before to discuss the agenda for the meeting. The most important agenda item is the speaking program. Whenever the subject had come up, Brandi had always talked about opening the program and welcoming everyone. Max is extremely glad that he can gently move her off that idea by announcing Nick Firestone as the emcee. Nick will open the program. But that wasn't the only part of the program that Brandi had expressed opinions about. She had talked about introducing the Tranquil Cove video, the Camp Quest video, etc. Now Nick would handle most of those duties. But the disturbing thing about Brandi envisioning herself as the factotum of the program is the obvious: she doesn't allow any role for Gupta.

"They're both co-chairs. There has to be a role for each of them," Max had explained on the call.

Max was sitting across from Gladys in her office. They had Margo on speakerphone.

"Absolutely," Margo's voice came over the phone.

"I'll have Nick introduce Brandi first. When she has finished her remarks, I'll have Nick return to the podium and introduce Gupta."

"Agreed," Margo's voice crackled in from the city.

"I just want to make clear that any time discussion of the program came up, Brandi positioned herself as dominating it. This might not jibe with what she has in mind," Max said.

"Well, that's just too bad. It's our program. We could expose ourselves to criticism if we omitted Gupta," Margo said.

"I'm just saying," Max added, "we should be prepared for some pushback."

"You just present it as a done deal and I'm sure Brandi will see reason. Anyhow, what is she going to say with Gupta sitting right there?" Margo said.

After goodbyes, Gladys punched the button on her phone to end the call. "You have your orders," she said.

Max returned to his cubicle satisfied that they had had this conversation. It didn't completely eradicate his unease about Gladys, though. She had said nothing. But he had brought the issue out into the open before both women. He is just praying that by presenting a united front to Brandi it will head off any possible objection.

■

At the Princess Diner, as they are finishing their lunches, Max pulls out his agenda to begin the meeting. He doesn't distribute copies to the women partly because it will be clumsy with lunch plates still in front of them but, mostly, because he wants to announce Nick Firestone's participation as a surprise. He'll give them their copies before they go.

"Since we've just enjoyed a delicious lunch, let's start with menu," he says as a segue. "The caterer has suggested seven passed hors d'oeuvres: assorted sushi, blue corn chips with avocado mousse—"

"Guacamole," Margo cuts him off, dryly. The two other women chuckle.

"Asian green curry crab cakes," Max continues. "Mini truffled grilled cheese, steak or chicken quesadillas—we get both," Max clarifies. "Sirloin cheeseburger, chicken and turkey sliders." Max looks up. "Sound good?"

"Yummy," Margo says. The two other women nod their agreement.

"Pre-plated on the tables will be an appetizer of a salad of Bibb lettuce," Max says.

"For the entrée, we're having swordfish brochettes," Brandi declares. "I already talked to Andy about it."

Another surprise from Brandi, Max thinks. Huddling with the caterer again.

"Swordfish?" Margo asks. "Do you think that's the best choice?"

"I love swordfish," Brandi says.

"I do, too," Margo counters, "But—"

"And it's the only thing besides steak that my husband will eat," Brandi continues.

"Do you think it will be…agreeable to most people?" Margo adds.

"There's a silent second choice if they don't want it," Brandi says.

"It'll be grilled on skewers?" Margo asks, skeptically.

"Skewers? No. Who said anything about skewers?" Brandi says.

"It's what brochette means," Max says before he can stop himself.

Brandi turns and fires skewers at Max.

The "emcee face" again. Fell right into that!

"You might ask Andy if they do grilled filet of swordfish," Margo suggests.

Brandi points a finger at Max. "Grilled filet. Got it, Max?"

Max makes a notation on his agenda. "Got it, Brandi."

The temperature in the room rises a few degrees in the silence that follows.

Margo breaks the tension with, "Good. That's settled. What else have you got, Max?"

"The question of emcee—is no longer a question. As of the other day, Nick Firestone has agreed to do hosting duties," Max announces.

There is a moment's silence, then Margo cries, "You got him! But how? I saw your email but, frankly, I didn't think that was going anywhere."

"It probably wasn't. But then Oscar Stratton got back to me. His wife is Nick's cousin. He made the call," Max grins.

"Congratulations, Max! Way to go!" Margo says.

"I watch *Top Dogs*. He's very good," Gupta says. "That's super, Max."

"I still want Joy Behar."

Everyone turns to look at Brandi.

"We haven't heard back from her management team," Max says.

"Have you followed up?" Brandi asks.

"Yes. I first called last Thursday. Nobody I spoke with knew anything about the letter but I was able to get the name of the person who handles her engagements. I was put through to his office but got his voicemail. I left a message. I called again on Tuesday and left another message," Max explains.

"Call again," Brandi says. "I have a feeling we'll get her. And when we do, you can call this Nick person and tell him thank you but we already have someone."

There is a stunned silence. Then Margo says cautiously, "We can't do that. Not after he's said yes."

"Why not? If we get Joy we certainly don't need two emcees," Brandi points out.

"Exactly," Max hastens to say. "If Joy's people get back to us, we'll ask her to attend as a special guest. Do ten minutes of comedy. That's her strong suit."

Brandi takes this in, not agreeing but not objecting. Looks of relief spread across Gupta and Margo's faces.

"That would be a coup," Margo says, not even convincing herself.

Having avoided that land mine, Max carefully presses on. "So, let's talk about the speaking program. Nick will open and welcome everyone—"

"I told you that I'm going to do that," Brandi cuts him off.

"Yes, you are. After Nick introduces you. It's better than having to introduce yourself. That's the traditional role of an emcee." *Uh-oh*, Max thinks. He didn't catch himself quickly enough. Was he going to get another "emcee face" from Brandi? But how else to handle these things with her? It's so hard to avoid telling her how things are done because there is so much that she simply doesn't know. Max glances furtively at Brandi and sees that, thankfully, she seems to accept this. He continues.

"Then Nick comes back to the podium and introduces Gupta who comes up—"

"Oh, no!" Brandi blurts. She turns on Max. "I told you how this is going to go. I said that she is not going to speak!"

"You don't get to say whether I speak or not!" Gupta says with uncharacteristic zeal. "I've had about enough of you!"

"But we haven't had nearly enough *from* you!" Brandi tosses back.

"I've fulfilled my commitment," Gupta says looking to Max for confirmation.

"That is correct," Max says to the ceiling, not that anyone's paying attention to him.

"Last time I looked, it's still just a pledge." Then Brandi commands Max, "Get an invoice out right away to our friend here."

"How dare you suggest—" Gupta begins.

"It's more than a suggestion," Brandi says with a taunting smile.

Max looks to Margo for support but she just sits there with a stupid grin plastered to her face. *Come on, Margo, where are you? You were doing so well with Nick and the swordfish. But now, when I really need you, when the time for us to stand together like we talked about yesterday has arrived, you're pulling a cocoon.*

"You are both co-chairs of the event," Max says. "An event, I would like to remind everyone, that is for the benefit of the National Cancer

Foundation. As our event, we intend to handle it properly and offer both of you the opportunity to participate in the speaking program. If either of you chooses not to participate, that's your decision. But we need to run this in an equitable manner."

"She has two tables in the room. Two tables! Maybe it'll be three. Out of what? Twenty-two! And she gets the same opportunity to speak as me? How is that equitable?" Brandi's voice has risen to a shout.

"Hey, hold it down over there, ladies." The voice comes from a table of three women sitting in a booth along the wall. "We're trying to have a peaceful lunch."

A chastened silence falls over Max's table.

"Meo-o-o-w," one of the women at the other table says and the rest laugh.

Brandi scoops her purse up off the floor and heads for the ladies' room.

Max calls for the check. They wait for it in silence. When it comes, Brandi has still not emerged from the ladies' room. Max stands and throws some bills on the table for a tip. Margo and Gupta get up.

"When I get to this event, I'm going to order a bottle of vodka and a straw," Margo deadpans. Nobody laughs.

Max goes to the register and pays the check. Margo and Gupta go past him out to the parking lot. When he exits, he sees Margo standing with Gupta next to Gupta's Smart Car. Max walks up to them.

"I'm sorry you had to put up with that," Gupta says to Max.

"It was inevitable," he replies.

■

When Max gets back from the Hamptons, he checks his email. There is one from Brandi sent earlier in the day to Oscar Stratton which she has copied Max on. Max now recalls that Oscar's wife, Charlotte, had introduced Brandi to Gupta at a party at the Strattons' apartment last year. That's how they had met and that is where Brandi had recruited Gupta to be her co-chair for *Festive in the Dunes*.

"I thought I had recruited an Escalade for a co-chair but ended up with a Smart Car—stupid! LOL," the email reads.

"LOL." Not familiar with text shorthand, the first time Brandi had used that in an email to Max he guessed it might mean "lots of love," which he thought completely inappropriate. Upon asking his daughter Gabby what it meant, she had told him "laugh out loud." Trying to find comedy in Brandi's missive he is, in fact, put in mind of several Disney cartoon characters. But not Mickey or Pluto—Maleficent, Cruella de Vil, Ursula the Sea Witch. Or, to cite another movie character, The Blob, growing in size and might with each hapless victim she consumes, leaving a path of destruction as she rolls toward the Southampton Pool and Beach Club and the sea.

Max deletes the email.

NINETEEN

At a meeting which was hastily arranged the day before, Max sits at a table in the firm's small conference room along with Brandi and the two principals of the PR firm. The purpose of the meeting is to make decisions about a live auction that Ross Flanders is proposing. Although Margo is responsible for Ross Flanders' participation, another appointment has prevented her from attending. Coming as it is a mere four days before the event, the meeting is not what Max needs thrown suddenly into his frantic schedule. However, he is not entirely unhappy about it being added to the evening. The committee never came up with live auction items on their own and it promises to provide decent ancillary income. Something that their silent auction certainly will not. That collection of laughable junk secured by the committee and breathlessly announced at meetings won't pay for the cost to have it sent back to the office. People sip coffee and make small talk waiting for the owner from the auction group to arrive.

When he does, Ross or Flanders, Max can never remember which is which, introduces him. "This is Jerry Steinkamp president of Steinkamp Promotions. Jerry, I'll let you explain your operation."

"Thanks. Good morning. First off, forgive me for being late. I hope I haven't inconvenienced anyone and I won't waste any more of your time. Steinkamp is a consignment house. We provide unique one-of-a-kind experiences for, in this case, your live auction."

Jerry passes out one-page slicks listing items such as "Hot Air Balloon Trip over the Loire Valley," "Two Tickets to 2014 Grammy Awards and After Party," "Three-Day Chinese Junk Cruise on South China Sea," etc.

"We have a worldwide clientele, are the number-one company in the field and do volume business with our various vendors. Because of that, you will notice that the stated prices of the individual packages listed on your sheets is very reasonable. That is our cost. All packages include air fare, accommodations and ground transportation. I will be the auctioneer at your event and will have several associates with me. I understand you are having a silent auction, too?"

"Correct," Max says.

"We can handle the checkout for that as well as the live."

"How does the consignment aspect work?" Max asks.

"We take our cost out of the opening bid. Anything over that, eighty percent goes to the organization and twenty percent is our cut."

Max has worked with consignment houses in the past and knows this is a good deal. No matter what the items go for, the foundation makes money. Max is relieved and has no objection. Not that anyone is asking his opinion. It appears that the decision to go ahead with this group has already been made.

"Any questions?" Jerry asks.

"How do we get started?" Brandi says.

"All you need to decide is where you want to set the opening bids," Jerry says with a grin.

A look of confusion crosses Brandi's face. "Aren't we going to use these prices on the sheet?" she asks.

Now Jerry looks confused.

After a pause, Max speaks. "I think we should add a few hundred dollars across the board. That way, should an item go for the minimum bid, at least the foundation makes something. My bosses wouldn't be very pleased with me as a fundraiser if I didn't insist on that."

A smile comes on Jerry's face. "I would tend to agree—"

"As if I didn't have anything to do with raising money for this event! Is that it?" Brandi growls across the table at Max.

There is abrupt silence.

"No, Brandi, I'm not saying that," Max begins slowly. "It's just that—"

"We'll use these figures," Brandi says to Jerry indicating the slick in front of her and looking pointedly at everyone in the room, defying anyone to challenge her. When no one does, she breaks into a big smile. "My girlfriends are going to love me when they see the excellent trips they can get for these prices!"

And that seems to be that.

One of the things Max has learned working charity events over the years is that people get involved with them for various reasons. There are as many reasons as there are people and each of them is as different as the people themselves. But one reason that is rarely present is charity itself. It seldom has a place at the table. Or even in the room. And if it does, it's over by the kitchen door.

TWENTY

Finally, Max sends the email to Brandi: "Seating chart and guest list attached."

■

It had taken all day to complete. The reason was because Gupta couldn't make up her mind where she wanted her people seated. It was only four tables but she dragged her feet the whole afternoon long. And when she did make a decision, she would call Max back and change things. He could have left her guests' names off the list and filled them in later but knew, somehow, that would amount to him offering up his ass to be kicked once again.

That wasn't all of it. Gupta had satisfied her $25,000 commitment by pledging a personal $10,000 silver table and another $10,000 silver table from a company through her husband, Bradley. She was also responsible for ten individual tickets at $500 through two companies that were also contacts of her husband. In addition, there were eighteen individual tickets which had come in from her solicitation list. So, on the face of it, she had more than met the commitment she had made when she accepted as co-chair.

However, it slowly became clear as she was agonizing over where to seat people that she was placing ten of the eighteen individual ticket buyers at her table.

For clarity, Max asked, "Just to be sure, you're putting ten individuals who bought their own tickets at your silver table?"

There was a pause on the line. Then, "It's not a silver table," Gupta said.

Then, it was Max's turn to pause. "You pledged a personal silver table when you agreed to co-chair."

"No, I pledged ten thousand. Which you're getting for the silver table from the company Bradley brought in."

"But I've been carrying you as a silver table this whole time on my weekly financial reports."

"That was your doing."

"You're listed in the program as a Silver Sponsor."

"I never told you to do that. And since this is going to be a full table, I'd like you to extend us the discount."

"So, this is a forty-five-hundred-dollar table?" Max asked. Individual tickets were $500 but there was a discount for whole tables. Max was pretty sure those orders were all unpaid pledges so he had no grounds to object.

"Yes," Gupta said. "And since Bradley and I are also sitting there, can you make that a table for twelve?"

"No problem," Max said. *The problem, Gupta, is that this event just got $5,500 lighter*! At least. He'd have to sit down and figure it out.

His feeling was that she still had hit her $25,000 commitment. Barely. He needed to just get through this stinking *Festive in the Dunes* mess and put it behind him. It's almost over. The event is already a success. Maybe no one will notice the shortfall. Can he get away with not sending out a post-event report?

■

Not two minutes after sending Brandi the seating chart and guest list, an email from her pops into his inbox.

"Please don't tell me you sent this to Gupta."

Max just stares at the message. A feeling of hollowness fills him as massive chunks of inner resolve break off and fall into a bottomless chasm. Should he go to Gladys with this? Miraculously, she happens to be in her office. But why? So she can, once again, provide him with her professional non-direction.

Max types his reply to Brandi: "Did not."

Her immediate comeback: "Don't."

TWENTY-ONE

Max makes good time and arrives at the office a few minutes early. On this day before the event, every minute will need to be carefully utilized. There is just so much still to do. Max is unaccustomed to working on a major event without help. Gladys had promised he would get the help he needed when the time came. Like most of Gladys's assistance, that turned out to be less than helpful. She had assigned a woman on staff to him to engage in any way he required. There were two problems with this arrangement. One, the woman had no event experience so there were very few things she could help with. The other was that her primary duty was assisting with the foundation's *Step Off Breast Cancer Awareness Walk* which was running concurrently. Normally she could spare no more than an hour a day for some data entry. So now, on the day that he had always used to take a breath and double-check all aspects of the event and tweak anything that was still needed, Max is staring down a long tunnel ahead of must-do jobs with just a glimmer of light at the end. His goal is to single-handedly run the gauntlet and reach that light—hopefully by a reasonable hour this evening. He girds himself for the day ahead and plunges right in.

First order of business is to triple-check the numbers on the seating chart and get it to the caterer by noon. He had given Andy Fox the setup and guarantee three days earlier, as required, but there had been changes as there always are. It doesn't seem like a challenging task but with his phone ringing nonstop and no one else to pick it up, it is.

Once that's out of the way, the biggest nut is dealing with the silent auction. Each item needs signage and a bid sheet. The bid sheets are a matter of making sure that the lot numbers, opening bids and increments are correct. The signage is something else. As committee members submitted auction items, they were required to also provide the signage—details about the item that would inform and entice potential bidders. Pictures, too, if possible. None of them did, even when Max asked for it several times. One of the "dead wood" told Max, when asked for the third time for information on an item, to "Google it" as if he didn't know what that was.

Hampering the process is the fact that the breast cancer walk is in full implementation mode and they are hogging both copiers. Max goes to Gladys to complain.

"*The Step Off Walk* is the Gotham Division's biggest event," Gladys explains. "It's always all hands on deck."

Max can only describe the expression on Gladys's face as a "dirty look" as if she is saying to him, "How dare you not only have the audacity to not get involved in the walk but to complain about the copiers."

"The Hamptons gala is also a big event," Max counters.

"Yes, it is," Gladys says with finality.

Max contemplates her Orwellian response. *All events are equal but some events are more equal than others.*

■

It is the middle of the afternoon before Max realizes how much time has passed. His phone, which has been relatively quiet for a bit, rings. He looks down at the caller ID. It's Gupta.

"Hi, Gupta."

"Is the seating done?"

"Yes."

"Can you send it over?"

Max closes his eyes. He knew this call was coming. He had no way to prevent it. Still, he was clinging to the thin sliver of hope that since he had spent so much time working on her tables with her yesterday, the angel of death would pass over him. He does not have the time and no longer has the will to continue refereeing his two harpy co-chairs. He lets the shit hit the fan.

"I can't."

"Why not?"

"Brandi won't let me."

"What?"

There is nothing to add.

"Is Gladys there?" Gupta demands.

"Yes."

"I want to talk to her. And Margo, too!"

"I'll have to set up a conference call. I'll call you back."

Max goes to Gladys's office.

"Gupta wants to talk to you."

"What's up?"

"She wants me to send her the seating chart."

"So?" Gladys says looking quizzically at Max.

"Brandi told me not to."

Gladys eyes grow wide as this sinks in.

"She wants to talk to Margo as well. I'm going to try to conference her in."

At his desk, Max explains the situation over the phone to Margo.

"I can't talk now, I'm going into a meeting," Margo says.

"Gupta is very upset. I think your talking to her might help."

"I can't. Just keep me posted," Margo says and hangs up.

Max returns to Gladys's office. "Gupta's on line two. Margo's in a meeting and not available."

Gladys looks down at the blinking light on her phone. Then, she says to Max, "Sit down."

"I don't have time for this now," Max says not moving from the doorway. "This event is entirely on my shoulders and I need to be accorded the opportunity to make it all happen. Please just let me know if I need to do anything."

Max does not wait for a reply and returns to his cubicle. Almost half an hour later, Gladys shows up.

"Send her the seating chart," she says and goes.

∎

Going on 11:00 p.m., Max is still working on the event documents. The office has long since cleared out and having use of both copiers, uninterrupted, is making things go faster. Out of nowhere, a forlorn-looking Aggie Potter stands at his cubicle, startling him.

"Aggie...I didn't know you were still here," Max says.

"Just clearing out my desk," she says.

"What do you mean?"

"The Camp Quest program has been canceled. Another victim of streamlining," she explains.

Max is shocked. He has heard nothing about it. Which he finds extremely odd since camp played a crucial part in publicizing his event in *Dan's Papers* and a camp kid is speaking at the gala.

"Is this a surprise?" he asks.

"Sort of," she says. "I knew something was up when none of the big bosses showed up at this year's planning meeting, but I didn't get the official word till this week."

"So that's it? There's not going to be camp this summer?"

"Poof," she says, gesturing with one hand.

"I'm so sorry," Max says.

"I'll be alright," Aggie says, sadly. "Good luck with your event."

Max hears Aggie letting herself out the front door and for some reason it reminds him of his hotel reservation. The foundation had agreed to pay for a hotel room for him after the gala. The drive from Southampton to New Rochelle is about two hours and, given that the event is slated to run until midnight, that would be too long a drive. The problem with accommodations in the Hamptons during the season is that all places require a minimum three-night stay. Max had already planned to take a room the night before the event which he would pay for himself. Knowing that he would be working late at the office, he wanted to be on the East End near the event to be assured of getting a good night's rest. Unfortunately that only amounted to a two-night booking. The nearest place to do that was Riverhead. Even at that, Riverhead is a good thirty-minute drive from Southampton. Max calls the hotel to tell them that he might be another two hours but to hold his room no matter how late he arrives. With that covered, Max sees the end of the tunnel and can almost feel the plump pillows with their crisp cases surrounding his weary head.

The night bell buzzes. Max gets up and goes to the front door. Through the glass he sees a skinny male messenger standing in the spill from the entry light. Max opens the door.

"NCF?" the messenger asks.

"Yes."

"Delivery for Max Short."

"That's me."

The messenger has a large square box on a handcart. Max leads him back to his cubicle and has him deposit it on the floor just outside. He follows the messenger back to the front, lets him out and locks the door behind him.

At his cubicle he takes a box cutter from his desk and cuts the tape sealing the box. He opens it. Inside are the bedsheets. On top of the bedsheets is a pair of pinking shears. Tucked under the pinking shears is an envelope with his name on it. Max opens the envelope and removes the paper inside. He unfolds it and reads:

My girlfriends and I never got around to this. I'm sure you'll do a better job anyhow. You are the pro!
LOL,
Brandi

Max looks down and sees Brandi's headshot which he used for the program smiling up at him from his desk. Max bends down, grabs the pinking shears from the box and raises them over his head, bringing them down, viciously stabbing Brandi in the throat.

TWENTY-TWO

TUESDAY, AUGUST 20, 2013

10:18 a.m.

NCF SUFFOLK COUNTY OFFICE

ISLANDIA, NY

DeMarco and Rooney stand at the front reception desk. Gladys walks up.

"I'm Gladys Ortiz."

DeMarco shakes her hand. "Detective Mark DeMarco. This is Detective Angela Rooney." Gladys and Rooney shake hands.

"We're with the Suffolk County homicide squad. We're investigating Brandi Napoli's murder," DeMarco says.

Gladys nods her head, somberly.

"We'd like to take a look at Max Short's desk and computer."

"Sure."

"If you'll just sign this consent to search report and show us his office, we'll be out of your hair in no time." DeMarco places the document on the edge of the reception desk and offers Gladys a pen. She takes the pen and signs.

"Take your time, Detectives. And if you need anything else from me, my office is in the back. Come on, I'll show you his cubicle."

■

DeMarco stands in Max's former cubicle looking down at the gash in the rubberized top of the desk left by Max having stabbed Brandi's picture. He feels it with his finger. Then he picks up the laptop on the desk and walks with it to the adjoining cubicle which is empty. He sits at the desk, opens the computer and powers it on. Rooney walks up.

"Take a look at this," she says. She is holding a jump rope.

DeMarco inspects it with his fingers. "Thick, natural fiber. Where'd you get this?"

"There's a whole bunch of them in a conference room back there," Rooney says.

"Let's take it. Go through his desk. We'll take the files and anything except paper clips. Also, grab the BlackBerry."

Rooney goes into Max's former cubicle.

■

At her desk, Carolyn Petrie speaks in a low voice into her phone. "There's a couple of cops here going through your cubicle and your computer."

Max stands in his living room on his cell phone looking through the sheer curtains. A New Rochelle police cruiser sits on the opposite side a little up the street. "They won't find anything."

"Are you sure?"

"Positive."

"That's good to know," Carolyn says with relief. Then, "How are you doing?"

"As best as I can."

"Found anything yet?"

"I've been to a few interviews. The minute I walk in, I can see it in their eyes. They weren't expecting someone my age."

"You'll be pleased to know Gladys is leaving."

"Oh?"

"Being forced out. They're combining the Suffolk and Nassau offices and she lost out to the other VP. Friday's her last day."

"Wow," Max says.

"Not really a big surprise. Things didn't go well for her after your
event. Quick as a bunny, Margo hijacked it away from her and is now
running it out of the Manhattan office. Heard they hired some poor
shmuck to work on it and Margo has him sitting right outside her door."

"That was her plan from the start," Max says.

"Of course it was. That bitch couldn't manage a bake sale. She was
just waiting for you to create a success so she could grab it."

There is murder in Max's eyes. "Yeah. But without Brandi, good
luck with that," he says with relish.

"Amen."

Then Max asks, "Has Gladys found anything else?"

"This you're not going to like. She got a good job as director of
alumni affairs at Stony Brook University."

"Typical. I've worked in this business long enough to know that
it's one huge cesspool and the biggest turds always rise to the top."

Carolyn chuckles. "Keep in touch."

DeMarco finds a letter on Max's computer. It reads:

Dear Gladys

This serves to provide you with notice of my resignation,
effective immediately. My primary reason for leaving is
Brandi Napoli. It is quite clear that she has no intention of

relinquishing her position with *Festive in the Dunes* and it is equally clear that you and Margo have no thought to replace her or rein her in. I cannot face the prospect of having to work with her for another year. By resigning it is my intention to rid that woman's voice from my life forever. I have nightmares about that voice. It just isn't worth it anymore.

Best of luck with the event moving forward. You are going to need it because it will be difficult to attract other volunteers given Brandi's dominance. When she first came on board she sent me an email telling me "I can work with anyone." Even if that were true, the real problem is there are not many people who can work with her.

Sincerely,

DeMarco closes the file and powers down the computer. He calls over the partition, "You about done?"

"Roger that," Rooney replies.

DeMarco picks up the computer and walks to the next cubicle.

Rooney is putting file folders in a cardboard box. "Not much except these files from the event." She grabs the BlackBerry and tosses that in as well.

DeMarco slides the computer into the box and picks it up. Rooney grabs the jump rope and follows him to Gladys's office. The two police detectives stand in the doorway of the office.

"All done," DeMarco says.

Gladys looks up from her desk.

Rooney holds up the jump rope. "I found a bunch of these in a room in the back. May I ask what they are for?"

"Our *Jump Rope for Hope* program," Gladys says. "It's a fundraiser and educational event we do in the schools in the fall and spring."

"Mind if I borrow this one?" Rooney says.

"There's always tons left over. You can keep it," Gladys says.

"May I ask you a question?" DeMarco says.

"Of course," Gladys replies.

DeMarco takes several steps into the office toward her desk. In a confidential voice he asks, "Did Max Short resign?"

"No."

"He never presented you with a letter of resignation?"

"Max Short was terminated."

TWENTY-THREE

The intercom on Max's phone buzzes. The caller ID displays "Gladys." Max picks up the phone. "I'll be right in," he says.

Max grabs a copy of the latest financial report that he printed out earlier, a legal pad and a pen and heads for Gladys's office. The figures are pretty impressive: $292, 010 paid and pledged. With a goal of $100,000 net, the event will clear double that. Max is in exactly the position that he wants—successful! And his success could not be timelier. Having been at the foundation for just over one year, Max has an inkling that Gladys is calling him in for his annual review. At his six-month review, which occurred after he was at NCF for eight months, Gladys's only serious point had been that she wanted him to become more connected to other staff members in the office. Given that he didn't work with any of them had made his lack of comradery understandable. Once immersed in the gala, it had been hard for him to work on that. He could start working on it now.

The experience was nothing short of horrible but there are now pluses to consider. Of course they'll never see Gupta again, which is a loss. But they had made new friends among Silver Sponsors and table buyers. If they could bring some of those folks on to a committee and clear out the existing "dead wood," Max would actually have people he could work with who had the potential to grow the event. And if Brandi knew that there were other people actively fundraising, she wouldn't feel so alone which would have to improve her disposition. Also, others' involvement would naturally rein in some of Brandi's overbearing tendencies. Along those same lines, he is now in a good position to request help for himself. Not part-time help from a staffer with no event experience but a full-time temp with demonstrated event experience to work with him for the final six weeks leading up to the gala. One bright spot of the recession is that there are a lot of people like that out there. Additionally, he is thinking of introducing honorees for next year's event. Oscar and Charlotte Stratton are high on his list. He brings the strength of his New York City corporate contacts and she brings the Hamptons social element. He plans to bring this up with Gladys now. Yes, the inaugural event had been a difficult birth but don't they often result in the most beautiful child?

He gets to Gladys's door.

"Come in, Max. Have a seat," Gladys says from behind her desk.

Max steps into the room.

"Close the door," Gladys says.

He does. Then he sees Midge sitting in a chair in the corner. She is a large woman. The biggest woman on staff. That's about all Max knows about her. Their jobs don't interact in any way. He doesn't even know her last name. *What is she doing here?* Max sits in a chair facing

Gladys's desk.

"Max, I think you are a very talented fundraiser," Gladys begins. "But there have been conversations regarding your continued service. Although your tenure here has been short, it has also been profitable and for that reason a decision has been made to offer you an unprecedented three-weeks' severance pay. I hope you find that generous. If so, just sign the agreement and leave it at your station." Gladys gestures to a manila envelope at the front of her desk. "Please take as long as you need to clear out your desk. I'll give you till the end of the business day."

Max feels like he's been kicked in the balls. He can't breathe. He fixes Gladys with a lethal stare. He envisions how good it would feel to rip off her face with his bare hands. Gladys looks back. She feels his contempt. She swallows hard. Tears spring to her eyes. Now he gets what Midge is doing here. Protection. In an office of all women, pick the one who most resembles a man if you're firing a man. Max stands.

"I'm sorry," Gladys offers, weakly. "It was simply decided that you are not a good fit for the foundation."

Max never takes his eyes off of her. He stands and picks up the envelope. "No, you're not sorry. But—"

Max turns and goes to the door, pulling it open. He thinks better of slamming it on his way out.

At his desk, Max sits with his head down until his hands stop shaking enough to do what has to be done. *Don't be hasty, don't be stupid. Copy all the event files to a removable device and wipe the hard drive. They will be able to recover the files but it will take some doing.* After he does this, he takes a Wolffer Estate shopping bag from his lower drawer and starts filling it with personal items. Then he remembers his ten dollars.

Gladys's assistant, Sue, had taken a collection in the office to buy Gladys and her fiancée Ingrid a gift to be given to them at a surprise shower to be held the following Monday. He had already signed the office card and wanted to get his hands on it and cut out his signature with a razor. He knew that wasn't realistic, but he was damned if he wasn't going to get his ten bucks back!

Max advances on Sue standing by her desk. "Give me my ten bucks back!"

Sue retreats a few steps. "What?"

Gladys steps out of her office and stands just feet from Max and Sue.

Max sees only red. In that instant, he can't even pull up Gladys's name. "For what's-her-face's surprise shower next Monday!" he shouts, jerking his thumb in Gladys's direction.

"It's been spent!" Sue stammers back, peevishly.

He can see she is only concerned that he spoiled the surprise. Max throws his arms in the air in disgust. Both women jump back in fear.

Max goes back to his desk to finish packing up. After a few minutes, Midge shows up. She's holding several dollar bills.

"This is all there was in petty cash," she says. "Eight singles." Midge places them on his desk. "And eight quarters," she adds, forming them into a low stack she places on top of the bills.

Max looks down at the money. He starts to laugh. "I just raised three hundred thousand dollars for these assholes and they can't even come up with a ten?"

Midge shrugs. "I'm sorry I had to be there," she says and disappears.

Max goes to Carolyn's cubicle to say goodbye. She isn't there. He returns to his cubicle, signs the severance agreement without reading it and collects his stuff. Max walks out the front door of the Suffolk County office of the National Cancer Foundation for the last time. He is filled with a sensation of intense relief akin to walking out of school on the last day before summer vacation. He doesn't imagine what lies ahead of him is going to a vacation. But at the moment he can't think about that. He just needs to savor whatever good feeling he can.

■

Max pulls up to his house and sees Patricia's car parked in the driveway. *What is she doing home? Did she tell me she was taking the day off?* Max parks alongside her car. He sits for a moment to collect his thoughts and prepare to face his wife.

He opens the front door. He walks in and closes it behind him. Patricia appears in the dining room.

"You startled me. What are you doing home?" she says.

Max stands with a queer look on his face. Then, "I was fired."

Not comprehending, Patricia says, "What?"

"I'm going to get them," Max says in a low voice.

"Who fired you?"

"Gladys."

"Your event was a success, wasn't it?"

"Yeah."

"What reason did she give?"

"I'm not a good fit."

"What the fuck does that mean?"

"I told you about that woman who tried to do a Hamptons event and it lost sixty-eight thousand dollars. Well, she's still got her job. You know why? Because she's a goddamn breast cancer survivor, that's why!"

Patricia's mouth drops open. She puts a hand to it and lowers her head.

"I raise three hundred thousand for them but I can't compete with her. I don't have tits! I'm going to sue the fucking shit out of them!"

Patricia raises her head, wiping away a tear. "Please…I can't deal with this now. I've got to go."

"Where?"

"I have an appointment with my oncologist."

Max and Patricia stand on opposite sides of an abyss. Neither can say a thing.

Then, Patricia finds her voice. "I'll be back to make dinner," she says. Patricia walks to the front door and lets herself out.

Max stands alone in the living room, shoulders slumped. At least he knows why she's home early.

TWENTY-FOUR

TUESDAY, JULY 23, 2013

9:00 a.m.

OFFICE OF GARY KEISSEL, ESQ.

MIDTOWN MANHATTAN, NY

Max sits across from the lawyer, a florid-faced man in his sixties with flowing white hair. The cuffs of his pale blue Supima cotton dress shirt are monogramed. They are also a little frayed.

"If I decide to take your case, my standard retainer is five thousand dollars which can be payable from the proceeds from the suit. So, go."

Max is momentarily tongue-tied. Although he practiced what he was going to say, he wants to make sure that what he says and how he says it are both compelling and complete. Keissel's abruptly diving in puts him on the spot.

"Until last week, I was employed by the National Cancer Foundation as an event fundraiser. My position initially consisted of starting a new gala event in the Hamptons. That event occurred two weeks ago on July thirteenth. The goal for the event was one hundred thousand net. The event raised over two hundred ninety thousand, producing net income of over twice goal." Max looks at Keissel who has no reaction.

Max wants him to understand the importance of what he has just said. "In the fundraising business, you're only as good as your last success. But being successful and reaching, not to mention exceeding your dollar goals is an unwritten guarantee of job security. At least until your next campaign."

The lawyer remains looking at Max, not responding.

Max continues. "There is a woman who works there who tried to start a Hamptons event for them three years ago and it failed miserably. Not only did it not raise any money, it lost sixty-eight thousand. She still has a job and I don't. The difference between us is that she is a breast cancer survivor and I am not."

"Hmm," Keissel ponders this. "What reason were you given for your dismissal?"

"I was told that even though my event was successful, I am not a good fit for the organization."

"Any idea what that means?"

"From the time I was hired until the day I was fired, I was the only man working in that office. Last month at a staff meeting, my boss, the vice president of the Suffolk County office, brought up the subject of noise levels in the workplace and how negatively they can affect performance. We all work in cubicles cheek to jowl and the partitions offer no privacy. She said that we need to keep our conversations as quiet as possible. Then she turned and made an example of me. She said that I, in particular, needed to tone down my 'big man voice.' She then suggested that when making and receiving phone calls I take my BlackBerry out to the parking lot."

Keissel purses his lips but, again, says nothing. Max is beginning to wonder if the man used to be a psychiatrist.

"I was humiliated that she would single me out in that way, using my sex against me in front of the entire female staff," Max says, hoping to drive the point home.

"Is this the woman who fired you?" Keissel asks.

"Yes."

"Did she also hire you?"

"Yes," Max says. Realizing that does not work in his favor he quickly adds, "I maintain that my termination, following successful job performance in contrast to a colleague's continued employment following her failure with the same assignment solely because of her medical condition, is blatant discrimination. On top of that, the reason offered for my termination of 'not a good fit,' is a further indication of a hostile work environment of *sexual* discrimination."

Keissel looks across his desk at Max for a long moment. "You should have been a lawyer, Mr. Short. Anything else?"

Max shakes his head.

"The fact that the woman who fired you also hired you throws out the sexual discrimination complaint. It might be true but it can't be proved." Keissel pauses and takes a deep breath. "As for the other? I can't take your case, Mr. Short. And I would sincerely suggest to you that no lawyer in New York State would take it because it's unwinnable. Not that you weren't discriminated against. I think you were royally screwed. But you, as a cancer-free man, suing the National Cancer Foundation because they fired you while choosing not to fire a female breast cancer survivor three years ago because she didn't do as good a job as you on a similar task? The optics alone are impossible! Employment in New York State is *at will* and you can be fired for no reason at all. I'm sorry."

TWENTY-FIVE

Patricia is on the bedroom phone. Max has gone in to the city to meet with an attorney and she takes the opportunity to make this call while he's out.

"Your father has been in a real funk since he lost his job. I was hoping you and Sarah might be free this Sunday for dinner. I know he'd love to see you both."

"We don't have any plans for the weekend. That should work," replies Jeremy, the Shorts' son.

"I'm inviting your sister as well."

"Cool. We haven't seen Gabby since Christmas."

"Five o'clock okay?"

"Sounds good, Mom."

SUNDAY, JULY 28, 2013
6:21 p.m.

The Shorts are gathered around the dining room table. Max and Patricia sit at opposite ends. On one side sit Jeremy and his wife, Sarah. He and Sarah have been married nearly a year. Across from them sits Gabby, Jeremy's younger sister.

"Tell me one thing you learned in school today," Jeremy says to Sarah. "When I was in grade school that's what my dad said to me every day when I came home."

"You weren't the only one. I used to get that, too," Gabby adds.

"I think that's a good practice," Sarah says. "Keeps kids on their toes."

"We should all ask ourselves that every day," Patricia adds. "Never too old to learn something new."

"I learned something new just the other day," Max says.

Everyone turns to look at Max expectantly.

"I learned that we live in a society that is ruled not by justice but by optics." There is a confused silence. Max continues. "Jeremy, you're the graphic artist, maybe you can tell me what optics means."

"Uh…You know, Dad. It's the way things appear."

Max snorts. "Well, everybody…It appears I'm fucked." There is a shocked silence. "Don't worry, I'm still going to get those filthy lying cunts."

"Max, I wish you wouldn't use that word," Patricia says.

"Why not?"

"It's an ugly word."

"Yes, it is. Which is why it is the perfect word to describe ugly people."

"Please let's not talk about those women tonight," Patricia pleads.

"Women?" Max says. "They aren't women. Women have minds and hearts and souls. Those three are nothing but genitourinary tracts. Cunts!" Max yells, slamming his hand down. Everything on the table jumps. No one knows where to look. "And I don't know how you can defend them," Max says, pointing a finger at Patricia.

"I'm not defending them!"

"I get fired after handing them a big success and all that you're bothered about is my using 'that word'?"

"I hate them as much as you do," Patricia says, her voice shaking with emotion. "More! It's because of them that I'm going to have to work for the rest of my life to support us."

Patricia and Max glare at each other across the table.

"But I also hate that word," she adds.

They continue to glare. After a moment or two, Max drops his gaze.

"Excuse me," Max says, gets up from the table and leaves the room.

■

Later, Jeremy, Gabby and Sarah stand with Patricia at the front door.

"Are you going to be okay, Mom?" Gabby asks.

"Don't worry about me," Patricia assures them.

"I've never seen him like that," Jeremy says.

"You know he can have a bad temper," Patricia says.

Jeremy looks at Patricia askance. "Not like that."

"You have to understand how shattering this has been for him," Patricia tries to explain.

"Who are these three lying—women? Is one that co-chair he mentioned? What was her name—Angie?" Jeremy asks.

"Brandi," Patricia corrects him. "Her and his former boss, Gladys, and another woman who works there, Margo."

"What happened?" Jeremy says.

"I can't go into all of it now. I'll call you both and fill you in."

"And keep us posted," Gabby says. "I'm worried about him." She glances up the stairs.

"Me, too," Patricia says.

■

Upstairs, Max sits in the bathtub, the steam from it permeating the room. He closes his eyes and tries to blank his mind.

Just let the hot water leach everything away—the booze, the bitterness, the rage.

The rage will not be so easily purged.

My kids were here for me tonight and what did I do? I pushed them away.

I am so proud of both of them. They have turned out so well. Jeremy's married to a great woman and runs his own business. Gabby's graduating next year and looking at grad school.

I have always done my best to protect them.

Their love and respect mean everything to me.

What do they think of me after that outburst? What's happening to me?

■

It was 1993. After having lived in New York City for twelve years, the Shorts had relocated to a co-op apartment in New Rochelle with the intention of raising a family. They had tried for a couple of years to conceive on their own with no luck. They were considering in vitro fertilization and surrogacy but were moved by new neighbors in their building who were adoptive parents. In speaking with them, the Shorts learned about all the children who were stuck in the foster care system waiting for someone to give them a permanent home. They applied for a license as foster parents and began their search.

At only the second agency which they visited they met Jeremy and Gabby. Brother and sister, they were born in Wheeling, West Virginia.

Having different fathers explained the fact that they did not physically resemble one another. The siblings had originally come to New York when a relative agreed to take them into foster care. After only a month, the woman decided that it was too much for her and they went into the system in New York. Their appearance confirmed for the Shorts what the agency had said about them having suffered physical abuse and malnutrition. Though six years old, Jeremy could have been mistaken for four. At four years of age, Gabby had a developmentally stunted vocabulary and rarely spoke. Almost more for those reasons than not, the Shorts were hopelessly smitten by the kids and decided to adopt. The agency, however, insisted that they take them in as foster parents first, on a legal-risk basis. This was done because, although the fathers were not in the picture, the rights of the mother, who was in a program for crack addiction, had not yet been finally determined.

"Given the mother's history of relapse, we have a high degree of certainty that her rights will be terminated but this is currently the only path for both the children and yourselves," the woman at the agency had told them.

Because of the abuse involved, a caseworker was assigned to them to help the Shorts cope. In addition to both kids being half-starved, Jeremy had multiple cigarette burns on his back. The mother denied any knowledge of how they got there. This further made her case shaky, indeed. At the same time, the Shorts were urged to get dual license status as adoptive parents in addition to being foster parents, so things could progress as smoothly as possible once approved.

Two other factors worked in the Shorts' favor: one was the children's ages and the other was that the agency would not separate the children in placing them. While most couples want to adopt babies, not older children, this was not a problem for the Shorts. Ultimately, they wanted two kids—a boy and a girl was perfect—and, they reasoned, having a two-year age gap between the kids would be easier on their nerves. Plus, they themselves were getting started late in the parenting game.

At first, Jeremy was very protective of his little sister and wouldn't let her out of his sight. Even with the Shorts, he always positioned himself between her and them. The caseworker had given the Shorts an ointment to use on Jeremy's burns. Both Patricia and Max had tried applying it at bedtime but Jeremy would not permit them to touch him. He refused to remove his pajama shirt.

The day word came that the mother's custody bid had failed and the kids were available for adoption was one of the happiest days of Max and Patricia's lives. When Max first told Jeremy that they were going to adopt him, Jeremy told him bluntly that that was not going to happen. When Max asked why, Jeremy told him he was not going to leave his sister. Max apologized for misspeaking. The Shorts wanted to adopt both of them.

One evening after the adoption had been completed, as Max was putting Jeremy to bed, Jeremy picked up the tube of ointment which he himself had been applying as best as he could to the burns on his back.

"Can you put some of this on my back?" Jeremy asked.

Jeremy took off his pajama top and lay face down on his bed.

Max took the tube and sat next to Jeremy on the bed.

"You let me know if I'm hurting you," Max said.

As gently as possible, Max rubbed the ointment into the angry wounds. Not only had Jeremy never let him do this before, he had barely let Max or Patricia even get a good look at his back. Max stared at the small, round reddish-black scars. Without warning, Max was overcome by the knowledge that whatever monster did this was hovering over the boy's thin back and shoulders just as he was now. *This was done by someone who was supposed to protect. Someone who had complete control.* Had Jeremy been tied up first? Perhaps. But maybe Jeremy submitted to it willingly in a deal to shield Gabby from threatened similar treatment. Max struggled to control his hands from shaking with anger. Either way it happened, his chest swelled with pride for the bravery and loyalty of his little boy.

"All set," Max said when done. He screwed the cap back on the ointment, set it on the bedside table and got up from the bed.

Then something happened which had never happened before. Jeremy sat up and as he pulled his pajama shirt back on said, "Thanks, Dad."

Jeremy had never called him "Dad" before. It hit him like a Mack truck. Max had never given it much thought. Never dared to ask Jeremy to call him Dad. The caseworker had warned them against pushing. Just let things develop, she had said. So he wasn't thinking about it. Wasn't anticipating it or yearning for it. He put no great stock in it. But when it happened it was like a thousand steeple bells in a thousand cathedrals all began chiming at once. He had to resist grabbing Jeremy and tossing him in the air. Hugging him as if some dreaded pox had passed—because it had. The months of strangeness and adjustment they had all worked through had finally paid off. They had turned a corner and there was no going back.

At the door, Max switched out the light. Then a second thing happened which had never happened before. Max said, "Goodnight, Son."

■

Anxious to put their high-rate tax dollars to work, the Shorts enrolled their kids in the local public school. It was very convenient, only a few blocks from their house. Jeremy was in first grade that September. At first, the school worked fine. Jeremy had a bit of a discipline problem—his teacher recognized his intelligence but commented on his need to focus his attention on the lesson being presented and not on doodling in the margins of his notebook.

Toward the end of the school year, Max got a telephone call at his office. It was Jeremy's teacher, Mr. Popandropoulos, or Mr. P as the kids called him. He told Max that he had the school psychologist, Dr. Patrick Kenner, with him. He put Dr. Kenner on the phone. Dr. Kenner informed Max that he was looking at a picture Jeremy drew that was very disturbing, very disturbing indeed. The psychologist went on to describe a battle scene with much blood, bodies cut in two, etc. He asked Max if he had ever seen any such pictures. Max answered, yes, he had seen similar pictures which Jeremy had drawn. Dr. Kenner asked Max what he thought of them. Max said that he had asked Jeremy what they were. Jeremy had told him that they were studying the French and Indian War in social studies and these were battles scenes.

Dr. Kenner told Max that, as a professional, these were not innocent drawings. These were very troubling pictures.

"Jeremy's very visual," Max said. "He draws all the time. Two weeks ago, we took him to the Museum of Natural History. On the way home on the train, he drew a picture of the building. From memory. It was quite accurate."

"What I am looking at is not an architectural rendering, Mr. Short. Frankly, it's a red flag."

"Of what?"

"I'm recommending counseling."

"For what?"

"ADHD. Attention-deficit hyperactivity disorder—"

"I know what it is."

"Based on his history of inattention in class, I believe it is a good place to start. With your permission, I'm also prescribing a course of Ritalin. I'm sending the picture home with Jeremy. I suggest you and your wife discuss this. I think you both need to consider what is best for your son. Please call me tomorrow."

∎

That evening after dinner, Max and Patricia sat Jeremy down at the table and pulled out the picture.

"Can you tell us what this is a picture of?" Max said.

Jeremy barely glanced at it. "It's the French and Indians fighting."

"But there are soldiers cut in half. And so much blood. Why did you make it so bloody?" Max asked.

"Look at the picture, Dad. The soldiers, they're French fries—with ketchup. I drew it after lunch. I was bored."

Max and Patricia both took another look at the picture. The French soldiers did have a decidedly julienne shape. They exchanged a look.

"No more drawing pictures in class—except if that's what you're supposed to be doing. Pay attention to the teacher and get your assignments done on time. And your mother and I don't want you talking to Dr. Kenner. If he approaches you or talks to you, you let me know."

"You got it, Dad."

The next day Max called Dr. Kenner.

"We've decided not to put Jeremy in counseling."

There was long silence. Then, "And why would that be?"

"We think putting a child that age in therapy can be a slippery slope."

More silence. "Well, Mr. Short, I assure you it will be a very slippery slope if he doesn't get the help he needs and ends up shooting his junior high classmates."

"That's not my son. I know my son. You don't. And we're not

giving you the chance. Stay away from Jeremy or you're going to have some problems of your own. Oh, and, no Ritalin. Have a nice day."

■

The following fall, Gabby entered kindergarten. Max walked her to school the first day. Thereafter, she would get a ride to and from school by a group of mothers who had organized a rotating car pool. Gabby was so tiny, it seemed impossible to him that he could let her walk into that big building all alone. But she was so eager and excited to be starting school she practically ran the whole way, chattering about making new friends. As soon as they got to the front of the building, she pulled her hand away from his and ran up the steps. "Bye, Daddy," she called over her shoulder.

At Halloween, they had a parade for all the kindergarten kids in their costumes. Gabby and Patricia had picked out a pale pink fairy costume with gossamer wings and a tiny sparkling crown. In the picture that Max took of her on the front stoop in her costume, her smile was so big and beaming he was sure he had never seen her smile like that before.

That evening, Max picked up Gabby at the house of the neighbor who minded her every day until Max got home. Gabby must have been watching for him because as soon as he pulled into the driveway she shot out the front door and got into the back seat of the car. This struck Max as somewhat unusual. Then he saw the woman motioning to him from the front door.

"I'll be right back, Gabby," Max said to her as he got out of the car. He walked up to the front stoop.

"I hate to have to be the one to tell you this," the woman began. "There was an incident at school."

"What happened?" Max asked.

"Their Halloween parade was to start right after recess. They had the kids get into their costumes before lunch. At recess, in the school-yard, a group of older girls surrounded Gabby and ripped the wings off of her costume. Then they pulled her crown off and threw it in the dirt. They put a witch's hat on her head and said that that was the right costume for her because she was as ugly as a witch."

In the car he racked his brain to think of the appropriate thing to say to his daughter. He almost started to talk about their plans to go out later trick or treating together. That's not going to happen now. *Goddamn those girls to hell!* They drove home in silence.

At home Max went to Gabby's room. She was sitting on her bed, so small and sad. She didn't look up when he entered. He went to the bed and sat.

"Am I ugly, Daddy?"

"No, baby, you're beautiful." He wanted to smother her in his arms and protect her from everything but she just sat motionless and he knew not to.

"Why did they say I'm ugly?"

"Maybe they're not very nice girls." Max felt impotent to do any-thing. "Do you want me to bring you your cookie snack?"

Gabby just mournfully shook her head.

"I'll be downstairs if you want anything." Then he got an idea. "What would you like for dinner?"

"Doesn't matter."

"How about macaroni and cheese?" Gabby loved his macaroni and cheese.

"Doesn't matter."

"I'll call you when it's ready."

Max left the door open and headed to the stairs. Before he could get there, her muffled sobs stopped him on the landing. Tears of rage sprung to his eyes.

The next day, Max kept Gabby home from school, deciding to let her play at the after-school neighbor's house. He had called in to work to say that he would be a little late. After dropping Gabby off, he walked up to school and straight into the principal's office. The principal, Mrs. Moses, a pale woman in her forties, reiterated what she had told him on the phone the evening before. The playground monitors had been spoken to.

"My son tells me they just stand around in groups and talk—they don't pay any attention to what's happening on the playground."

Mrs. Moses's nostrils flared. "As I said, they have been reprimanded and will be expected to be more diligent moving forward."

"I want their names," Max demanded.

"I'm not giving you their names," Mrs. Moses said starchily.

"I want to speak with them personally and let them know how traumatizing this was for my daughter."

"I can't do that."

"Why?"

"I have a duty to protect my staff."

"And no duty to protect the children in this school?"

"It's my understanding that your daughter was not physically harmed."

Max looked at her. There was a sneer on her face!

"If you were a man, I'd punch you for saying that."

Mrs. Moses recoiled slightly. "If you were a real man, you wouldn't threaten a woman."

Max continued to stare at her. Then he turned and walked to the door and opened it. He turned back. "Since I'm not a real man, you'll forgive me for not holding the door for you." He slammed it hard behind him. The glass in the door shattered as he walked away.

That was the last straw. The Shorts pulled their kids out of public school and enrolled them in St. Vincent's Academy in the next town over. When it came time to send their kids to high school, the public school was not an option either. Having Jeremy and Gabby pass through a metal detector every day was not the kind of environment that the Shorts wanted for them. They enrolled Jeremy in Fordham Prep. It sits adjacent to the Jesuit university of the same name in the Bronx. It even offered courses at the university for prep school seniors which Jeremy was eventually able to take advantage of. They sent Gabby to the Ursuline School in New Rochelle. The combined tuitions put a strain on the Shorts' budget given that they were already paying school taxes for a high school they chose not to use. But they considered it a worthwhile sacrifice. If you can't provide a safe place for your kids that challenges them academically and gives them a leg up in this world, what the hell good are you?

■

The water in Max's tub has gone cold.

I have always done my best to protect them.

Maybe what I most need to protect them from now is me.

■

The large house is silent and dark. Its massive square rooms possess no elegance or charm. In better times it would have been regarded as baronial. Now, however, the absence of light makes it gloomy. More, it makes it sinister.

Abruptly, Gladys darts through a shaft of light pouring in through one of the tall, bare windows. She is naked except for a petticoat like the one a young girl might wear under a party dress. She is gone as quickly. He follows. It amazes him that he knows the house so well. Even in a hall cut off completely from light, he knows every turn. He stops and listens. Faintly, very faintly, he can hear her breathing. It comes in irregular bursts. *She is trying not to cry*! *Haha*! He moves closer. Now he can hear rustling like from a rat in a bread barrel. He moves in. She is at the cupboard with her back to him. Then she senses him. She spins around, losing her balance and crashes back into the louvered doors of the cupboard, a can of tomatoes in her chubby hand. He grabs the tomatoes from her. She flinches. He comes very close—face to face. He lays the can of tomatoes against her cheek.

"No tomatoes for you," he hisses.

Her composure breaks. "Please…please—"

"They're my tomatoes," he says. "Everything here is mine."

"But I'm so hungry. Please."

Her face completely dissolves in hot tears.

He feels a rush of intense pleasure watching her crack. Adrenalin explodes through his body gushing up into his skull. He could snap her neck with one hand! He throws his head back and roars with laughter.

■

Max is jolted awake. Did he yell out in his sleep? He looks over next to him and Patricia is asleep, undisturbed. No, it was part of his dream. His tee shirt is wet with perspiration. He stares at the ceiling.

Ever since he was fired he has had such dreams about work. Not always about Gladys. They could be a mash-up of one or two or all three of them. Mostly they are berating him, hounding him. The dreams are vague, never clear or specific and, upon waking, they melt away like filthy snow in the morning sun. But this one was so—real. He looks down. His hand is still cupped as if around a can. And Gladys's face is still in front of him—quaking, breaking, deliciously so! But her face is also a mirror. He sees himself as he never has before. His cruelty is so aware and self-satisfied he longs to wallow in it. He sees both Gladys and himself at once. And both of them terrify him.

MONDAY, JULY 29, 2013
9:47 a.m.

Max opens his eyes. After a moment, he realizes he is alone in bed. He listens. The house is quiet. He turns to look at the bedside clock. He has slept later than usual, even for being unemployed. Patricia has obviously left for work. Without waking him to kiss him goodbye. Obviously. Max gets out of bed. He goes downstairs. The kitchen sink and counter are piled high with dishes from dinner the night before.

The wall phone rings. Max walks to it and picks it up.

"Hello."

"Mr. Short, this is Rob Pierce."

The name means nothing to Max.

"From Chase Bank."

"Oh, yes."

Delicately, Rob says, "Do you still work for the National Cancer Foundation?"

"Well, I, uh…Just recently, I left there."

"New job?"

"Not yet."

There is a pause. Then, "I'm calling to tell you that your application to refinance your mortgage has been declined."

Max shuts his eyes tightly.

"Mr. Short?"

"I'm here."

"You'll be receiving a letter in the mail within five business days but I wanted to let you know as soon as I heard."

"Thank you. Thank you for calling."

"Have a nice day." *Click.*

Max continues to hold the receiver in his left hand. It is shaking.

He brings his right hand up, cupping the top of the receiver. Slowly and deliberately, he replaces the receiver on its cradle.

TWENTY-SIX

WEDNESDAY, AUGUST 7, 2013

8:07 a.m.

SHORT RESIDENCE

NEW ROCHELLE, NY

Max is on the back porch watering plants in window boxes attached to the porch railing. Patricia walks out.

"Can you look at something for me?" she says.

Max puts the watering can down on the picnic table in the center of the porch. Patricia hands him a piece of paper. Max takes the paper and looks at it.

August 7, 2013

Ms. Audrey Kimchi
President
National Cancer Foundation

Dear Ms. Kimchi

I am writing to inform you that I recently received a "Summer of Hope" solicitation letter from Gladys Ortiz, the Suffolk County vice president of NCF. Why on earth would I respond to any kind of request from her?

This is the same woman who fired my husband after he had successfully planned and produced your recent Hamptons gala, *Festive in the Dunes*. She provided no support to the event or to my husband, even though it was a Suffolk County event. Instead, she completely abdicated her responsibilities for it to a volunteer and a staff member from your New York City office—a woman who was not my husband's supervisor! Ms. Ortiz was frequently and mysteriously out of the office, denying my husband the opportunity to strategize with her. When asked, her assistant was never able to say where she was or when she would be back in the office. Where was she? What was she doing? I do know she is engaged to be married and I can only imagine that planning her wedding was what was occupying all of her time.

The reason she gave my husband for his termination was that he was not a "good fit" for your organization. That, at least, is true. My husband has a long and successful record as a fundraiser working for effective and reputable nonprofits. As a breast cancer survivor, I am telling my doctors, friends and other patients to avoid your shoddy institution and direct their charitable giving to worthy cancer organizations.

In closing, please see to it that Ms. Ortiz finds the time to remove my name from her solicitation list.

Sincerely,

Patricia Antol Short

"Is she still the president there?" Patricia asks.

Without looking up from the letter, Max nods his head.

"Feel free to add whatever you like," Patricia says. When Max does not respond, "If you think it's okay, I'll add the address and mail it from work."

Max looks up, tears standing in his eyes. "Thank you."

"I thought it might help get the bitch fired."

Max smiles. He goes to Patricia and enfolds her in his arms.

"I have a late meeting. I might not be home till around nine. Don't wait for me to eat."

"I'll wait."

They kiss.

Patricia takes the letter from Max and turns. Max watches her go back into the house.

TWENTY-SEVEN

Patricia walks through the front door. She closes it behind her. She hears activity in the kitchen and sniffs the aroma coming from there. She walks to the sofa and throws her purse down on it. Today's paper sits on the coffee table. "Hamptons Socialite Murdered," the headline reads. There's Brandi's picture, the same headshot that was on Max's desk. She heads back for the kitchen.

Max stands at the counter tending to a large electric skillet. Patricia walks up to him and puts one arm around his waist. Max turns to her. They kiss. She plucks a fried potato from the baking pan next to the skillet and takes a bite.

"How was your day?" Max asks.

"Not bad. How about yours?" Patricia says moving to the stove. She lifts the lid on a pot.

"It was—pretty good, actually."

"Homemade béarnaise sauce, frites, filet mignon," Patricia says looking to the steaks on the counter. "Are we celebrating something?"

"Having to go in on a Sunday, you deserve a nice dinner. Those Yankees work you too hard."

"That the only reason?"

"I saw those steaks in the freezer and decided to put them to use."

Patricia walks to the table and picks up the open bottle of wine there. "Isn't this the wine the kids gave you for Father's Day? I thought you said you were going to save it for a special occasion."

Max doesn't respond as he scoops potatoes out of the skillet with two wooden spoons and adds them to the others in the pan.

"I heard about Brandi Napoli," Patricia says to his back.

Max turns to her with the baking pan in his hand. "Wasn't that something?" Then he turns back to the oven and opens it. "Dinner will be just a few minutes," he says sliding the pan into the oven and closing the door.

"I'll change and be right down." Patricia goes.

■

Having finished dinner, Max and Patricia sit at the table. Max splits the end of the wine between their glasses.

"Do you think she did it?" Patricia asks.

"Gupta? I don't know. God knows she had a motive. But…somehow I can't picture her doing it."

"Not the murdering kind?"

"Who really knows what kind anyone is? Especially if pushed."

"Maybe she had help," Patricia offers. "Or maybe she hired someone."

"Could be."

"If it wasn't Gupta, it'd have to be someone with a good reason."

"A woman like that? People would have to get in line," Max says with a short laugh.

"Now that she's dead, she's a woman?"

Max wags a finger at Patricia. "Don't get me started."

There is silence as they sip their wine. Then a mischievous smile crosses Patricia's face.

"Maybe it was you."

"Me?"

"You certainly have motive."

Max considers this. "Granted."

"And opportunity. You're not working. You could have driven out there."

"The paper said the murder likely occurred in the early evening. You'd have known if I was gone."

"It happened on Friday."

"So?"

"I worked late Friday."

"Oh, right."

"So, ladies and gentlemen of the jury," Patricia says, ticking off on her fingers, "we have motive, opportunity and…what's the third thing?"

"Means."

"Well, anyone with a knife—you could have driven out there, slit her nasty throat and been home in time for the ten o'clock news."

"Or, perhaps it was you. Can anyone confirm you worked late Friday?"

Patricia thinks. Then, "No."

"I have witnesses to your saying you hated her."

"Among others," Patricia objects.

"Maybe you're not finished. If I was the suspicious type, I'd check our EZ-PASS account."

"Maybe we did it together. The cops said they weren't sure if it was a lone killer."

"And it was such a lovely night for a drive."

"Would you crack under interrogation and turn on me for a plea deal?"

Max considers this. "No, I suppose not."

"The beauty part is," Patricia says, "as spouses we can't be made to testify against each other."

Max smiles and raises his glass. "I'll drink to that."

Patricia gets up and walks to Max. She leans in to him firmly placing her hand under his chin, turning his head toward her. She kisses him hungrily. After a moment, she pulls back, holding him in her gaze.

"Are we celebrating something?" Max asks.

Patricia walks to the other end of the table and turns back to him. She gives him an enigmatic smile. Then she turns and leaves the kitchen and heads up the stairs. Max watches her go. Max gets up and follows.

TWENTY-EIGHT

TUESDAY, AUGUST 20, 2013

5:36 P.M.

SUFFOLK COUNTY POLICE DEPARTMENT

HOMICIDE DETECTIVE SQUAD

RIVERHEAD, NY

Nancy Perkins sits behind her desk in her office. DeMarco and Rooney are seated in chairs opposite.

"Find anything?" she says.

"This," DeMarco says passing a piece of paper across to her. "It was on his computer."

Perkins takes a minute to quickly scan the letter. "It might indicate intent but we'll need a lot more. Anything else?"

Rooney holds up the jump rope. "There were a bunch of these in a conference room. They hand them out at jump rope events that are held in schools. We're going to run it by ME Bellows to see if it's consistent with the ligature marks on the victim's throat."

"No bloody pinking shears absent-mindedly left in his desk by chance?" Perkins asks dryly. Not getting an answer and not expecting one, she continues, "How did your outreach to New Rochelle go yesterday?"

"They're having a patrolman go by his house this week on the pretext that there have been break-ins in the neighborhood," DeMarco says.

"Good. Let's keep them on him. And if Max Short sets foot on Long Island, let's use this to have a little chat," Perkins says, handing the letter back to DeMarco.

TWENTY-NINE

Max sits at the kitchen table drinking coffee and reading the newspaper. The doorbell rings. Max gets up and goes to the front door. He opens it. Standing on his stoop is a uniformed police officer.

"Good morning," the policeman says. I'm Officer Stone with the New Rochelle police department." He shows Max his badge. "I hope I haven't disturbed you."

"Not yet," Max replies.

The officer forces a smile to show that he gets Max's little joke.

"How can I help you?"

"We're talking to people in the neighborhood to alert them to a recent rash of car break-ins. Are you aware of this?"

"No."

"Well, good to know your car hasn't been broken in to," the

policeman says, jerking his thumb in the direction of the car in Max's driveway.

Yes, that's my car and my license plate, Max thinks, trying not to betray his annoyance.

"Have you noticed any unfamiliar persons around the neighborhood?" Officer Stone asks.

"No. When do these break-ins occur? At night?"

"Some," the policeman responds. "But many are reported by people arriving home from work in the evening. May I ask, are you often home during the day?"

Yes, Officer, I'm fucking unemployed! Max wants to scream. *Put that in your goddamn report.* "Yes," Max replies.

"We would be very appreciative if you would let us know if you do see anything suspicious," Stone says, handing Max his card.

"Certainly," Max says.

"Thank you. Have a good day." The officer turns to go but then turns back. "And if you see our squad cars around more than usual, it's on account of the break-ins."

Max nods. He closes the door. Max walks to the living room window and looks out through the sheer curtains. The policeman walks across the street to his squad car and gets in. Max stays at the window for several moments watching until the squad car pulls away.

"So I'm being watched," Max says softly to himself. "Watch away, you won't see a thing."

THIRTY

Max stands at the bathroom sink shaving. Noise from the television in the bedroom comes through the open door.

"We have an exclusive News Twelve update on that murder in Southampton—"

Max turns his head to listen. He turns off the faucet and puts down the razor. He walks to the door to the bedroom, shaving cream covering half of his face. The news announcer continues.

"As previously reported, socialite Brandi Napoli's body was found on a Southampton beach over a week ago with her throat slashed. An anonymous tipster has called a producer at this station to report that the victim's tongue was also cut in two—that is to say bisected—by what this individual claims were pinking shears. Suffolk County homicide detectives have refused to comment."

"So, this is an uncorroborated story at this point?" her co-anchor adds.

"At this point, yes," she says to him. She turns back to the camera. "We will keep you up to date on further details as they emerge."

Max steps back into the bathroom and picks up his razor. He looks at himself in the mirror for a long moment. Then he turns the water back on and continues shaving.

THIRTY-ONE

The security guard comes down the hallway. A large ring of keys jangles from his belt. He checks office doors, making sure that they are locked. He comes upon one that is open.

"Locking up," he calls in, taking the keys from his belt.

No answer.

"Hello. Anybody here?"

Still no answer.

"At least you could turn out the light," he mumbles under his breath. He hits the switch just inside the door and extinguishes the overhead fixture in the office. This reveals a light coming from the open door to the connecting office. The guard trudges to that door and reaches in to snap that light off as well, but suddenly jumps back, his keys crashing to the floor.

Gladys Ortiz sits at her desk, unmistakably dead.

GLADYS

Born in Brentwood, NY thirty-some-odd years ago to parents from Puerto Rico, Gladys Ortiz is the vice president of the Suffolk County office of the National Cancer Foundation, a position that she has held for eight years. She is of medium build with dark hair and eyes. She currently lives in Commack with her fiancée, Ingrid Casales. She is also working to finish her thesis for a master's degree from Stony Brook University on the north shore of Long Island. She completed the course work years earlier and the deadline for her thesis is fast approaching. It's now or never.

As a boss, she has two shortcomings. The first is that she is, most of the time, an absent boss. She's usually in the office in the morning. That's the time to get her because come lunchtime she disappears, often never to return. Her assistant either can never say or has been instructed not to say where she is and when or if she'll be back. It makes things difficult for staff. You don't get much feedback from an empty chair.

The other problem is that she is a weakling and that is very dangerous in a boss. She is intimidated by everyone and anyone. She's always saying, "Get along—if you want to keep your job." Unfortunately, for her staff to keep their jobs they also have to do them. So they can't afford to wait for her to make a decision because she won't. A decision is a very scary thing for Gladys Ortiz. Someone may not like it. What then? And if she ever she finds herself in that situation, she is not above pushing the blame onto an underling—or them under the bus. Technically, she isn't a liar. If you ask her if she will back you up she'll say, "I'm right behind you." And when you are in the midst of the fray and turn around to look, she is indeed behind you. Very far behind you.

THIRTY-TWO

"Congratulations."

Max looks up from his desk. Gladys stands at the entrance to his cubicle.

"Thanks," Max says. "For what?"

"For getting your two co-chairs last Thursday night to agree to work together. How did you do it?"

"I stressed the importance of the success of the event in helping NCF fight cancer. I have found if you can get volunteers to focus on the bigger picture, it helps them to move beyond their pettiness."

"Sound policy."

"Keep your fingers crossed. The event has a long way to go and their individual orbits could collide again."

Gladys's expression grows less sunny.

Max realizes he should stifle himself from always feeling the need to undercut a positive with a cautionary comment. It doesn't move him up on the likeability ladder. It's just he prefers to keep things in perspective, for himself as well as others.

Gladys is holding a copy of the last financial report. "I see the Lawrences have made a ten-thousand-dollar gift. How did that happen?"

Joan Lawrence is on the Suffolk County board of NCF. When Max first started, Gladys had suggested that he reach out to her. The previous year, she, along with a couple of other volunteers had staged a small event for the chapter. It had been in the form of a potluck supper which they had prepared. They sold fifty-dollar tickets and raffled off several donated items. The take was very insignificant—not something Max would normally waste his time on. But Gladys wanted him to see if he could revive it. At that point, progress on the gala was in its early stages and such an event should not demand too much of his time. Max wanted to show his new boss that he was a team player, so he agreed to contact Joan. She had come into the office one day and they met to discuss the event. In the course of introducing himself, Max told her that he had been hired to start a new gala event in the Hamptons. At the mention of that, Joan's eyes had lit up. She said that she and her husband were looking to buy a place on the East End. Most of their conversation then revolved around what Max was planning for the Hamptons. At that point, little had been decided so there was not much to tell. Gladys had told him that the Lawrences were well-to-do. The fact that they were looking to buy in the Hamptons seemed to confirm that. Eventually, the potluck supper idea didn't pan out. However, Max definitely made note of Joan's interest in the gala.

"As I told you, when I first met with Joan, she expressed a special interest in the Hamptons gala. So, once everything was in place, I sent her a letter over Brandi's and Gupta's signatures inviting her participation as a Silver Sponsor. A week later, their family foundation check arrived in the mail," Max says with pride.

Gladys takes this in, nodding her head. Then she walks away without comment.

Max grabs a piece of paper off his desk and walks over to Carolyn's office. She is in.

"Got a minute?" Max asks.

"Come on in."

Max enters and sits in the chair opposite Carolyn's desk.

"What's up?" Carolyn asks.

"I was hoping you could tell me."

"About what?"

"Our fearless leader."

"What did she do now?"

"It's what she hasn't done," Max says. "My first week here, I met with her and she gave me a list of people she said she could approach about participating in the gala."

"Is that the list?" Carolyn asks, pointing to the paper in Max's hand.

Max hands the paper to her.

Carolyn peruses it. "She's mentioned some of them to me, too. But I don't know them or have any idea what their stories are." Carolyn hands the paper back to Max. "Has she given you an update on any of them?"

"She hasn't talked to any of them yet. Originally, I understood she didn't want to approach them prematurely. But everything's been in place for several weeks now—the date, the venue, the giving levels. What is she waiting for?"

"Have you asked her?"

"Every time we meet. She just says she hasn't had the chance."

"I feel for you but I can't say I'm surprised."

"Do you know Joan Lawrence?" Max asks.

"She's on the board," Carolyn replies. "What about her?"

Max tells Carolyn about his history with her, concluding with, "Last week, I got Joan's family foundation check for ten thousand dollars."

"Congratulations."

"Thanks. The thing is, Gladys just asked me how that happened. In a very suspicious manner, I might add. When I told her, she said nothing. And she didn't look too happy about it."

"You're messing with one of her board members."

"She told me to work with her. You'd think she'd be happy."

"You showed her up," Carolyn says. "I hate to say it but I think our boss has a chronic case of the *mananas*."

"And where does she go every afternoon? She's never around. Sue never knows."

"Working on her thesis?" Carolyn says, slyly.

"Or fucking her girlfriend," Max retorts.

Carolyn laughs. Pause. Then, "Do you have a fact sheet for the event?"

"Yeah."

"Shoot it to me. I'll talk it up when I'm meeting with my corporate contacts and see if there's any interest."

"Thanks," Max says.

"I wish I could do more."

THIRTY-THREE

At the meeting by the pool at Brandi's, Gladys is anxious to talk about her contribution to the silent auction. Given that it is the only concrete addition she is making to the gala, Max is fine with letting his boss lead off the meeting with it.

"She's a very well-known artist on Long Island," Gladys says brightly.

"Never heard of her," Brandi says, taking a long slug of her mimosa.

"What's her name again?" Gupta asks.

"Agnus Aucklander."

Gupta furrows her brow, thinking. Or making a show of it. She says nothing.

"What does she paint?" Margo says.

"Landscapes. Mostly Long Island beachscapes," Gladys says.

"So, realism," Margo says.

"Um...yes. She's going to be choosing one from her collection with a market value of at least ten thousand dollars," Gladys adds enthusiastically. "So, we can start the bidding at what...nine thousand?"

No one has anything to say to that.

She reconsiders. "Or maybe we should make it eight?"

"I think we should start lower," Gupta quickly interjects.

"Seven," Margo says.

"Six," Gupta counters.

"We don't have to decide today, girls," Brandi says, clearly bored.

"It's just that it's so tough to nail that kind of thing down," Gupta says.

"So true, so true," Margo adds.

"She has quite a following on the Island," Gladys says defensively.

Yes, but this is the Hamptons, Max thinks, *and although the East End is physically on the Island, it ain't the Island.*

"Where's her studio?" Gupta asks.

"Hampton Bays," Gladys says.

"Isn't that somewhere in Queens?" Brandi quips.

Gupta and Margo cackle.

Margo quickly tries to steer them to higher ground by piously intoning, "Artwork is so subjective."

■

Driving out to the meeting, Max had decided he was going to hold his tongue when Gladys presented her auction item. Having had sufficient experience with auctions, he was well aware that artwork at a general goods and services auction seldom went. People weren't there to purchase art. Perhaps if it was a work by a very famous artist people might try to snag it at a good price to turn around and sell it for more. And while he hates to admit it, he agrees with Margo—art is subjective. But Gladys is so sure that this is going to be a big money-maker for NCF.

Max wants to prepare her for the fact that her expectations might fall short. But he does not want to be the one to deliver that message.

.

At one point, Brandi gets up saying, "I don't know about anyone else, but I'm hot. Let's continue this inside." She heads for the French doors.

Once inside they gather around the table in the kitchen and the meeting continues with a conversation about possible masters of ceremonies.

"I want Joy Behar," Brandi proclaims.

"Do you have a way to reach out to her?" Max asks.

"Isn't that your job?" Brandi shoots back.

"I'll find out the name of her management company and send them a letter."

"What about Derek Jeter?" Gladys says.

"That's thinking outside the box," Margo says.

"I love Derek Jeter," Brandi enthuses.

Max fixes Gladys with an icy stare. She may be his boss, but she has just crossed a line she should not have crossed.

.

When he first started at NCF, Gladys had managed to get out of him that his wife worked for the New York Yankees. It was something that he preferred to keep quiet. It had happened to him numerous times before at previous jobs where superiors would use that knowledge to try to get things from him. Get things out of Patricia, to be more exact—Yankees tickets, memorabilia, promotional tie-ins, celebrity appearances, you name it. And they were shameless in their pursuit, usually trying to make Max feel that his job was in jeopardy if he did not produce. Like he was not doing his part because everyone was expected to bring whatever they could to the table in support of the cause. But it wasn't about what Max could bring to the table, it was what his wife could bring to the table. He was the employee not her. She didn't have to bring anything to the table. And if what he brought to the table wasn't enough for them, they could fuck off!

At the respiratory/digestive disease job, his boss came to him one day and asked if Patricia would be able to secure Yankees tickets for an upcoming gala for the Washington, D.C. office. He and his counterpart there were talking about trading auction items—they'd get a D.C. item in exchange for a New York item. With sufficient notice, Patricia was usually able to do that so Max told him she probably could. His boss told Max he would let him know if they decided to go ahead with the swap.

Several weeks later, his boss came running up to Max in the late afternoon in a sweat. "Where are the Yankee tickets?" his boss demanded.

Max was confounded. "What tickets?"

His boss had never followed up with him about tickets. The guy was ready to piss his pants. The executive director from D.C. was on the phone! Their event was that night! His boss ran to his office telling Max that he had to get right back to D.C. and tell them how to get the tickets. Within seconds an email from his boss bounced into his inbox with the email address of the D.C. executive director.

Max felt he had no choice in the matter. To challenge his boss in the state he was in would not be a good idea. Max picked up the phone and called Patricia at work. He explained the situation. He was sorry. Could she turn around a request that fast? Patricia had been remarkably calm. She couldn't get physical tickets to D.C. but she could email a voucher that would have the information for the winning bidder to use to claim them. Max thanked his wife. He apologized again. He hung up the phone, furious. From that moment on, Max vowed he would never let himself be put in a similar situation again.

■

Max continues to stare Gladys down.

"I'm sorry, Max. I totally forgot or I never would have mentioned Jeter." Gladys turns to the others. "Max's wife works for the Yankees," she explains.

Oh, that makes it all better, you dumb cow. If she really wanted to explore getting Derek Jeter, she could have come to him and discussed it in private. But drop it in front of everyone!

"Holding out on us?" Brandi chides.

Margo turns on Max with an expectant look. "Well?" she says drawing the word out to three syllables.

"Well, what?" Max retorts, straining to keep his voice neutral. Max clears his throat. "Let's talk videos, shall we?"

■

"What about Derek Jeter?" Max mimics Gladys in a mincing voice.

"What!"

That evening over dinner, Max is telling Patricia about his meeting.

"Everyone loved the idea. I was speechless. I just looked at her. She got all twitchy and acted like the idea had just come to her out of the blue. Like she had momentarily forgotten that you worked for the Yankees," Max says.

"I hope you squelched it then and there," Patricia says.

"It won't come up again."

"It better not."

"Then, by way of explanation, Gladys told them that you work for the Yankees."

"Oh, no. We can't go there!"

"Don't worry. This isn't going anywhere."

"From what you've just told me it sounds like Brandi's going around behind your back. What's to stop her from going to the

Yankees?"

"Nothing. But if she does, it'll have nothing to do with me and nothing to do with you."

"But if people at work find out my husband's with NCF—"

"Does anyone there know?"

Patricia thinks for a moment. "No."

"Good. Keep it that way."

Max gets up. He picks up his plate, reaches across the table, places Patricia's plate on top and takes them to the sink.

"I don't trust people in your business," Patricia says.

"Me neither. Unfortunately, I have to work with them."

"There are people at work who would love to use something like this to get me pushed out," Patricia says.

Max turns from the sink to look at his wife. "Even if it isn't true?"

"That doesn't matter. Once painted as a potential problem it doesn't go away."

Max turns back and continues rinsing the dishes. He throws over his shoulder, "Do you want coffee?"

"No. I'm not going to be sleeping well now as it is."

THIRTY-FOUR

FRIDAY, JUNE 28, 2013

8:59 a.m.

NCF SUFFOLK COUNTY OFFICE

ISLANDIA, NY

Max pulls into the parking lot and turns off the engine. He spies Gladys's Jeep parked there.

Good, she's in.

Max gets out, locks the car and heads into the low brick building. He goes directly to Gladys's office. He needs to tell her about the blowup between Brandi and Gupta at the diner the day before. She won't be happy, of course. But he had done nothing inappropriate to spark it. He and Gladys and Margo had all agreed prior to the meeting that both Brandi and Gupta should have roles in the speaking program. When he had tried to go over the program, Brandi had gone ballistic. Brandi's notion that Gupta doesn't deserve to speak is utter nonsense and Max is actually glad it's now out in the open. *You first need to identify a problem in order to solve it.*

Max gets to Gladys's door and looks in. She is not in her office. He glances over to Sue's desk and sees her computer dark and her sweater hanging on the back of her chair. She's not in yet. Max goes to his cubicle. The red message light is blinking on his phone. He sits and picks up the handset and goes into his voicemail. The first message is from Brandi.

"If you ever do anything like that to me again, I'm going to Margo and Gladys." The venom cuts through her booze-warped voice. "I told you how the program is going to go and I'm telling you again—she is not going to say a fucking word! Understand?"

Max thinks about how best to deal with this. Clearly Margo has no intention of standing up to Brandi. And Margo is not his supervisor. Gladys is. He doubts that she will stand up to Brandi either but he has to let her know what's going on and let her hear for herself Brandi's abusive behavior—the threat, the language. Max saves the message. After listening to his other messages, Max sets his phone for voicemail. He gets up and again goes back to Gladys's office. She is now sitting behind her desk.

"Good morning," Max says.

Gladys looks up. "How did your meeting go yesterday?"

"Haven't you heard?"

"What?"

"I thought maybe Margo would have said something. I was going over the speaking program. When I got to the part about Gupta's remarks, Brandi blew a gasket. Started screaming that Gupta wasn't going to speak. Gupta, of course, started yelling back."

"That doesn't sound good," Gladys says.

"It happened in a diner. Can you come to my desk? I want you to hear something."

Gladys gets up and follows Max.

"I thought the meeting was scheduled for Brandi's."

"She moved it. She was having her floors done."

They get to Max's desk and he plays the voice message back for Gladys on speakerphone.

At its end, Max says, "How do you think we should respond?"

"I don't think we should."

"I think she needs to understand that I am not an independent contractor doing things willy-nilly as I please. I work for NCF and I report to you and I work with Margo and we all decided on this course of action."

"This event is doing so well and we are so close to success, this is no time to start parsing things that aren't going to matter in the end."

"As my supervisor, Gladys, I would really appreciate it if you would explain the situation to her."

"I wasn't there. I can't speak about things I didn't witness. For all I know, Gupta said something to provoke her."

"I told you what happened. Margo can confirm it."

"Maybe you should ask Margo to speak to Brandi."

As if! She clammed up the moment Brandi started in and didn't so much as let out a peep. Why would she say anything now?

"Mary Shelley would be jealous," Max says.

Gladys looks at him, perplexed. "How's that?"

"We've created a monster. Brandi. The eight-hundred-pound gorilla."

Gladys gives him a weak smile. She points to the blinking red light on his phone. "You have an event coming up, mister. Pick up your messages." Gladys goes.

THIRTY-FIVE

Max hurries to finish up the work he needs to get accomplished. This evening is the second kickoff event which Ross Flanders Public Relations has organized. It is scheduled for 6:00 p.m. at the MacKenzie-Childs shop in Southampton. As busy as he is with the gala, this pointless event is not what Max needs.

Whoever heard of holding a kickoff reception the week of the real event? Kickoffs are held months before. The one in the city made sense. Not that it generated a single ticket sale. But it gathered people together to learn about the gala and NCF. It helped put the event on the map and on people's calendars. But holding a kickoff right before the main event accomplishes nothing. People who are coming have already ordered tickets; those who haven't aren't coming. The worst part is, though Max has had nothing to do with planning it, he has been charged with picking up the wine which Gupta has gotten donated by Wölffer Estate Vineyard in Sagaponack. It will take him about an hour to drive from Islandia to Southampton. Sagaponack is another twenty-five minutes further—without traffic. A July evening in the Hamptons without traffic? Dream on!

He stops by Gladys's office on his way out. He raps on her open door. She looks up.

"Oh good. Sit down for a minute," she says.

"I can't. I've got to get out to the kickoff event in Southampton. I have to pick up the wine."

Gladys looks confused. "Call me from the road," she says.

That is something Max is not going to do. Calling while driving is not only dangerous and stupid, in New York it's illegal. In all of his years working in the not-for-profit industry, he had received some pretty high-handed directives but he had never been told to break the law in the commission of his job. *This makes a first and new low-water mark. Go NCF!*

After a few minutes on the road, he reconsiders. If he doesn't call Gladys after she told him to, he's going to hear about it. He can hardly spare the time but he pulls into a service station and calls.

"Hi. It's Max."

"Listen, I can't talk right now. It's not that important. We'll talk tomorrow."

Max drops the hateful BlackBerry into the console between the seats.

■

He makes it to Route 27 in good time but that's when the funeral procession commences. Max wonders why people spend millions of dollars to own homes out here. It's impossible just trying to get around. How is this in any way relaxing? Sure, you get to lie on the beach. You need to because by the time you get out here you're a nervous fucking wreck.

Max anxiously watches the dashboard clock rapidly tick away the minutes while the miles roll under his wheels agonizingly slowly. For a good part of the journey he is right behind Betsey Johnson in a convertible. Not that he's such a celebrity whore that he recognizes her, especially from the back. But her New York vanity plate is BETSEY and her flaming tresses blow in the breeze. Who else could it be? At one point, Betsey makes a right turn off of Route 27 and Max is overcome by sudden sadness. Not because he misses Betsey Johnson but because she has reached her turnoff and he still has miles to go.

His BlackBerry rings. He picks it up. It's Margo. He lets it roll into voicemail.

"Wondering where you are. Please call in."

He drops the phone back in the console. Since he is practically at a standstill he could safely call her back but decides he will wait until he gets to Wolffer and has picked up the wine. No sense subjecting himself to her outraged huffing and puffing before he has to.

When he finally makes it to Wolffer it is 5:45 p.m. Not only was the traffic crawling the entire way, but once here, there is some confusion about the wine donation. It is the regular manager's day off and he didn't leave any message about it. Certainly they make charitable donations, an efficient young woman behind the desk informs him. They are a very socially conscious business. They keep a running ledger of all donations and there is nothing entered for the National Cancer Foundation and, no, the name Gupta Ritter is not familiar. Max even offers to buy the two cases of wine and figure it out latter. At that point, the young woman says that she will have the wine put in his car if he will leave his contact information. Max hands her his business card with sincere gratitude. Then he calls Margo.

"Where are you?"

"I'm at Wolffer."

"Oh, for heaven's sake!"

"Twenty-seven is a parking lot. Do you know any side roads that will get me back to Southampton quicker?"

"I do but I can't possibly give you directions. We'd never see you again."

"Okay. Well, I'll get there as soon as I can."

■

By the time Max gets back to Southampton, it is going on 7:00 p.m. Thankfully the traffic on Route 27 heading west was somewhat less congested. There are no parking spaces anywhere on either side of the street near MacKenzie-Childs. He considers double parking, putting on his blinker and carrying the two cases of wine into the store. But the street is narrow and that will undoubtedly cause a very public traffic jam right in front of Margo and company. The mere thought of the scene that would cause keeps him cruising on. He finally finds a spot about a block and a half away. He dons his black linen sport jacket and lifts one of the cases out of the car. It is a sultry evening and the sun is still bright. He immediately breaks into a sweat and within a half a block droplets of perspiration are freely dripping from his brow staining the lid of the wine case in his arms.

Max enters MacKenzie-Childs. Mercifully the air conditioning is doing its job. No one takes notice of his entrance. Which is hard to miss given that there is almost no one else there. Brandi is standing in the center of the small store speaking to Ross/Flanders. Gupta is talking to a young woman who Max assumes is the one from the PR firm with whom he has spoken a few times on the phone. Margo is chatting with a woman Max does not recognize.

Max sees the skirted table that is serving as a bar at the rear of the shop with a uniformed bartender behind. He carries the wine there. Clearly the man has already been pouring wine. There are several bottles of both white and red open on the bar. The bartender reaches over and takes the case from Max, putting it on the floor behind the bar.

"There is another one in the car. I'll get it," Max says.

"Here," the bartender says, "take the handcart." He points to it behind him.

"Thanks," Max says going around the table to retrieve it.

Max returns with the second case and hands it to the bartender. Margo is there having her chardonnay replenished.

"Where did this wine come from?" Max asks.

"The liquor shop next door," Margo says evenly.

There is no hint of recrimination in her voice. No outrage. No condescension. *She's on her best South Fork behavior tonight.*

The woman Margo was speaking with when Max first walked in is right behind her proffering her glass for a refill. Margo doesn't introduce her and Max doesn't ask. He takes a glass of red from the table and roams the shop feigning interest in the over-decorated, over-priced items on display. Mostly Max is shocked by Margo's calm demeanor. Not only Margo, but the whole party. In fact, it's as solemn as a wake. Unlike some of his family's Irish Catholic affairs that were downright raucous compared to this. This is like a viewing where everyone is being quiet so as not to wake the dead. Max wonders if that's where the term came from. As Max considers the situation, he decides being late is not such a bad thing. They have wine and he gets to endure a curtailed purgatory in this birdbath.

At one point, two young men enter the shop. One has a camera. The other carries a notepad and pen. They take a few pictures of Brandi and Margo. They snap a few of Gupta. They even take one of Max, the guy with the notepad getting Max's name and title at NCF.

Then they depart as quickly and unobtrusively as they came. Max walks up to Ross/Flanders.

"Who were those two?" he asks.

"They're from *Dan's Papers*."

"*Dan's Papers*? What are they doing here?"

"Brandi told me to call and make sure that they covered the event."

Max is mystified. He thinks he must be misunderstanding what the man is saying. *Why would she want them to cover this?* He decides to not pursue it.

■

Within an hour, the party has run its course. Ross/Flanders helpfully offers to take the two unopened cases of wine and bring them to the Southampton club on Saturday.

Max's main concern is Brandi. After the scene in the diner and the hostile voicemail she left him, he is anxious about facing her. However, he had observed her during the reception and she seemed to be in a reasonably good mood. She was calm. She was laughing. He even saw her and Gupta conversing at one point. He knows he needs to try to mend bridges and decides that there is no better moment.

"Brandi, may I have a word with you?"

She glances around the room. "Follow me out."

They stand on the sidewalk in front of the store. The sun is setting and the air is pleasantly cooler.

"Brandi, I want to apologize about the meeting at the diner the other day. I realize now that I should have spoken to you privately first. But I want you to know that Gladys and Margo and I did discuss how to handle the speaking program and it was a decision we all agreed on. Gupta is a co-chair of the event. She is listed on the invitation as such and she will be listed in the program distributed at the event as well. In addition, as of the other day, she has more than satisfied her commitment to raise twenty-five thousand dollars. It was not a decision that I made in a vacuum."

"The woman is a disgrace," Brandi says in a calm almost plaintiff voice. "How dare she cause a public scene like that? She humiliated me and she humiliated Margo. I would think that NCF would want to treat her in as low a profile manner as possible."

Max can't believe his ears. Brandi just said that Gupta started it? He is momentarily speechless.

With that, Margo walks out of the store with Gupta. Margo eyes Max talking to Brandi with deep suspicion. Brandi has her back to them and does not turn around. Whether she is aware of their presence or not, Max can't tell. The two women walk off together in the other direction.

Max finds his voice. "You two seemed to be very cordial at the reception inside."

"Of course I'll be cordial to her. It's just…I don't care what she does now," Brandi continues, sounding deeply hurt. "She didn't do the job she promised and she doesn't merit the same recognition as me."

■

This is one of the most challenging aspects of this business. No two volunteers are of equal ability when it comes to fundraising. A few of them love it and pursue it with gusto. Brandi being an excellent example. However, most hate and fear it and need to be dragged kicking and screaming all the way to the finish line. The problem comes in when you have volunteers of different abilities performing the same role. You can't give them different goals based on their abilities. It has to be standardized. Max likes to think of it as establishing the "floor." When he creates job descriptions for volunteers, he gives the same goals to all volunteers recruited to the same role. That's the "floor." Having established that, all volunteers are encouraged to do as much as they can. In the case of *Festive in the Dunes*, the "floor" for both Brandi and Gupta had been $25,000. There is an adage in fundraising: "One third of volunteers will do what you ask, one third will do more than you ask and one third will do nothing." In over twenty-five years at this job, Max has found that to be pretty much true. You could heap additional kudos on the volunteer who exceeded expectations but you could not denigrate the volunteer who only met the basic requirement or even fell through the floor and ended up in the basement. Another adage in the business is: "Praise and honor for all volunteers."

When at the heart disease organization, Max had started a women's lunch with two women board members. The original idea was to honor several women who had demonstrated "heart" in their lives and through their work. Lauren Bacall had been one; Kitty Carlisle Hart another; Mary Tyler Moore a third. They were not conceived as revenue-generating honorees. Several years in, Max became acquainted with a woman who was the head of a large retail firm and had recruited her as a lunch honoree. Coming out of the business world, he had a feeling that she would naturally assume that she was expected to raise money. In fact, she proceeded to do so. Max said nothing to dissuade her. Well into the campaign, she asked him what the other honorees were doing along the lines of fundraising. She received weekly financial reports that identified all gifts with the names of the contacts who had brought them in. Her name was all over the place. Her sister honorees not. Max fibbed and told her that it was the expectation that all honorees contribute to the fundraising effort but, in the current crop, the others were not as able as she. The woman was no fool and instantly saw through his subterfuge and vain attempt at flattery. After a moment considering a response, she merely dismissed it with a wave of her hand. She continued fundraising, taking the event to new heights. Good thing. If she had not chosen that path, it could have been ugly and rightly so.

■

A sudden gust of salty breeze buffets Brandi and Max as they stand outside MacKenzie-Childs.

"I don't understand what I've done to deserve this kind of treatment," Brandi continues, almost pouting. "And I'm sorry, but I have to put my foot down. I will introduce Gupta as a co-chair at the event but she most certainly will not get up to speak," she adds with finality.

■

The following afternoon Max sits in Gladys's office.

"Brandi's playing the victim."

"How so?"

"She's twisting the whole thing around. She's saying that Gupta started the scene in the diner."

Gladys just looks at him noncommittally.

I know, you weren't there and can't comment.

"I told her that you, I and Margo had all decided that Gupta needed a speaking role in the program," Max informs her.

A look of irritation tinged with fear comes over Gladys. "I heard you were very late getting to the event," she responds, incriminatingly.

"The traffic on twenty-seven in the summer is impossible. You know I left here at two thirty."

"You should have had Gupta pick up the wine on her way from Amagansett."

"She didn't offer and I was told that it was my responsibility."

"I can't help you there," Gladys says smugly.

No, you can't help me anywhere, can you?

"I also heard that you and Brandi had a loud argument out on the street afterward."

"It wasn't a loud argument. It was a conversation. Who told you that? Margo?"

"Um-hum," Gladys says, nodding her head with a grin as if she's caught him red-handed.

"You shouldn't take everything Margo says as gospel."

"Are you calling her a liar?"

"I'm saying she has a vivid imagination and an uncontrollable need to constantly stir the pot."

THIRTY-SIX

WEDNESDAY, JULY 10, 2013
11:10 a.m.
SOUTHAMPTON POOL AND BEACH CLUB
SOUTHAMPTON, NY

It is the final on-site walk-through before *Festive in the Dunes*. Brandi and Gupta are in attendance. So are Margo and Gladys. Carolyn Petrie and a half a dozen other women from the office are there as they will be working the event in various capacities. Andy Fox is also there. He is wearing a rumpled, ill-fitting sport jacket which looks like the ones restaurants with jacket requirements give to men who show up without one. His arms are dangling down several inches below the cuffs like an organ-grinder's monkey. *Is this his idea of looking professional?* Max thinks, going over the audio-visual needs for the event with the AV vendor.

■

Brandi had secured AV services through a contact of her husband's. As is the case with most of the other benefits Brandi brought to the

195

event, this arrangement came with a price beyond what will eventually appear on the invoice.

At one of the first committee meetings, Brandi had announced that all committee members needed to be in the loop on all correspondence regarding the event. This is not how Max usually did things. His motto regarding that was "need to know." And most members of this particular committee didn't need to know much since they contributed so little. All the same, Brandi's directive had caused a torrent of feedback on most of his emails. Sometimes someone took issue with how he was proposing to proceed. Sometimes someone simply didn't like or understand the way he was expressing himself. Responding to it all had become exhausting and non-productive.

On reflection, Max had come to realize during the course of this Hamptons event that he had been lucky. For most of his career, he had run corporate events. In that scenario there is an honoree or honorees and a chair or co-chairs. These people were president or CEO-level individuals from companies who were involved to display that they are good corporate citizens. You met with them once at the beginning of the campaign, got their leadoff five-figure gift and a commitment to raise the additional suggested amount. That was it. You never saw them or spoke with them again until they showed up at the event. You did liaise with a senior-level person to ensure the fundraising was on track. In terms of every other aspect, they could care less. They left you alone to do your job. *Festive in the Dunes* is a very different animal. Every committee member is involved in every decision. The problem is most of them bring nothing to the table but their opinions.

Since Brandi had secured the AV company, they were eager to please her. Max had his initial meeting with them at the club to go over what would be needed. Although Max neglected to ask them to send their proposal only to him, it would have made no difference.

Brandi knew the meeting was taking place and was expecting to see the quote. As is usually the case, the initial estimate was high. Over $8,000. The budget which Max had created allotted $2,500. Brandi exploded. She sent Max an email chewing him out. She copied everyone. Max's reply was that this was a process and the first quote was the beginning not the end. He would now work with them to remove or modify elements to get the cost within range. Naturally, this did not suit Brandi or anyone else. Especially Margo.

At the next committee meeting Margo, like the Grand Inquisitor, solemnly declared, "The way you do these things is you tell them right off how much you have to spend." All nodded their acceptance of this universal truth, signing off on Max's auto-da-fé.

Of course, this is precisely what you don't do. If you tell a vendor how much you've got to spend, the quote will come back—surprise, surprise—that very amount. Then, you have no opportunity to negotiate. Negotiate what? The quote's on budget. You also forfeit the chance to see the full-blown, top-drawer proposal. That educates you as to what they have to offer. Knowledge is power. *Never give away your bargaining position.* Max wasn't going to argue the point with Margo, the damage had been done. Most galling of all was Gladys's response.

"You should talk to Dana Daniels, she might give you some tips. She's had experience negotiating with vendors."

You mean Miss Colossal Fuck-Up to the tune of minus sixty-eight thousand dollar? You think she will be able to school me? Really?

■

"How's it going over there, Max?" Brandi calls out from the other side of the club. "We don't need a Cecil B. DeMille production, you know."

The AV guy gives Max a sympathetic look. He has, obviously, worked with Charm Girl before.

"We've got it, Brandi," Max calls back.

■

Later, Max is seated at a table with Brandi, Gupta, Margo and Gladys. They take up the subject of centerpieces. Margo had found painted tin beach pails online and had ordered two dozen—one for each of the twenty-two expected tables with two extra, just in case. Max had purchased toy shovels and pinwheels to have sticking up from the pails. They discuss how best to prop up the shovels and pinwheels. They consider filling each pail partially with sand.

Agreement all around the table.

Max chokes out, "Or, how about—?"

He has no idea what to suggest. He just knows that while they may say that they'll all pitch in filling the pails with sand, it's going to end up being solely his responsibility. It can't be done until the day of the event. None of these women are going to be out on the beach, in the heat, scratching around in the sand in their party clothes. The NCF staff who will be working the event are all women and they will, likewise, balk at having to do this. He has no doubt that Gladys will take their side. With everything else that is already on his plate, day of, he doesn't need this.

They all look at him, waiting.

"Tissue paper," he says. *When in doubt, tissue paper to the rescue. Women can't resist it.* "We'll put a piece of florist's foam on the bottom to stick the pinwheels in then stuff the pails with colored tissue paper to prop up the shovels."

They look back at him as if amazed by the simple beauty of the suggestion. Does he detect slight irritation that none of them had thought of it?

"That should work fine," Brandi says flatly. It passes by virtue of no contest.

They move on to the auctions. Max goes over the silent auction items. He says that he and Mary Taylor are speaking later in the day to set opening bids and bid increments. Gladys adds, excitedly, that she is meeting with Agnus Aucklander the next evening at her studio when Agnus will select the painting to be donated.

"She has promised that it will be valued at no less than ten thousand dollars," Gladys says. She also shares that Agnus will be attending the event as her guest.

Brandi talks about the live auction. "They're all trips and fabulous one-of-a-kind experiences," she says.

"How about putting Agnus's painting in the live auction?" Gladys ventures.

There is no immediate response.

"Given its value, I don't think it belongs with the silent auction items," she continues.

"Given it's not a trip or experience, it doesn't really fit with the other live auction items," Margo says. "You said that this artist is attending as your guest? What if it doesn't go? Or doesn't go for as much as she thought it would?"

Gladys lets out a slight laugh and opens her mouth as if to speak but doesn't.

Margo changes the subject. "At the women's lunch in the city, we do a balloon auction. I'd love to do something like that at the gala."

"What is it?" Gupta asks.

"An announcement is made from the podium that for a thousand dollars individuals can make a contribution in support of Tranquil Cove. If interested, they are asked to raise their hands. Staff go around and get their credit card information and tie a balloon to their chair, recognizing them as donors," Margo explains.

After a moment, Gupta speaks. "I don't know if this would work, but what if we did something like that in support of Camp Quest? You know, adopt a camp kid."

Not to be outdone, Brandi quickly jumps in. "Each table would be in support of a particular kid."

"We could put a kid's picture by each pail on the tables," Gupta continues.

"I love it!" Margo says. She turns to Gladys. "Can it be done?"

"Of course," Gladys says, without batting an eye.

A queasy feeling swells in Max's gut. He immediately senses that the practicality of the idea is a bridge too far. One of those last-minute, tacked-on elements that falls into his lap and threatens to overload, short-circuit and doom his chances of pulling off the event success-fully. But he says nothing. Then.

■

When they get back to Islandia, Max follows Gladys to her office.

"This adopt a camp kid idea, is this doable?" he asks.

"Why not?"

"To use kids' pictures and names we're going to have to secure written permission from their parents, aren't we? We had to do that for the camp kid that was profiled in the *Dan's Papers* article. It took some time to turn around. And that was only one kid. For twenty-two? How can we do that in the time left?"

"That's what the Internet is for," she says.

"What do you mean?"

"I'll pull pictures of kids off the Internet. Make up names. Print out pictures."

Initially, Max is relieved that Gladys is handling this. But he is still uneasy about it. He heads for his cubicle, then changes his mind. He goes to see if Carolyn is in.

"I just needed to share the latest," he says, sliding into the chair across from her.

"Tell. Tell."

"As of today, we are doing a balloon auction at the gala to support kids for Camp Quest. There will be a picture of a kid at each table and the people at that table will be asked to donate to support that kid's two weeks at camp."

"Sounds reasonable," Carolyn says.

"Except there's no time to get permission to use real camp kids' names and pictures, so Gladys is going to pull pictures of kids off the Internet and make up names for them."

"You jest."

"'Fraid not."

"Well, she's the boss. If she wants to do it, I don't think there's much you can do about it. Any blowback is on her."

"That's what worries me. This is my event and this could conceivably come back to bite me in the ass. I really don't trust her."

"Go back to your desk, send me a memo detailing this conversation with the date. I'll acknowledge by return email, then we both have evidence."

"No. I don't want to get you involved."

"We can worry about that if and when."

"Thanks, Carolyn. I honestly don't know what I would do if you weren't around."

THIRTY-SEVEN

Max is glad to see home as he pulls into his driveway. It has been a stressful day. What with all the back and forth with Gupta over the seating, he didn't get out of the office until almost 6:00 p.m. Traffic on the Northern State got unusually heavy shortly after crossing into Nassau County and it had taken him over an hour to get home.

Patricia's car is not there, meaning that she isn't home yet but should be shortly. *It'll be deep freezer diving for dinner tonight.* No sooner has he stepped from his car than his BlackBerry rings. It's Gladys.

"Hi, Gladys."

"I'm at Agnus Aucklander's studio. The painting is awesome! Agnus just finished framing it. We're sure it's going to bring in at least ten thousand. The frame alone is worth that much," Gladys gushes.

"That sounds great," Max says feigning as much enthusiasm as possible.

Max walks into the house. He drops his briefcase on the floor and walks into the kitchen. He stands next to the kitchen counter, sliding over a pad of paper and a pen in case he needs to make any notes.

"Now, I want you to expand the signage for the piece," Gladys continues. "Agnus just gave me lots of biographical stuff. I'll forward it to you to use."

"Fine. I'll get on it tomorrow," Max says wearily. The end of the tunnel which he caught a glimpse of leaving the office, recedes further and further away.

"Mary Taylor is with me. She wants to talk to you."

Mary has had some experience working on auctions for her kids' school and for her church. Max finds her to be knowledgeable and he is glad for the support with the auction. She had even made herself available to go out to Southampton with him for a site visit. Gladys hands the phone to Mary.

"Max, I just wanted to talk to you about what we should list as the value and the opening bid."

"Is it really worth ten thousand?"

"Agnus has set the value at sixty-five hundred."

"For the painting?"

"Yes."

"What about the frame?"

"Let's just leave it at sixty-five," Mary says.

"Sounds good. What should we open with?"

"I've consented to be the reserve bid at two thousand. It's a little low but we don't have anyone else and that's what my husband and I agreed we could do."

"Thank you, Mary. Hopefully that will get us off to a good start and bids will grow from there," Max says cheerfully.

Mary doesn't say anything to that.

Gladys is back on the phone. "I still think we should put it in the live auction."

Gladys heard Margo's response to this very issue yesterday, along with Gupta's and Brandi's tacit concurrence. Now she's trying to corner Max when he's alone. He thinks a moment before he speaks. "What does Agnus think?" As hot as she is on the subject, as hot as she is to make her sole contribution a smashing and very visible success, he's sure that Gladys has brought this up with Agnus.

"She's not sure…"

Max is eager to end the call.

"Anything else?" he says.

"I want something in the speaking program about Agnus. She'll be there so we can have the emcee introduce her. I'll forward you bullet points and you can make it flow."

"That is a terrible idea, you pathetically dumb bitch! I don't have the time for this now! Why have you waited until the last moment to dump all of this useless shit on me?" is not what Max says. What Max says is, "I've already sent Nick Firestone his script. I'll have to give him changes on site. He's probably already marked up his script. It might not be easy for him to incorporate the additions."

"He's an actor, he's used to adapting," Gladys says and hangs up.

Max puts the BlackBerry down on the counter and walks to the living room. He goes to the window and pulls back the sheer curtain. He sees Patricia pulling into the driveway.

Time to hit the freezer, he thinks, heading for the cellar door.

THIRTY-EIGHT

A dark scarlet plume of arterial spray decorates the curtains covering the windows behind Gladys Ortiz. Black rivulets of dried mascara stain the cheeks of her upturned face. Her eyes stare sightlessly at the ceiling. Her throat is ripped open. Her jaw is slack, mouth open. Her tongue, like Brandi's, is cut in two bearing the distinctive serrated pattern left by pinking shears. It protrudes obscenely like a butchered slab of meat escaping from an overstuffed sandwich. Her splayed legs display the crotch of her beige pants stained dark and wet where she pissed herself. A team of forensic officers carefully examine her body and the surrounding area. A police officer stands guard at the office door. Detective Mark DeMarco and Detective Angela Rooney approach the officer, brandishing their IDs. The officer steps aside and lets them pass.

"The neck wound looks consistent with the one on Brandi Napoli's neck," Rooney says. She looks down to Gladys's feet in flip flops. "Ankles zip tied. Same. Same mutilation of the tongue. Only difference is her left wrist is zip tied to the arm of her chair. Why not the other?"

"So she could write something?" DeMarco speculates. "Use the computer? What's the security guard's story?"

Rooney references her notes. "Slow day. No Friday classes in the summer. A handful of students using the library."

"Which is where?"

"Downstairs. Didn't see or hear anything unusual. Of course he did admit to listening to music on his earbuds. Oh, and New Rochelle police report Max Short's car has not been in his driveway since earlier this morning—"

DeMarco's phone rings. He answers it. "DeMarco." He listens for a moment or two. Then, "Thanks." He disconnects. "A squad car has picked up a partial on their license plate reader at a stop light on Sunrise Highway in Bay Shore heading east. The first three letters, CBN, match Max Short's. It was on a silver Volvo like his. When they circled around to confirm the full plate, the vehicle was nowhere to be found. If it was him, it's feasible we could put him at Stony Brook at the time of the murder."

"But if he committed the murder and was heading home, he'd take the Northern State or the LIE," Rooney reasons aloud. "Why would he drive to the south shore and why would he be heading east?"

DeMarco glances over at Gladys Ortiz's bloody corpse behind her desk. "I'd say this gives us cause to ask him those questions in person. Doesn't he have a son who lives on Long Island?"

"Dix Hills," Rooney says. "I remember that because when I moved here, I looked at a place there but it was too far in."

THIRTY-NINE

FRIDAY, AUGUST 30, 2013

6:46 p.m.

JEREMY & SARAH SHORT'S RESIDENCE

DIX HILLS, NY

DeMarco and Rooney are in their car parked across from the house.

"How long should we just sit here?" Rooney asks.

"The BOLO on him is still active. If there's an update, we'll get a call. In the meantime, this is the best place to wait."

"He could be in the house."

"Could be but where's his car?"

With that, DeMarco looks in his rearview mirror and sees Max's car driving up the street behind them. "Isn't that considerate of him not to keep us waiting?"

DeMarco and Rooney watch Max pull into the driveway. He switches off the engine and gets out of the car. DeMarco turns to Rooney and nods. Rooney opens the passenger door and gets out of the car.

Max walks up the path to the front door. He rings the bell. After a moment, the door is opened by his daughter-in-law, Sarah.

"Max Short?" comes Rooney's voice from behind Max. Max turns and both he and Sarah look at Rooney standing ten feet away on the path.

"I'm Max Short."

"Detective Angela Rooney with the Suffolk County homicide detective squad," she says, holding her badge up high in front of her.

"What can I do for you, Detective?"

"We're investigating the murder of Brandi Napoli. We understand that you worked with her when you were with the National Cancer Foundation."

"That's right."

"My partner and I would like to ask you a few questions." She turns and points to the car parked on the other side of the street. DeMarco sticks his arm out the window, smiles and gives a cheery wave.

"I only know what I read in the paper and heard on the news. I no longer worked there when it happened."

"I know but you did work with her for about a year and you might be able to add bits of information that could prove helpful."

Max puts his head down and thinks.

"We haven't had the opportunity to speak with you before this and we thought, since you happen to be in the neighborhood...Our boss is a real stickler for thoroughness and we'd love to be able to tell her we closed this loop."

Max still debates this in his mind, turning to look at Sarah.

"You could follow us to the local stationhouse. I promise you we won't take up any more of your time than is absolutely necessary," Rooney says pleasantly.

"Is Jeremy home?" Max asks Sarah.

"No. He's not back from his meeting." Pause. "I can come and wait with you, if you want."

"No, that's okay. Just please call Patricia and tell her I am at the Dix Hills police station meeting with Detective Rooney and—" he turns to Rooney, questioningly.

"Detective DeMarco," Rooney fills in.

"Tell her not to worry," Max continues. "I'll call her when I'm out. I've been told it shouldn't take long."

"Sure, Max. I'll call her," Sarah says.

∎

At the stationhouse, Rooney and DeMarco enter a small windowless room with a table with several chairs around it. DeMarco holds the door for Max who enters, looking around.

"Have a seat," DeMarco says, pulling a chair out for Max to sit. Max sits. DeMarco closes the door.

"What brings you to the Island today?" DeMarco asks.

"I was helping my son put up shelves in his home office."

"He gets to work from home? That's nice."

"He runs his own business. He's a graphic designer."

"Gets to be his own boss, too? I'd say he's doubly blessed. I tell you from working in homicide, you'd be amazed how many people off someone who they work with."

"That wouldn't surprise me at all."

DeMarco gives a short laugh. "So did you get all the shelves up?"

"Mission accomplished."

"Did it take long?"

"We were done by two."

"Heading home after this?"

"I'm spending the night."

"Where were you coming from just now?"

"I grew up near here. North Babylon. When we finished with the shelves, I took a drive down to have a look at my old house."

"Around two o'clock?"

"Yes."

"The old neighborhood, eh? Still know people there?"

"No."

"You didn't talk to anyone?"

"No."

"Just sat in your car looking at your old house?"

"For a while."

"It must have been for quite a while. North Babylon's only twenty minutes from here. You pulled up to your son's house about quarter to seven."

"Belmont Lake State Park is two blocks away. I went there. Walked the nature trail. Sat on a bench by the lake and watched the rowboats. Fed the ducks. Then drove to an old haunt for supper. I discovered it's sometimes best to let old haunts remain in your memory."

DeMarco laughs. "I hear ya."

"It's the Lemon Street Diner in Bay Shore, Detective. You can confirm with them that I was there." Max glances at his wristwatch. "You said you wanted to talk to me about Brandi Napoli?"

DeMarco produces a newspaper and tosses it on the table in front of Max.

The headline screams: PINKING SHEARS MURDER MYSTERY. Again, there is the picture of Brandi.

"We withheld the detail about the pinking shears. Someone leaked it to the press. It's something only the killer would know. I'd call that boasting."

"I heard about it on the news," Max says.

"That was a pretty nasty trick she pulled on you with those sheets right before your event."

"She was a nasty person."

DeMarco glances at Rooney. "There was another murder today. Very similar and should prove to be identical. Gladys Ortiz was found at her desk at Stony Brook University with her throat slashed."

Rooney and DeMarco watch the shocked look on Max's face.

"Gladys is dead?"

Rooney produces the jump rope and tosses it on the table in front of Max. "Look familiar?"

Max stares at the rope. "It's a *Jump Rope for Hope* which NCF gives out at their events."

"That's where we got this," Rooney says. "There's a whole bunch of them in a room at your old office. Brandi Napoli and, likely, Gladys Ortiz were garroted with ropes just like this rendering them unconscious before their throats were cut."

DeMarco places both hands on the table and leans in close to Max's face. "But first you waited for them to come to. Where would be the fun if you couldn't see the terror in their eyes?"

Max meets DeMarco's glare calmly. "You have quite an imagination, Detective."

DeMarco straightens up. "This, I didn't imagine."

DeMarco reaches down into his briefcase on the chair next to him and pulls out a sheet of paper. "We found this on your NCF computer." DeMarco reads Max's letter aloud.

"Dear Gladys

This serves to provide you with notice of my resignation, effective immediately. My primary reason for leaving is

Brandi Napoli. It is quite clear that she has no intention of relinquishing her position with *Festive in the Dunes* and it is equally clear that you and Margo have no thought to replace her or rein her in. I cannot face the prospect of having to work with her for another year. By resigning it is my intention to rid that woman's voice from my life forever.

"Gladys Ortiz told us you were fired."

"That's right."

"You never presented her with this letter?"

"No."

"Why write it?"

"I was having a bad day. It cheered me up."

DeMarco looks hard at Max. *"Rid that woman's voice from my life forever.* Maybe Brandi Napoli's voice wasn't the only one you wanted to silence. Maybe Gladys Ortiz's voice, too. I bet having to listen to her tell you that you were fired couldn't have been enjoyable. You wanted to shut her up. Slashing her throat and cutting her tongue in half with pinking shears for good measure would shut her up nicely, wouldn't it?"

Max looks steadily back at DeMarco. "Detective, am I free to go?"

DeMarco studies Max for a moment. Then, he walks to the door and opens it. He gestures through it with an open palm. Max gets up from his chair and walks out of the room.

Rooney looks at DeMarco. "Cool customer."

∎

Outside in the parking lot, Max gets into his car. He sits for a moment looking through the windshield. A smile spreads across his face.

Two down. One to go.

FORTY

Seated around the conference table are Margo, Gladys and Max. It has been one week since Max started at NCF and this is the first planning meeting of the proposed Hamptons gala. To this group has been added Ricky Colon, the Manhattan director of social events and Max's counterpart at that office.

For the past fifteen minutes they have been engaged in the sole task of trying to identify individuals who might be approached to serve on an event committee. Max has scribbled the name of every suggested candidate, spelling it phonetically if unfamiliar. It's a very short list.

"I have someone," Margo says potently. Her eyes gleam as she waits for all heads to turn in her direction. Clearly, she has been holding back until the sense of futility in the room had reached the desired point before dropping this bombshell on the table.

"I can get Jean Shafiroff to chair the event," Margo avows. It is not a mere suggestion. It is not a fond hope. It is a stated fact. "I've already spoken to her about it."

"Jean's tops," Ricky says with relief—clearly not a member of his stable.

The name means nothing to Max. Gladys's blank expression registers the same.

"I have to wait until after July twenty-first to officially ask her. That's the date of the Southampton Hospital Gala and Jean is on the committee. She's much too busy now."

Max considers that this development means that there can be little forward motion on the event for the next month. The date and the venue will be contingent on Jean's okay. He can still do research on venues, caterers, musicians, masters of ceremonies, etc. And if Jean is truly a lock, it'll be worth the wait.

"She sounds great," Max says.

"Google her," Margo says.

Max does. The first thing that strikes him is the number of sites on which her name turns up. He clicks on a few of them. They all tell the same story—education and marital status, followed by a litany of causes and events that she has supported, chaired or otherwise been involved with, including Southampton Hospital. Max is also impressed by the number of organizations that have honored her over the years. *She's definitely a player.* This is good. Players have quid pro quo.

Players go to a lot of events and support a lot of charities. Many of these events have honorees and chairs and co-chairs who form the event's leadership. When someone you know is being honored at or chairing an event and they ask for your support, you do so because of your relationship with them. Then, when you are being honored at or are chairing an event, you turn around to these same people and get them to support your event. It usually works very well but not always.

Sometimes players get played out. Max remembers meeting with the CEO of a major communications company once who had been recruited to chair an event which Max was running. The CEO explained that he was happy to do anything that was asked of him except submit names of people from his universe for solicitation. He told Max that the only reason he had agreed was because they had gotten the one person in the world to recruit him to whom he could not say no. But as for soliciting friends, colleagues and vendors, he could no longer do that. One acquaintance had recently told him that when he saw him coming down the street, he crossed to the other side "because every time I shake your hand, it costs me five thousand dollars."

Max doesn't get the impression that is the case with Jean. For one thing, she is considerably younger than that CEO and second, she is very active in both New York City and East End philanthropy. She should have many people who owe her.

After that meeting, every time he runs into Margo in the Manhattan office, he asks if she is still pursuing Jean. "Like white on rice," is her reply. It gets to the point that when he sees her, he doesn't have to say anything. "Like white on rice," she calls out.

THURSDAY, AUGUST 9, 2012
10:04 a.m.

Six weeks later, the same group is gathered around the table in the conference room at the Manhattan office. They have met twice in that time. On both occasions, the agenda was the same—identify volunteers for committee recruitment. A significant number of names emerged, some pie-in-the-sky, some realistic, all dead ends. The Southampton Hospital Gala had been one week before the last meeting. It had been too soon then to expect that Margo had spoken to Jean and when she made no reference to it, Max decided to let it slide. But it is now three weeks since the gala and Max intends to bring it up at the top of the meeting. Margo beats him to the punch.

"Bad news, dears," Margo begins, staring at some spot on the highly polished surface of the table. "Jean has accepted to chair Southampton next year."

Silence all around. Ricky Colon looks pissed.

Max almost asks when next year's Southampton Gala is scheduled for but stifles himself. It is a desperately stupid question. No, not desperate. Pointless. Much more pointless than desperate. What is the woman going to do? Clone herself to chair two events in one summer? Max feels like a kid who has been told about a wonderful new ice cream flavor but when he asks for a scoop, is informed it is sold out. He doesn't know what he is missing but, illogically, it only makes him miss it more. When Jean seemed in the bag, he could afford to regard her critically. *Sure, she's good but I've known better.* Now that he's denied the chance to work with her, he envisions her as some magical creature. She is a goddess who, with the mere snap of her well-manicured fingers, has money managers up and down Route 27 dumping their ducats into coffers at her feet. Max looks across at Ricky's irritable expression and now he is pissed. *How dare she turn us down! Who does she think she is?*

Having absorbed the shock and disappointment of Margo's news, Max switches into survival mode. He needs to get over this. *Who needs Jean Shafiroff anyhow? She's probably not all that great. In fact, she's probably a hideous crone. A hideous crone who would have made my life miserable.* Max decides he has dodged a bullet. What a relief! From that moment forward, Max will always think of Jean Shafiroff as a hideous crone.

"I'm sorry. I really thought that was going to work out," Margo says.

MARGO

Margo Schumacher is a Jewish sixty-one-year-old little brown wren of a woman. That does not mean she is meek. On the contrary, she is very vocal and has an opinion about everything. And that voice! Margo has a pseudo-British accent like a 1930s Hollywood star. It is pure studio diction class. Hyde Park via Flushing Meadow. She acquired it while married to one of Her Majesty's loyal subjects and living in England for a few years before dumping him and returning to the States with a handsome settlement.

In truth, her assertiveness is just a tactic to try to hide the fact that she is extremely insecure. With good reason. As senior vice president for development at NCF, she has oversight of all Gotham Division fundraising activities and events. This encompasses Manhattan, Brooklyn and Queens, along with Nassau and Suffolk counties and New Jersey. Like many not-for-profit organizations, NCF omits the Bronx because, well, "there's no there there." And Staten Island is another country. But Margo is in way over her head. Having been at the organization just over a year, she's desperate to score a success to justify her continued employment until she can retire.

Holding a new event among the one-percenters in the Hamptons was her idea. One was tried before but the less said about that the better. Since she has a home out there and a Manhattan apartment, using contacts from both she is sure she can make a success of it. At least that's how she sold it to the president. Deep down, she knows that she is like the waitress who keeps assuring you that she'll be right with you but brings nothing to the table because she hasn't figured out how the kitchen works. That is why hiring the right person to run the event is so crucially important. A seasoned professional with a sound track record for running events. Someone who really knows how to get these things done. Margo has bluffed her way into every job she has ever had and then found people to surround herself with whose work she could take credit for. After a few years, but not too long, she'd resign and find another place to land. Since no one she worked for ever really knew what she couldn't do, references were never a problem. But on her own? Impossible!

Like most national nonprofits, NCF is organized regionally with separate chapter offices. These operate as silos with no crossover of staff, implementation or revenue. The Hamptons being geographically in Suffolk County, this new event will be run out of that office. At first Margo was unhappy about this. But she was able to obtain the concession that all details would be cleared with her in advance of any decisions and she would participate in all meetings and conversations of her choosing. Upon reflection, this arrangement suited her nicely. Once the event was a success, she would claim it as her own and no one would dare contest her. Certainly not the mealy-mouthed vice president in Suffolk, Gladys. And if the thing flopped, it wouldn't be a black mark on her record. That bitter harvest would be dumped on Gladys's head.

FORTY-ONE

Max pulls the seat belt across his chest and buckles it for his drive out to the Maidstone Club in East Hampton. Earlier in the week he had confirmed an appointment there for a site visit to check it out as a possible venue for the event. He had spoken with the general manager, Ken Murphy. It was not Ken with whom he would be meeting. Ken had explained that he would be out of the office on Thursday and he had arranged for assistant manager Mick Conklin to meet with him. The meeting is scheduled for 11:00 a.m. The drive from Islandia to East Hampton takes close to an hour without traffic. A weekday morning in September does not portend heavy traffic. Just the same, Max is leaving a little early to ensure not being late. He has never been there and wants to avoid any delaying surprises.

Since the disappointing news about Jean Shafiroff nearly two months ago, Max has been working on securing a venue. Without a confirmed gala chair, he cannot lock in a specific date so he is working with any Saturday in June, July or August. He has seen several places, most of which don't cut the mustard for various reasons.

One was East Hampton Point. The club had a capacity of 200 persons seated for dinner. There was also an outdoor deck for cocktails prior to dinner. Although it was not on the ocean, it's location on the eastern shore of the bay afforded it a beautiful sunset view. Max had created a budget that would net about $160,000 based on 250 paying guests. Even factoring in people who pay for their seats but, for one reason or another, don't attend—Max needed space for 220. Although the manager assured Max that she could squeeze in a couple more tables, Max felt it was cutting it too close. On top of that, seating was in two separate rooms on two different levels. Without video monitors, half the party would not be able to see or hear the program.

Wolffer Estate Winery in Sagaponack was certainly desirable. It was like being in a Tuscan villa. The problem was it only seated 175. There was a stables/polo grounds area outside where a tented event could be held. The tent could be sized to accommodate as many guests as needed. The caveat was that they only did three tented events a year and, though she wasn't sure, the manager thought that they were already spoken for. She said she would check the calendar and get back to him. He wasn't holding his breath. The night after his visit, he had a dream that they did hold the gala in a tent on the stables/polo grounds and everyone was screaming at him that the place smelled like horse shit!

Another possibility was a tented event at another location. Tented events are very popular in the Hamptons for reasons that were becoming apparent to Max. There were precious few establishments that had the capacity to hold larger parties.

He had contacted a caterer who advertised off-site services. He met her at her office and she drove him out to a place called Mecox Farm in Water Mill or Bridgehampton. The towns along Route 27 all run into each other. The "farm" was a flat, grassy field surrounded on three sides by a body of water. A large event tent was already erected alongside a smaller kitchen tent.

"What if it rains?" he asked. "This field will be one huge mud pit."

"A guaranteed rain date is built into the contract," the caterer had responded.

Max had had experience with rain date events and was not eager to go there. Besides, the only other event Max had done in the Hamptons had been a tented event for the respiratory/digestive disease organization he had worked for and, after that experience, he had vowed never to do one again.

Doing a tented event in the Hamptons requires permits. Lots of them. There's a permit for the event itself. Beyond that, there's a permit to run water to the site, there's a permit for trash removal, there's a permit for portable lavatories, there's a cooking permit, there's a music permit, there's everything but a permit permit. All of these permits need to be obtained from the town of Southampton. To say they are none-too-eager to hand them out is an understatement. Coming from outside the community and not knowing anyone at city hall doesn't help grease the wheels. It also didn't help that Max inherited the event from another staff member who left just before it. Many event staff keep lots of details in their heads. When they're gone, it's impossible to know what has been done and what hasn't. Documentation is sketchy. Even things that appear to be confirmed need to be double-checked.

On top of that, the man who owned the ranch where the event was scheduled to take place got himself in trouble with the local authorities. He had booked an event for a children's charity that was staging a kids' carnival. Apparently city hall had not been accurately advised about the nature of the event and when they saw it, they were not amused. Max saw the picture in *Dan's Papers* that accompanied an article about the carnival. A giant clown head loomed above garish rides in an otherwise sylvan field. They couldn't do anything about the event in progress without appearing like ogres, but Southampton put a moratorium on events in the field for the rest of the summer. This was four weeks before Max's event! Max called the owner in a panic and demanded that he do something about it. The owner assured Max that it was not a big deal and not to worry. But he did worry. His boss worried. Board members worried. He was expected to somehow make Southampton change its mind even though everyone knew that was out of all of their hands. Finally, after over a week, the man called Max to tell him that his event was still on. Max suspected that the resolution had something to do with money changing hands but that was not his concern.

However, that was only the beginning of his woes. Most charities are stupid cheap. They only look at the bottom-line cost of doing something without considering the best and most efficient way. Someone involved with the organization got a restaurant to donate the food. They weren't catering the event, they were only donating the food—raw! Another group had been hired to cook the food on site. The restaurant was not delivering the food. It had to be picked up.

Max was required to drive to MacArthur Airport in Ronkonkoma and park his car in the overnight lot. He then walked two blocks to a rental office where he had reserved a refrigerated truck. He drove the truck to the restaurant which was a few towns east of where the event was being held. By the time he had loaded the food into the truck, it was the middle of the afternoon. The event was set to start at 6:00 p.m. and Route 27 had turned into its usual parking lot. Max crawled back to the event to be greeted by his red-faced boss demanding an explanation for what he had been doing for so long. Max was going to mention the traffic but if his boss hadn't figured that situation out by now he never would.

When the event was over, Max and the rest of the staff had to completely clean the site and return it to the condition it was in prior to the party. This entailed bagging up all trash and recyclables. All materials and unredeemed auction items were put in individual staff members' cars to be brought in to the Manhattan office. By the time they were finished, it was after midnight and Max was bone-tired. He had gotten the foundation to agree to reimburse him for a motel room on the Island for the night. However, the motel was in Riverhead, a good forty minute drive.

When he got there, he pulled up to the office entrance which was behind a half-wall that separated the motel property from the road-way. Because he was tired and not completely familiar with judging the truck's width, he hit the wall, taking out a good-sized chunk. When Max explained to the man behind the desk what had happened, he was shocked the man seemed unconcerned. When Max got to his room he figured out why. The place was falling down all on its own. The ratty carpet emitted a foul smell. There was a serpent-sized rust stain in the bathtub. The soap by the sink was not only not wrapped but had bubbles on its surface from the previous guest.

Although the motel did not charge for the damaged wall, the truck rental company was not so forgiving. Since Max had not been authorized to take out collision coverage on the truck, (he'd been told to "drive carefully") there was more than a few hundred extra on the bill. So, between that, overnight parking, gas, and the motel, the foundation ended up paying a hefty fee for their "free food."

Good. Serves the assholes right!

■

So far, Max's first choice is the Southampton Pool & Beach Club. The L-shaped floor plan consists of a bar and a dining room. Using 60-inch round tables, seating in both areas can accommodate up to 240 guests. The elbow of the L is a large square area where the band can be set up along with a podium and microphone. It also allows ample space for dancing. Speakers participating in the program are visible from both seating areas. The bar area is dominated by a large oval bar which divides the room, providing space to set up silent auction tables on the other side of the bar from table seating, as well as at the rear of the room. There is a central lobby area that Max sees as a perfect place to set up auction item checkout. There is a front deck for registration and a full, deep rear deck overlooking the ocean for the cocktail reception and after dinner. Max is hoping once he has checked out the Maidstone Club, he will be done with venue search.

Frankly, Max was surprised when he was told by Ken Murphy that the exclusive golf club did do outside parties. So was Margo when Max told her.

"I had no idea. This could be a huge coup. When's the meeting? I'll join you there."

As he drives through the Pine Barrens heading for the East End, Max feels vaguely irritated that Margo will be waiting for him. He knows that, ultimately, site selection would be made by whoever chaired the gala. Margo will voice her preference, of course. But he has been doing this solo for so long he feels strongly that he doesn't need anyone else to check out the club. It puts him in mind of how he always thought co-anchors on television news broadcasts looked like they dearly wished the other one wasn't there. His boss at the heart disease job once referred to him as "the lone ranger." Max wasn't sure if the man meant it as a compliment or not but Max took it as such.

Having reached the Hamptons but not yet East Hampton, Max sees a police blockade ahead. A police officer is waving all eastbound traffic to make a left onto a side road. Max has no choice but to follow the line of cars being diverted. He figures that there will be other police along the way at some point directing traffic back onto Route 27. Max continues to follow the traffic. The line of cars wends its way through open fields. One by one cars ahead break away from the group, turning onto side roads. Max figures that these drivers have no need to return to the highway. He remains with the pack because— well, he has no other choice and has no idea where he is or how to get back to the highway. The pack continues to dwindle as individual cars peel off. Now there are only two cars in front of him. Now one. When that car turns onto a side road, he is tempted to follow it but has no idea if it will lead him back to Route 27 or plunge him further down the rabbit hole. He pulls off onto the shoulder.

The beauty of driving in the Hamptons is that Route 27 is the yellow brick road. So long as you follow it, it will lead you to the fantasy destination of your choice. That is to say, to virtually every town in the Hamptons all the way to Montauk Point. The curse is, if it is jammed up, as it is most times during the summer or there is an accident or detour as there is today, you're screwed. In that case, there's no way to get there from here. There are year-round residents who do know how to navigate the side roads. It suddenly occurs to him, it being September, every other motorist who had been diverted from Route 27 must have been of that group.

Max had not programmed the address of the Maidstone Club into his GPS before he left Islandia. He figured once he got to East Hampton, he'd pull over and enter the address to get directions from the highway to the club. He decides the time to do that is now. He reasons that as long as he has been driving in basically an easterly direction, he must be parallel to East Hampton somewhere to his south.

Into his GPS, Max enters: 50 Old Beach Lane, East Hampton, NY. He waits as the GPS finds his location and plots his route. "No match" is the message that comes back. Max double-checks the address. It looks right. He reenters it as: 50 Old Beach Ln., East Hampton, NY. Again, he gets the message "No match." He enters: Fifty Old Beach Lane, East Hampton, NY. "No match." He tries: 50 Old Beech Lane, East Hampton, NY. "No match." 50 Olde Beach Lane, East Hampton, NY? "No match." He looks at the dashboard clock. It reads 10:36 a.m. He still has over twenty minutes to get to the club on time. He decides to call the club, tell Mick that there was a detour off of Route 27 and he's lost. He would set his GPS for East Hampton and get directions from Mick to the club from the highway. He'd also ask Mick to explain to Margo if she was already there.

"Good morning, Maidstone Club," a woman's voice comes over the phone.

"Hi. My name is Max Short from the National Cancer Foundation. May I speak to Mick Conklin?"

"Mr. Conklin is not here. Hold on." The woman puts Max on hold. After about thirty seconds, she comes back on. "Good morning, Maidstone Club."

"This is Max Short. You put me on hold."

"Oh, yes. You were asking about Mr. Conklin. This is the clubhouse. He doesn't work here. Let me try the pro shop for you. Hold on."

Now Max is on hold for about a minute before the woman comes back on.

"He's not at the pro shop. No one's seen him this morning."

"I have an appointment with him for eleven o'clock. I wanted to let him know I might be running a bit late." Stony silence greets this. "Do you happen to see an appointment listed for this morning with the National Cancer Foundation?"

"I don't keep Mr. Conklin's calendar. Hold on."

Max looks out through the windshield at the bucolic splendor all around him but the anxiety seizing his bowels makes it appear to be an eerie photographic negative.

"Is there anything else I can do for you?" the woman's voice comes back over the phone.

"I'm on my way there now. Can you give me directions to the club from route twenty-seven?"

More silence. Then, "I'm afraid I can't and I'm here all alone so there is no one I can ask." She is well trained. She doesn't hang up on him. But he can almost see her withering expression on the display screen of his phone. *Game, set, match.*

He is about to ask her if she sees a small woman in the vicinity who looks like her head is about to pop off but thinks better of it. "Thank you very much for your help."

Max doesn't have Margo's cell phone number and she had never asked for his. All he can do is get to East Hampton as quickly as possible. There has to be someone there who can give him directions to the Maidstone Club. Max enters "East Hampton" into his GPS. The device plots his course. When the map comes up on the screen, he is amazed to see that he is out near Sag Harbor! *How the hell did I get all the way out here?* Even at its widest point a car ride from Long Island's north to south shores takes about half an hour. At its easternmost end, the Island dwindles to what amounts to two overgrown sandbars. Max is back on Route 27 in no time.

Finally in East Hampton, he pulls into a gas station across from the firehouse. He glances at the dashboard clock: 11:14 a.m. He picks up his BlackBerry to call the club to see if Mick Conklin has made it in. Before he can dial, the phone rings. It's Margo.

"Where are you?" her voice demands over the phone.

"I'm in East Hampton across from the firehouse."

"What are you doing there?"

"The police detoured everyone off twenty-seven. I don't know the side roads out here. I got lost. I don't have your number."

"Nor I yours. I had to get it from Gladys."

Oh, great! And I know you didn't just ask for my number. You went into all the details, in Technicolor, of why you needed it.

"No one here knows anything about this meeting!" Margo fumes. "Who did you talk to?"

"Ken Murphy. But the meeting isn't with him. It's with his assistant, Mick Conklin. When I called earlier, he wasn't in."

"This is not how things are done," Margo grumbles.

"My GPS can't find Old Beach Lane. Can you give me directions from here? Let me just get there and I can straighten this out."

Margo gives Max directions to the club from the firehouse. "It's only two minutes away. I'll keep a lookout for you," she says. "What kind of car are you driving?"

"A silver Volvo wagon."

There is pause and then Margo says, more to herself, "This is so wrong."

What's wrong? My car?

■

"Mr. Short." Mick Conklin walks to where Max and Margo are seated in the lobby of the Maidstone clubhouse. He holds out his hand. "Mick Conklin."

Max stands and shakes his hand.

"I'm so sorry for the mix-up. It's completely my fault. I got Ken's message but put it on my calendar for tomorrow by mistake."

"Don't apologize. I finally got here, so it's all good." Out of the corner of his eye, Max sees Margo standing next to him twisting her lips impatiently. "This is Margo Schumacher," Max says, turning slightly in her direction. "She's also with the foundation."

Margo's hand shoots forward. "Margo Schumacher, senior vice president for development, National Cancer Foundation," she says, showing Max how to properly introduce her.

Mick smiles, vaguely puzzled, as he takes her outstretched hand.

"I understand you had some trouble finding us," Mick says to Max.

"My GPS couldn't locate an Old Beach Lane."

"That's because it's not a municipal road. It's the club's private driveway. Sorry about that. Happens all the time."

"I had to lead him in," Margo explains.

"So you're planning an event for next summer?" Mick says to Max.

"Yes."

"Tell me about it as we walk."

Max explains that they are planning a seated gala dinner-dance for approximately 220 guests. They don't have a date yet but are looking for a Saturday evening.

"Max will be handling the details but I will be overseeing everything from our Manhattan office," Margo adds.

They have arrived on the second floor.

"This is the barroom. If you're doing cocktails, this is where that would happen."

They are standing in a big, high-ceilinged rectangular room. There is a large mahogany bar on the left side of the room backed by an enormous mirror set in an ornately carved mahogany frame. The room is ringed by mahogany wainscoting above which are colorful but conservative-striped papered walls. Enormous double-hung windows on two sides overlook a hole of the golf course situated on a bluff above the sea. The impression is very clubby and very masculine.

Margo spies pamphlets neatly spread out in small piles on a massive oaken library table spanning the center of the room in front of them. She walks to the table and picks one up. It is a program for the local chapter of a national charitable organization's golf outing being held that very evening. She turns to Mick. "You do golf events for outside organizations?"

"Nine per year. I'm filling slots for next year's calendar now."

"How does one go about booking one?" Margo asks.

"Send a letter to the golf chair, Tommy Wolfensohn. The ballroom's this way," Mick says heading toward a pair of double doors beyond the bar.

Max and Margo follow. Margo sidles up to Max, putting one hand on his arm.

"Imagine little old me at the Maidstone Club," she coos in his ear, hunching up her shoulders and beaming girlishly.

The ballroom is an elongated two-story-high room with chandeliers, decorated in shades of cream.

"We can do one hundred eighty in the ballroom at round tables surrounding a dance floor. If needed," Mick goes to a double set of pocket doors at the back of the room and pulls one side open, "we can do another hundred in the terrace room."

Max walks up and looks into a lower-ceilinged room overlooking the ocean. He turns back to the ballroom. If they set the podium at the far end, then people sitting in the terrace room will be able to see and hear the speaking program. "Do you have a podium and a stage?"

"Both. The stage is eight by eight—only good for speeches. If you're at all interested, you should send a query letter with all the details to Penelope Dickerson. She's the house committee chair. They have to approve all outside ballroom events. They can't take any action until you have a date but it's a good idea to get in the queue." Mick hands Max a sheet of paper. "The best way to start is to pick a menu from one of these packages. That way, we can get back to you with total costs which will include the reception foods, dinner, liquor and wine so you can make a decision."

Max looks down at the paper in his hand. There are three packages listed with prices per entrée: fish, chicken and beef. This is a new one on him. Usually you give a desired price range and how many guests you expect and you sit down much closer to the event to choose a menu. But, when in Rome…

"Are we locked into these packages?" Max asks.

"No, you can choose one from column A and two from column B later and the costs will be adjusted accordingly. This is just to get started."

■

Outside in the parking lot, Max says to Margo, "I'll type up my notes and send them to you. When I've heard back about the menu, I'll let you know."

"We're not doing that nonsense with the menu, now! And you're not picking the menu at all. It's not how it's done."

"That's not how it's usually done but it seems that's the way they do it."

Margo closes her eyes and shakes her head. In disagreement or disbelief, Max isn't sure which.

"Can you tell me where the office for *Dan's Papers* is? I'll be needing to make an appointment with them soon," Max says.

"You'll pass it on the way back. I'm going that way, you can follow me. It's in a house with a front porch. It'll be on the left. I'll honk my horn as we pass. I'm in a, um…silver SUV."

Max gets into his car and watches Margo as she crosses the parking lot to hers and opens the door. She puts one foot in and hoists her small frame up into the high cab. Max can't fail to notice that the car is gray.

FORTY-TWO

TUESDAY, OCTOBER 23, 2012
11:10 a.m.
NCF, MARGO SCHUMACHER'S OFFICE
MIDTOWN MANHATTAN, NY

"We've got five acceptances for this Thursday's recruitment meeting," Max says.

Max is seated in a chair opposite Margo who sits behind her desk. Margo is regarding herself in the mirror of a compact that she holds in her hand. With the other hand, she is using the pad to apply makeup.

"Do you want me go over the list?"

"That's not necessary."

"I have to say, Ricky really has been very helpful in getting this pulled together," Max says.

"That's nice." Margo makes a gargoyle face as she juts her chin out to smear makeup on it. "You're going to be asking these women to do what, again?"

"Just to put forward the names of people with places in the

Hamptons who they know and can approach about serving as chair of the gala committee."

Margo dabs a bit more on her brow. "That's it?"

"That's it."

"Sounds like an elaborate waste of time." Margo puts the pad in the compact and snaps it closed, dropping it into her purse on top of her desk.

"I've seen it work."

"You've got them in a room. Why not ask them to be on the committee?"

"Because we explained that's not the purpose of the meeting. I think pulling a bait and switch is not going to get us very far."

"Just like the not very far we're at now? What are you going to do if this doesn't work?"

"Well, uh…Gladys says she has some people she can ask—"

"Gladys! She's a nothing. Nobody likes her, you know. After her last Hamptons fiasco—I wasn't here but I heard it was *très* embarrassing."

"I'm just going to stay positive," Max says.

There is a pause before Margo replies. "I can't. You've been here since June. It's the end of October. If you had the stuff we thought when we hired you, you would have made something happen by now. It's been very disappointing and I have to tell you that I no longer have any faith in this gala."

"Are you still coming to the meeting?"

"It's on my calendar."

Max stands. "Good." *Or not if that's your attitude. In which case I can't believe you would want to miss catching me as the Hindenburg going down in flames.*

FORTY-THREE

It is the first gala planning meeting with Brandi as the new chair. It's two weeks after the recruitment meeting at which she volunteered for the job. In attendance are Max, Gladys and Brandi. Conspicuously missing is Margo. The three sit at the conference table in silence, each engrossed in their cell phones or Blackberries.

"I have no message from Margo," Max says. "Gladys?"

"No."

"Me, neither," Brandi says.

"Well, I think we should go ahead. We can fill Margo in when she gets here," Max says.

"I'd like to start off by making it clear that I don't like bait and switch," Brandi says, giving Max a hard look.

The term strikes Max. It's the one that he had used in discussing the recruitment meeting with Margo. But that hadn't happened. They stayed on agenda and Brandi volunteered.

"What do you mean?" Max asks.

"I agreed to chair the gala event, not a golf event. I certainly never agreed to chair two events."

"I don't understand."

"Margo called me yesterday. She asked me if I would like to chair a golf event. She said that you two had discussed it."

Max is dumbfounded. He looks to Gladys who is picking a piece of lint off her jacket.

"The only event that I have responsibility for is the gala. Ask Gladys."

Brandi does not ask and Gladys does not offer.

"You and Margo need to start talking to one another because I have no intention of being the victim of your dysfunction. If that's the way it's going to be, I'm out of here." Brandi looks from Max to Gladys and back. Neither responds. "You and Margo are like an old married couple. You never talk to each other, is that it?" Brandi shakes her head derisively.

■

After the meeting, after Brandi has left, Max and Gladys remain in the conference room.

"What's she trying to pull?"

"What do you mean?"

"With this golf event."

"It must be a Gotham Division event."

"She never talked to me about it." Max picks up his BlackBerry. "I'm going to call her."

"Max!" Gladys barks. "Put down that phone."

"That's obviously the reason she didn't come to the meeting. She couldn't face us knowing Brandi was going to tell us what she's up to."

"What Margo does is none of your business."

"She tried to hijack my volunteer!"

"Don't make me write you up for insubordination."

An incredulous grin crosses Max's lips. "Insubor—"

"That's what it is! Margo is your superior. She doesn't answer to you and you have no right to question her."

"Clearly Brandi wasn't too happy."

"Brandi is chairing your gala. That's all you need concern yourself with."

■

The next day, as always, Max types up his notes on the meeting and sends it out to Brandi, Margo and Gladys. He omits any mention of the golf event.

FORTY-FOUR

Max is sitting at his desk, on the telephone.

"Morning, Mick. It's Max Short at NCF. How was your Thanksgiving?"

"Uh, good."

"I've got a gala meeting coming up and I think we are getting close to making a decision about the venue. I was hoping that we could talk about some dates."

There is a pause on the line. Then, "We have a policy here at Maidstone. We only do one event per year per organization."

Now, there is a pause on Max's end of the line. "Uh, what does that mean?"

"NCF has already booked a golf event for July."

"Through who?"

"Margo Schumacher."

That sneaky bitch!

Flummoxed, Max grasps for something to say so as not to sound like a total ass. "Oh, yeah. What date is that again? I may have gotten my wires crossed."

"Hold on." Mick puts the phone down but the line is open. Max hears the garble of office voices and noises in the background. Max feels like a fool. He should have known. *"Imagine little old me at the Maidstone Club."*

Mick picks the phone back up. "It's scheduled for the nineteenth."

Max pretends he is just now seeing it on a calendar. "Ouch. There it is. Totally missed that. Sorry for the confusion, Mick."

"No problem."

"Yeah, well. Sorry for the call. Have a good day." Max hangs up the phone. *Dammit! Insubordination or no, Gladys needs to know about this. I hope she's in.*

Max gets up and heads for her office.

FORTY-FIVE

"I don't understand what Margo's doing."

"What do you mean?"

"I just got off the phone with the Maidstone Club. I was calling to give them our proposed dates to find out about availability. The guy told me that they only do one event per year per organization and Margo has already booked a July nineteenth golf event."

"I don't follow," Gladys says, her brow furrowing.

"Maidstone was my contact for the gala. When Margo found out I had an appointment there, she invited herself along."

"So?"

"That's when she found out that they did golf outings. Apparently she went ahead and booked one without saying anything to me."

"I'm afraid I don't know anything about that," Gladys says, helplessly shrugging her shoulders.

That's why I'm telling you about it! "I've already emailed Brandi and Gupta that both Maidstone and the club in Southampton are options. Now Margo's stolen Maidstone out from under me."

Gladys just looks at Max questioningly, not saying anything.

"You were there at the last meeting when Brandi told us that Margo was trying to get her to chair a golf event. Thankfully, Brandi had no interest. But, clearly, Margo was attempting to steal my co-chair and now she has stolen one of my venues. It seems she is doing her best to sabotage our event."

Gladys looks off into the distance as if conjuring a replay of the scene. "That's not how I remember it," she says, slowly.

Max can't believe this obfuscation. "How do you remember it?"

Gladys bolts up in her chair like a daydreamer rudely elbowed awake. "You need to direct all of your energies into getting this event pulled together and making it a success. Nothing else. This gala is very important to Margo and there is no reason in the world why she would want to undermine it. And you do need to work with her."

Walking back to his desk, Max reflects on his conversation with his boss. He hadn't had any specific anticipation of the outcome. He just felt strongly that he needed to make her aware of what Margo was doing. What struck him most was her complete lack of outrage. This is her chapter's event. Where was her sense of ownership, her sense of pride? She twisted herself into a pretzel to avoid any trace of that. Maybe she doesn't care. Or maybe just about her own neck.

FORTY-SIX

It is the first meeting with both co-chairs since Brandi recruited Gupta. Neither Gladys nor Margo was available to attend, so it is just Max and the two women. The number one item for discussion is venue selection. In light of their schedules, the women have agreed that the two best dates for the event are Saturday, June twenty-ninth or Saturday, July thirteenth. Originally, Max had planned on presenting the two dates, along with the Maidstone Club and the Southampton Pool and Beach Club as options. He had reported back to both women about both clubs, indicating them as at the top of the list in terms of being able to accommodate the size event that they are planning. Brandi and Gupta are familiar with both venues. However, now that Margo has snatched away the Maidstone Club, Max has to present the Southampton club as the only option. Although he would love

242

to, he can't go into the real reason for why the Maidstone Club is not available. You learn early on in this business that you lie to protect the reputation of the organization if you want to last. That means lying to protect the reputations of the people who work there. Especially if they are superiors. You don't want volunteers to start to get the notion that they are devoting their time and money to a charity that can't stand up to scrutiny. Max hates this part of the job. He just closes his eyes and plows forward.

"First off, I have to report that the Maidstone Club is no longer available to us."

"What!" Brandi says.

"Unfortunately, when I got back to them, it was already booked for both of our dates."

There it is. The big lie. And a dangerous lie, Max well knows. In a community like the Hamptons it could be uncovered as easily as flipping a horseshoe crab on its back. If one of the women casually mentioned to someone that they couldn't get Maidstone for either of their dates because it was already booked and this someone happened to be a club member who told them in no uncertain terms that they have the latest events calendar and there are no events scheduled for those dates, Max's boat would be scuttled. Or if the women, being passionate about having the event at Maidstone, suddenly came up with another date that worked, Max would be sunk. Still, if he is not going to expose Margo's duplicity, he has little choice.

"Have you talked to Margo?" Brandi says.

"I'm dealing directly with the club," Max responds.

"Not fast enough," Brandi reprimands him.

"I called as soon as we picked dates," Max says simply, striving to not sound defensive.

Brandi greets this with a frown but says nothing.

"About the dates," Gupta says. "I'm thinking that the twenty-ninth is the Saturday before the Fourth of July. People could be going elsewhere or already have plans. I think we should avoid it."

"I agree," Brandi says.

"Plus, July is the start of the Hamptons high season," Gupta adds.

Blessed consensus! How rare and wonderful! "So, July thirteenth it is?" Max says.

Both women nod.

"The Southampton club is fine with me," Gupta says.

"Me, too," says Brandi. Turning to Gupta, "Maidstone smells musty."

Max wishes that had been Brandi's first word on the matter but he is glad it is her last. Max loves when decisions are made. Maidstone Club, dead and buried. Onto Southampton and beyond!

■

Later Max is on the phone filling Margo in on the meeting.

"So, you're going to be in that shitbox by the sea?" she says rhetorically and lets out a dirty laugh.

"It's what the women want."

It's been almost two weeks since Max got the word about Margo booking a golf event at Maidstone. They have not spoken about it. She certainly has not apologized about doing it without informing him. This conversation is as close as it has come. The "shitbox" comment—that's gloating. Whereas Max previously felt that he and Margo were reluctant partners, he now feels that they are rivals. She has the Maidstone Club. If her golf event can become the breakout Hamptons event for NCF that she has been lusting for, attracting all the "right" people and spawning endless annual ones to come, great. If not, she is still calling the shots on the gala. Still pulling the marionette strings and claiming any success as her own. She can't lose. And if she can't lose, is it even possible for Max to win?

"I'm just glad we were able to make decisions and move forward," Max says.

"Good luck," Margo says and rings off.

FORTY-SEVEN

The elevator for the penthouse is clearly identified with a sign on a metal stanchion. It has been specially keyed for the evening to go directly between the street and the penthouse. Once the doors close, off it goes.

The elevator doors open into the foyer of the apartment. A coat rack with hangers is positioned off to one side. There are about two dozen coats there. *It's still early*, Max thinks.

He spots Margo standing at the entrance to the living room. He walks up to her. "Good evening."

Margo turns to him. "Oh, good, you're here. There's someone I want you to add to the invitation list for the gala. Charlie Marder. He is the owner of *the* landscaping company in the Hamptons. It's in Bridgehampton. Google it."

246

"Sure, Margo. Does he do your place?"

"Of course," Margo says absently, surveying the crowd.

"I can draft a personal letter for your signature asking for his support. Do you think it would be appropriate to suggest he consider a premium table?"

"I told you just to put his name on the list!" she retorts.

"If you're a client of his, a personal appeal would be the most persuasive."

She continues to scan the room, not turning to him. "He did do the original landscaping on my place when I first moved in. He's frightfully expensive. I had to drop him." Pause. "With the recession, a lot of people did," she adds, almost to herself.

Max is feeling déjà vu. Another Jean Shafiroff. Max doesn't know whether to disdain Margo or pity her.

"He should have been on the invitation list for tonight," Margo snipes.

Max does not respond to that. It's his turn to survey the room.

"Let me know if he responds," she instructs him. "I'll follow up," she says, turning and giving him a conspiratorial smile.

Margo, Margo. Always with your nose to the glass, looking in.

"Is everything alright downstairs?" she asks, clutching a stem glass of white wine, her knuckles white to match.

"Seems to be," Max answers.

"Looks can be deceiving."

Margo is riveted on a group in one corner of the living room. Max follows her gaze.

"Ceci Bombeck," Margo says without being asked. "Chair of the Manhattan Special Events Committee."

Max sees a well-groomed woman in her sixties, animatedly holding court with a group of several women, one of them being Brandi.

Max studies Margo looking at Ceci with a blend of fear and longing. *She wants to be part of that group. Desperately. But she dares not approach. Why?* Then Max notices Ricky Colon standing not too far away. He, too, has eyes only for Ceci. *The Queen Bee has her drone protecting her!*

Brandi rushes up to Max. "There was no save the date card in Ceci's goodie bag. What happened?"

"I thought you gave them cards to stuff in all the bags," Margo says accusingly.

"They asked for seventy-five cards. I gave them one hundred fifty, just to be safe," Max says. "How many bags did they prepare?"

"They told me two hundred fifty," Margo says.

"Two hundred fifty? You couldn't get a hundred fifty in this apartment," Max says.

"That's not helpful," Margo sniffs. "That explains it," she continues. "There are one hundred bags without cards. If they didn't segregate them and are randomly handing out bags—"

"Oh, shit, here comes Ceci," Brandi says. She turns on Margo. "Handle it!" she says and walks off.

"I heard you hired the public relations firm which made the snafu," Ceci huffs, walking up to Margo. "You begged me to come tonight and then—this? All I can say is I am very glad my committee has nothing to do with this event." She gives Margo a stern look. "And I promise you, Margo, they won't!"

"Ceci, please…I'm sure there's a reasonable explanation."

"I doubt it. But call me in the morning." Ceci turns to go.

"Stop at the registration table on your way out. They have plenty of cards," Margo says hopefully.

Ceci just looks at Margo for a moment. She rolls her eyes and walks off.

■

The next morning Margo calls Max to say he needs to call Ceci.

"About what?"

"The missing save the date cards in the goodie bags! You need to explain."

"It sounded to me last night that she wants to hear from you."

"I shouldn't have to do it. The way she spoke to me, as the senior vice president for development for the foundation, it's not right. She just wants me to grovel."

"I don't think hearing from someone she doesn't know is going to satisfy her," Max says with soft guile. "It's your blood she wants to savor, Margo. Under the circumstances, no one else's blood will do," he wants to tell her but refrains. Instead, he adds, "It might just make her even angrier."

There is a pause on the line. Then, "You should have stayed down at the front desk all evening to oversee that everything was done correctly!"

"That was not my responsibility! It was the responsibility of the idiot PR firm which you hired!" he almost yells back at her. He says, "I had volunteers there last night who I needed to attend to."

"Well...What's her number?"

Max can't believe his ears. "I have no idea—"

"You should! You should know these things. You've been here long enough. The honeymoon is over. You need to educate yourself about the organization that you work for!" Margo hangs up.

FORTY-EIGHT

"How's that golf event going?" Brandi is looking at Margo with a sly smile.

Margo looks up from the papers on the table before her. "Beg pardon?"

"Your golf event. The one at Maidstone."

Margo looks back at her blankly. "I don't know anything about it," she says shrugging. "Maybe Max knows." She turns and gives Max an expectant expression.

Max is dumbstruck. She is disavowing any knowledge of the event she schemed so recklessly to create, almost torpedoing *Festive in the Dunes* in dry dock. Margo knows all about it. She just wants to be identified with it about as much as Peter did with Jesus when fingered by a servant girl.

.

Max had met Melinda Jenkins. She's the woman Margo had hired to run the golf event. Her cubicle was in the large room near Max's in the Manhattan office.

"Hi, I'm Max," he said standing at the opening to her cubicle.

"Melinda," she said swiveling around in her chair and offering her hand. "You're running the new Hamptons event."

"Yeah. I'm in the city mostly one day a week."

"I hear it's going well."

Max could see the trace of envy in her eyes. He had heard the scuttlebutt, still he had to ask. "How's the golf event going?"

"Better, now. It's hard to get something new started when you're all on your own."

He could have commiserated but decided that was not what she needed to hear. She told him that her committee consisted of doctors from an oncology practice in Hicksville in Nassau County. They had pretty much filled out one course but they probably would not be using the second eighteen holes. The club had been very understanding, though, and were not going to be charging them greens fees for the second course. Melinda was trying to be upbeat and even made an attempt at perky but was clearly coming across as someone who had been abandoned. Her face conveyed the frozen fear of a lone survivor in a rubber raft in shark-infested waters. Though Margo's name never came up, it was clear who had put her there. She finally admitted that they would be lucky if they broke even. There was a picture on her desk of a man and a young boy smiling on a sunny beach. Max hoped that she had not left a good job or turned down a good offer in order to take this position. Once this was over, by the savage rules of the nonprofit jungle, she'd be back on the street looking for a job and trying to put a positive spin on why her tenure at NCF was so brief. As he left, Max told her to let him know if he could be of any help.

Margo's great coup! The Maidstone Club! The right Hamptons event attended by all the right people! In reality, what she got was not a New York City event in the Hamptons during the season but a Hicksville event on the East End in the summer. And by the look of it, *little old me* won't be showing her face at the Maidstone Club after all. Either one of them!

Although Max had been working with her less than a year, he is certain that her entire professional career has been one long game of pin the tail on the donkey. She's got the pin. She has the tail. Now by using blind instinct and a soupçon of luck, she's sure to nail the sucker this time. However, like that kid's birthday party favorite, when you proceed solely on that basis there's no way you can win.

■

Max looks across the conference table at Margo's beady eyes waiting for him to respond to Brandi's question about the golf event.

"From what I've heard, it's moving along."

Brandi gives a sickly sweet smile. Brandi doesn't want to know how the event is going. She's probably already heard things. She just had a few minutes until the meeting began and decided to limber up her nasty.

"Okay, ladies, shall we get started?" Max says.

FORTY-NINE

Once the women have finished gushing about the annoying adopt a camp kid balloon auction which has now been tacked on at the last minute and is providing for Max another hurdle on his way to putting this goddamn gala in his rearview mirror, Max endeavors to pull the on-site walk-through meeting back on the rails.

"Let's talk seating," he says.

Brandi had given him a number for the individual guests she is expecting outside of her full tables. She had also given names for these guests but the two don't compute. It seems he is missing some guests' names.

Max has always done his seating on index cards. He had learned this valuable lesson from the first boss he had had at the consulting firm. With guests' names coming in a constant stream, and changing, and tables changing, etc., it is the only way to keep the process fluid and you from jumping out a window. Nothing is committed to a list until the seating is finalized, often the day before the event.

The first time he had gone over the seating with Margo, she seemed to be delighted with the process.

"Oh, you have cards for every table!" she had said.

"And every individual."

"The significance of the different colors?"

"Different giving levels," Max had said.

"Very clever."

Over time though, Max had noticed as the event grew more and more successful, Margo seemed to grow more and more resentful. He knew how important the success of the gala was to her. Max would have thought she'd be happy. And she seemed happy—with the event. It was him she was not happy with. Her negative attitude toward him seemed to increase in direct proportion to the dollars raised. She was jealous. And with reason. She had had no impact on the gala's success. The few efforts she had made were all duds. What was he supposed to do? Make the event less successful? In a strange way, though that would certainly not make her happy, he feels that she might be nicer to him. Maybe nicer was not the right word. Kinder? No. More understanding. Failures are most comfortable with other failures.

"Can we go over the people that you are expecting?" Max says to Brandi.

"Sure."

Margo glances around and then looks hungrily across the table at Max's open portfolio. Max notices this out of the corner of his eye while facing Brandi seated next to him. Margo needs something to write on. She wants a piece of paper. Well, he's not going to offer her one.

"There's Jim and Ellen Whitcomb," Brandi begins.

Margo grabs a cocktail napkin from the center of the table and Max's pencil, without asking. She starts scribbling on the napkin.

"Bob and Fiona Powers…Tim and Candy Rodriguez…Mike and Karen Weaver…uh, oh, Phil and Pearl Battersea. That makes one table," Brandi concludes.

"Are you getting any of this?" Margo says, pushing the napkin across the table at him. Max glances down. She has shredded it into an illegible wad in her fevered attempt to catch Brandi's guests. Max resists the urge to swipe it to the floor. He ignores it.

"Got it," Max says, gesturing with a small stack of index cards in one hand. "Just a few more," Max says holding out an index card. Before he can ask his question Margo snatches the card from his hand and rips it in two.

"Stop with these stupid cards," she grumbles, throwing the pieces down on the table between them like some kind of challenge.

Max picks up a blank card from his portfolio, retrieves his pencil from in front of Margo and rewrites the names on it. He shows it to Brandi.

"Are they coming?"

"Yes," she replies.

Max produces another card. "And them?"

"Yes."

Another card. "How about them?"

"Yes."

One last card. "Them?"

"Yes."

"Those are my questions for now," Max says.

"There are more. I'll email you the names, grouped by table," Brandi says.

"That would be great."

Margo sits hunched over, the big loser at this hand of cards.

∎

As the last matter of business, Max leads the group out onto the back veranda. It extends the entire length of the club and affords a dramatic view of the narrow white sand beach and the blue-white waves pounding the shoreline. It is a sublime day. Azure blue sky above. Not hot. A strong offshore breeze fills their nostrils with a clean, salty ambrosia. Between the wind and surf, Max must raise his voice to be heard.

"For the last forty-five minutes of the party, the club will have a bonfire going on the beach."

"Beautiful," Gupta says.

All nod in silent agreement.

"I know," Brandi says. "We should have tiki torches on the beach."

Thank you, Brandi. One more last-minute element to contend with. Who's supposed to go pick those up, as if I don't know?

"Purrfect!" Margo declares. She turns to Max. "Put that down, tiki torches."

FIFTY

The night bell buzzes. Max gets up and goes to the front door. Through the glass he sees a skinny male messenger standing in the spill from the entry light. Max opens the door.

"NCF?" the messenger asks.

"Yes."

"Delivery for Max Short."

"That's me."

The messenger has a large square box on a handcart.

At his cubicle, Max takes a box cutter from his desk and cuts the tape sealing the box. He opens it. Inside are the bedsheets. On top of the bedsheets is a pair of pinking shears. There's also a note.

I can't deal with this shit, now!

Max kicks the box hard across the floor. He sees his hotel room in

Riverhead receding further into oblivion.

.

Much later when he has finished with everything else, Max looks down at the box of sea-themed linens. The whole thing is so pathetic. He considers not cutting them up. He can always say that he had left the office before the messenger got there. But the messenger service will show that he received the box.

Shit!

That wouldn't go down well. They might even fire him over it. He's come so close to success with this project, he can't allow that to happen. He can't let Patricia down. She's worked too hard—they both have. He can't let something like this spoil it now. An existential morass squats over him like a sumo wrestler, weighing him down. He feels crushed like a bug. What a ludicrous position to be in. What a comical situation it is for a grown man to be cutting up bedsheets alone in the middle of the night in order to hang on to a stinking job! And what a ridiculous job it is. Running charity events for a living? How did he ever get into this! It's comic alright. The way a sad sack clown is comic. He feels like crying.

"Fuck!" he screams at the top of his voice. It is a primal scream. It dispels the weight. He takes in a deep breath. He holds it for ten seconds. He slowly lets it out. An old acting exercise that has always had the effect of calming him down. He'll show them. *These will be the goddamndest best top cloths they ever saw. Those bitches' eyeballs are going to fall out on the floor*!

He has to figure this out.

The tables are 60-inch rounds. If he cuts the sheets into 60-inch squares, they'll cover the tops with the four corners hanging over a little. Right! He hauls them into the conference room where he can lay them out on the floor. On a counter in the conference room is a metal tape measure which they use to cut lengths of pink ribbon for the breast cancer walk.

He lays the first sheet out on the floor. Starting from the bottom corner, he measures 61 inches across. He wants to leave a little extra around the sides. He marks the spot with a pencil. From here, he measures 61 inches up. He marks that spot. To complete the square, he measures 61 inches up on the other side. He uses the edge of the tape measure to draw lines connecting the pencil marks. He double-checks that all sides measure 61 inches. He picks up the pinking shears and trims around the perimeter of the square, just inside the pencil lines.

This is a pain in the ass and will take forever!

The process requires him to crawl around the entire square. Not only is that hell on his knees with the hard asphalt tile floor, but the sheet keeps slipping around like some demon earthworm. This will not only take forever, by the time he gets to the event, he'll have to trade in his sport jacket for a straitjacket! There has to be a better way.

He removes the second sheet from the box and ponders. He lays the sheet on the floor and repeats the process of measuring out a 61-inch square. Instead of the pinking shears, he takes a large pair of scissors from a can holding pencils and markers and foot rulers. He uses this to cut the square from the bedsheet. Then, he folds the square in half, diagonally, forming a triangle resembling a pyramid with only two 61-inch sides to trim. His fear is that the pinking shears will seize up attempting to cut through the double thickness of sheet. To his amazement and immense relief, the shears seem to work better on the two-ply material than they did on the single. This works much better, but before he's through he is already planning how to attack the third sheet. With this one, he folds the square diagonally in half and then in half again. This forms a smaller triangle with only one 61-inch open side to trim. Will the shears be up to taking on four layers of sheet?

Max moves along the 61 inches like a hot knife through butter.

Triumphant, Max works the shears in the air like the talking jaws of a hungry carnivore. "Bring it on!" the beast says.

Emboldened, with the fourth sheet, he decides to see if he can rip the squares out. Starting at one mark, Max makes a small three inch cut in the sheet. Then he grabs both sides of the cut and pulls outward. The fine percale material rips straight and true! Max feels vindicated. He has come up with a method to dispose of this heinous task expeditiously!

Still, by the time he has created twenty-five top cloths, folded them back in the box and finishes loading everything into his car, a deep-rose-stratified dawn beckons him east. Never before in his professional career has he had to pull an all-nighter leading up to an event. Hell, even in college he retired cramming before a test in sophomore year. Being sufficiently prepared in advance for a challenge in order to allow for a good night's sleep has been his mantra since he was a teen. People who pulled all-nighters before an event were amateurs.

■

He is reminded of a volunteer with whom he had worked when he was with the heart group. She was on the committee for the women's lunch. She was rich but you'd never know it by looking at her. She wore her salt and pepper hair in a long braid down her back over clothes that looked like she had been wearing them since she got home from the Woodstock Festival. She coordinated the event's silent auction. She had a crew of friends who helped her. Max had seen these women setting up on several occasions. They all looked like damaged goods to him—you know, women who walked around with wary, worried expressions like they were expecting at any moment for a ton of bricks to fall on their heads. You'd have to be damaged goods to follow this nitwit around. She would gather her crew at her Park Avenue apartment the night before the lunch to organize all of the items into packages like some overgrown sorority girl running a Greek mixer. As they finished a package, she would call Max's assistant, Maria, and give her the information so Maria could create a sign for that package with a lot number. Then Maria would email the sign to the volunteer for her approval. The process started in the late afternoon but went on for hours. For one event, it was pushing midnight and Maria's phone never stopped ringing. Max was done with what he had to do but he was not going to leave Maria there alone. Finally Maria showed up at his doorway in tears.

"She keeps changing her mind. She makes me do signs over and over again."

Although staff fundraisers are always supposed to handle volunteers with kid gloves, Max decided it was overdue time for him to set her straight. "Finish the sign you're working on and then we're going home. If she calls again, put her through to me."

She called again.

"Yes?" is all the woman said in a tentative voice once put through to Max. She was good at pushing around Maria. She was good at pushing around her damaged-goods friends. She never wanted to have to talk to Max. He would not be pushed around and she knew it. She would undoubtedly report him later. So what? She'd complain about him regardless.

"Maria is finishing up the last sign. Don't pester her anymore. And don't bother to call again because we're leaving. I'll see you tomorrow. Goodnight."

After the event Max told his boss what had happened and pleaded with him to cut her loose. He swore he could make up any difference her lack of participation might cause.

"How much has she pledged to this year's lunch?" his boss had asked.

"A five-thousand-dollar table."

"That's your answer."

So typical of the type of small-minded thinking that pervades nonprofit management. Don't alienate the donor! She's loaded. She might make a big gift one day. Or at least pay off her pledges. It was how people like her held charities hostage. She was certainly wealthy. Aside from the Park Avenue apartment, she claimed to have places in Martha's Vineyard, Aspen, a ranch in Montana and a home in the Hamptons. That last was probably in Montauk but she just told everyone it was the Hamptons.

■

Outside, Max pulls his inventory list from his pocket and gives it one more double check. It is lengthy and exhaustive. Max looks into the packed cargo area of his car. Has he forgotten anything? It is so hard to do this alone. Usually he would work with someone else when packing for an event. One would read items from a list while the other verified and boxed them. Having to do it alone was like having to play both roles in *Waiting for Godot* because the theater company couldn't afford to hire two actors. And about as absurd.

This is also the first job he has ever had where he works out of a cubicle instead of an office with a door which he can close. Is he going backwards in his career? Or is it just the rest of the world?

He glances over at the building's front door. He has locked it. He slams the hatch of his Volvo shut. It rings in his ears like the slamming door of a roller coaster car. He climbs in the front seat and pulls the seat belt across his chest like a thrill ride's safety bar. He turns the key in the ignition. There's no turning back now. *Festive in the Dunes, here we come!*

■

Max had turned off his BlackBerry last night after business hours so that he could work undisturbed. Gladys knew he was at the office and could reach him on the office phone, if needed. Fortunately, she had not bothered him. Why? At that point, what's been planned for is in the mix and nothing that hasn't is going to be added. The only important thing is that every detail is accounted for and shows up on site. He turns his BlackBerry back on as he heads out. It rings a few times on his drive to Riverhead. He ignores it as he always does while driving.

■

The hotel in Riverhead has been open less than a year and is a vast improvement over the Bates-like motel he had stayed at when working for the respiratory/digestive disease foundation. He closes the door to his hotel room behind him. He is so overtired, he feels on the verge of hallucinating. He only has eyes for the plump white, almost erotically enticing bed before him. He pulls off his clothes and pulls back the comforter. His BlackBerry rings. It's Margo. He doesn't answer. For the first time, he notices that she has left him fifteen messages since last night. He doesn't need to be talking to Margo. He needs a few hours of sleep after which he'll shower and change and head out to Southampton. There'll be plenty of time out there for Margo to discuss with him anything she wants. He turns off his BlackBerry and pulls the covers over his ears.

FIFTY-ONE

"Max!" Margo's shrill voice comes from a near distance.

Max is just getting out of his car. He looks across the car's roof. Margo is stomping across the parking lot toward him.

"We need to talk!"

"Sorry, Margo, CVS was all out of tiki torches."

This stops Margo in her tracks, confused. Then, "I'm not talking about tiki torches!" she brays at him like some diminutive drill sergeant. She continues toward his car. "Where have you been? What have you been doing? I've been trying to reach you since last night."

Max opens the station wagon's hatch and indicates its contents with open palms. "Preparing everything for the event—auction signs, bid sheets, check-in lists—"

"Your phone was turned off. That's unacceptable!"

"I was at my desk all night. You could have called me there."

"How was I supposed to know that?"

By using your head for something else but a place to hang your earrings. Max does not respond. He begins pulling items from the trunk and placing them on the ground.

"Gupta's had a complete meltdown! A complete meltdown!"

"I called and told you about that yesterday. You said you were too busy to get involved."

"You didn't explain the magnitude of the problem properly."

Max continues to pull items from the car.

"And, you didn't handle it properly."

"I had Gladys speak to her."

"Gladys!" she spits back, derisively.

Max keeps unloading the car.

"It's no way to treat a volunteer. You know, given her age and the quality of her contacts, she could prove to be more valuable than even Brandi!"

Max looks toward the club. "Do they have handcarts in there?"

"Oh, stop with all this! We need to put our heads together now. This needs to get fixed. What are you going to do about Gupta?"

"I'm going to see that this event goes off without a hitch. That's the job you hired me to do, yes? Now, excuse me. I'm going to find a handcart."

Max leaves Margo sputtering on the asphalt.

■

The club had to wait until after their regular lunch shift was over and those members had departed before they could begin setting up for the gala. To Max's eyes, it appears nothing has been done. In fact, that's pretty much true. He had called for setup volunteers to arrive no later than 2:00 p.m. A quick glance around reassures him that they had adhered to that. These were all staff members from the Suffolk County office. Their assignment for this part is generalized setup. Unpack everything as quickly as possible, identify where it needs to go and make sure it gets there. Unfortunately, since the catering staff had not yet put up any tables, there are a lot of people just standing around looking to him for direction. They only have four hours to pull it all together. With a sinking feeling in his gut, Max wonders if it can be done.

He finds one of the younger women from the office who had always struck him as someone who doesn't mind getting her hands dirty. "Have you seen any hand trucks around?"

"No, but I'm sure the club must have something. What do you need?"

"Get a hand truck and someone to help you. Go out to my car and start bringing everything in."

"Okeydokey."

Having arranged for that, Max considers the next task in order of importance. The silent auction.

When Max first heard about the members' lunch delaying their getting started, he was immediately concerned there would be sufficient time to set up the auction. Although their auction is small and crappy, procured mostly by the "dead wood" committee, setting it up will take time. First, the club needs to provide tables with skirts. Then the volunteers need to create "pop-ups": empty boxes of various sizes on which to display items. Max had brought a good supply of boxes which he had collected over the past few weeks. They were unassembled and flat; he brought along tape so they could be reassembled. Once this is done, the tables need to be covered with decorative cloth. Max had picked up several bolts of a shiny material from a shop in the garment district on W. 36th St. in the city. The signs describing each item had to be found, put in frames and paired with appropriate items. Then the corresponding bid sheet for each item had to be inserted into a clipboard with a pen (tied to the clipboard; these pens have legs) and placed accordingly. Given that the tables are not yet up and the materials have yet to be located, this activity needs to be kick-started posthaste!

Max goes in search of Joseph, the banquet captain. He has been given his name but has never met him or spoken with him. Max stops a waiter and asks him where he can find Joseph. The waiter points to a tall Caribbean man standing in the middle of the frenzy in the main dining room in a wrinkled and sweat-stained tee shirt. Max walks up to him.

"Hi, I'm Max Short," he says to the somewhat distracted man.

Joseph turns immediately to him and offers his hand along with a genuine grin. "Good to meet you, Max. What can I do for you?"

Max is so glad he didn't call him Mr. Short. A good sign. "Did you get my floor plan?"

"Right here," Joseph says, pulling a sheet of paper from his pants pocket, folded in thirds. He unfolds it and holds it out so they can both see it.

Max points to the back of the bar area. "This is where we're setting up the silent auction. We need those tables in place right away."

"I'll take care of it," Joseph says to Max. Then he turns and calls "Hector" to a man across the dining room and walks away.

Max wonders if Mary Taylor is here. She should be. She, too, had been concerned about the time factor in setting up the auction. Max walks back to the bar area. He finds Mary standing there alone and forlorn with her arms hanging at her sides like her prom date just left for the parking lot with her best friend. She's also overdressed.

Attire for the event had become a more complicated matter than Max was used to. Attire at these special events can be of concern to some women. Many of the events that Max had run over the years had taken place in the city. Attire on those invitations had been listed as "Black Tie" or "Business Attire." Ironically, both of those designations best address male attire but it is never men who are unsure of what to wear. At those events most women wore cocktail dresses. Even in the case of a "Business Attire" event, if women are coming from the office, unlike men who will simply show up in their suit, women will always change into a cocktail dress. Most women who attend city events know this. Once in a while Max would get a call from a woman asking him what she should wear. His response was simple and reassuring—a cocktail dress. Sometimes an old guard grand dame would show up at one of these events in a long gown but that was rare.

Festive in the Dunes was a bit more problematic. It was considered a gala event which suggested more formal attire. But it was a party in the Hamptons at a beach club at which people would be invited down to the beach after dinner to sink their toes in the sand. The question of how to best describe suitable attire started to take up an inordinate amount of time. Max counted at least three meetings when they discussed this without reaching a solution.

"Casual?" he had offered.

"People will wear shorts," Brandi said.

"Casual chic?"

"People will wear nice shorts."

Round and round they went, coming up with all sorts of risible and ridiculous suggestions. Absent telling men to wear "Khakis with a Button-down Shirt" and women to wear a "Killer Sun Dress," there seemed to be no solution.

On a phone conversation with Margo right before one of these meetings, she had presented her remedy to Max. "Cruise wear."

"Cruise wear?"

"Yes. It implies casual yet upscale. It's the perfect description for what we want. Bring it up at the next meeting. It'll resolve this."

At the next meeting, Max dutifully offered, "Cruise wear?"

"Cruise wear!" Brandi exclaimed. "Definitely not. I don't want someone showing up in a pink blazer like that woman from *Gilligan's Island*."

Max threw a sideways glance at Margo who had no reaction and offered no defense of her "perfect" idea. She seemed preoccupied with an invitation proof in her hand.

Of course you won't say one word, Margo. You'll just let Brandi murder your child in front of your eyes.

In the end, they took inspiration from the name of the event and decided on "Festive Attire." It looked good on the invitation but had not satisfied a lot of women's concerns about what to wear as evidenced by the number of calls Max got.

Among them, Mary Taylor. "What does festive attire mean?" she had called to ask Max.

Max felt he needed to be very careful in answering her question. Brandi had made it clear that she wanted a dressy crowd. If Max gave Mary a wrong cue and she came underdressed, not only would Brandi be pissed that the silent auction chair was inappropriately attired, but Mary would be mortified. Given that she was on Gladys's board, that would not be a good thing for Max.

"A cocktail dress?" she said with more than a hint of suspicion of Max's answer.

"Sure. Something summery."

There was a pause on the line. She was probably already uncomfortable discussing her wardrobe with a man. She was not about to start describing the options hanging in her closet for his recommendation.

Max could understand her predicament. Her husband was a successful businessman. They were solidly affluent. They had a beautiful home on the Island's north shore. It was in a desirable neighborhood but it was not the Hamptons. Mary suffered from a syndrome common to many Long Islanders that Max thought of as "jitney envy." It stems from having to watch the Hampton Jitney roll past you on its way to greener pastures. Even though you lived in the Land of Oz, you did not live in the Emerald City. So, no matter where else you lived, it was all Munchkinville by comparison. He had seen it in Mary's eyes the day they had driven out to the club for a site visit. Peering out of the car window up at the tall hedges encircling so many estates, Max could tell they made Mary feel small.

■

So, she has overcompensated. Her dress is nice but wrong somehow. It strikes Max that the problem is the color. Black and red. Not summery. The hose with the dressy black pumps is also a mistake. As is the too-good jewelry. She looks like a guest at a wedding and not a Hamptons wedding, either. She doesn't exuded festiveness. She looks embalmed. Max walks toward her feeling guilty but also not. This, like so many other elements of this event, had been taken out of his control.

"Max, where is everything? The items. The signs and bid sheets. When I got here, I couldn't believe that the tables weren't even set up."

"Everything is being brought in from my car. I had to pack up last night by myself so things are everywhere. I didn't have time to mark the boxes. I'm sorry but you'll have to sort through them."

"Okay…" Mary says dubiously.

Two waiters walk into the bar area carrying a long six-foot table. "Where do you want this?" one of them says to Max.

"Right over in that corner. Then the others next to it along the windows with two protruding forward."

"Big F," the guy says.

Max doesn't understand. "Excuse me?"

The waiter pulls out a copy of the floor plan and points to the table setup for the silent auction. "Looks like a big F," he says.

"Oh…yes." Max laughs. "Exactly."

Max turns back to Mary. "There are two bolts of fabric you can use to cover the tables once you have the pop-ups in place. Is anyone helping you?"

"Gladys is. And she said she can pull a couple of other people over."

"Good. If you need me, I'll be around."

Now Max needs to find Carolyn. Max had sat down with Carolyn last week to recruit her as his on-site assistant. This is the job that, in previous places where he had worked, his actual full-time assistant performed. Since he had no such person at NCF, he turned to Carolyn. Not only was she sane, she was one of the few people he felt that he could work with under the stressful conditions of an event. Thankfully, she agreed. He hadn't used the term "assistant" in speaking with her. She outranked him on the organizational chart and, though he knew she wouldn't give a shit, he felt more comfortable with the term "right hand." Being left-handed, Carolyn instead dubbed herself his "Gal Friday." He sees her unpacking a box in the main dining room over by the sliding doors to the front deck.

"Carolyn."

She looks up.

Max walks up to her. "I want to go over the staff volunteer jobs with you. Let's go in the other room where we can hear ourselves think." Carolyn follows Max into the lobby, which is where the club has their registration desk. This is where the silent auction closeout will be later. Max walks up to the registration counter and lays his portfolio down on it.

"By four o'clock, the setup should be done and the rest of the volunteers will be arriving. At that time, I'd like you to convene a meeting with everyone to go over the various job descriptions. I haven't had the chance to talk to anyone. I've sent them their specific job descriptions but that doesn't mean they've even looked at them or brought them with them."

"Aren't there some people coming from other offices?"

"Yes. Two people from Brooklyn and one or possibly two from Queens. They're all new to the organization. That's why they're coming—to see how an event is run."

"At least they won't have bad habits."

Max starts to reply but says nothing. He takes several stacks of papers from his portfolio and lays them out in individual piles on the counter. He hands Carolyn a sheet of paper. "This is a list of all the volunteers with the jobs assigned to them next to their names. These," he points to the nine separate piles on the counter, "are those job descriptions. Each is marked with an individual's name so it's easier when handing them out." Max hands her another sheet of paper. "This is the volunteer schedule with time frames for when each of these activities needs to take place. As you can see, there is some crossover with people who have more than one job. If I'm free, I'll come join your meeting."

"Wow, you really do know what you're doing."

"I hope so. Any questions?"

"Is there a staff table?"

"Yes. I'm glad you asked. Table number five in the back of the main dining room. Tell everyone that when they are not working, they are welcome to go there and enjoy themselves."

"Just not too much?"

Max shrugs. "The least of my concerns."

■

"Max!" Margo shrieks at him from across the dining room. "The Tory Burch bag is missing!"

Kidnapped? he thinks. He walks up to her. The bag is one of a few items that Margo procured for the silent auction. That, along with two tickets to *The Book of Mormon* and a book and framed poster by some East End denizen and artist.

"I personally handed it to you in my office last week."

"Has everything been opened?" Max asks.

"Everything. It's nowhere to be found!"

"It has to be here somewhere. I remember seeing it last night."

"All of these boxes should have been marked for what's inside. This," she spreads her arms to encompass the entire room, "is utter chaos!"

"I'm sure it's here. Let's give it a few minutes before we panic."

"What if it's not here? It's a very expensive item. What if you didn't pack it? You'll simply have to drive back to your office and get it."

An hour out and who knows how long to get back here, if ever, to pick up some purse that'll bring in two hundred bucks if we're lucky? Max looks up and sees Nikki. She is a stunning African American woman who works in the Suffolk County office. The bag is slung from her shoulder and she is modeling it for some of her co-workers. Max points in her direction.

Margo turns and sees the Burch bag. "Well," she says with a smile of relief, "at least there's someone in the Suffolk County office who has taste." She heads off toward Nikki.

Max notices the looks on the faces of women who have heard Margo's remark. They whisper to each other as she passes. They snicker. Max knows what they are saying. He has surreptitiously heard them in the office when Margo's name has come up. "Maggot" is what they call her.

3:00 p.m.

Right on time, Max sees Brian DiPalma walk into the dining room. Not the famous Hollywood director but the head of the AV firm which Brandi has secured through her husband. Max walks up to him.

"Hi, Brian." Max points to the cleared space at the front left side of the dining room where electrical cables lay on the floor. "Is this going to be enough space for you?"

Brian looks at the space. "Yeah, I think so."

The club had let his crew in the evening before to lay their cable around the perimeter of both the dining room and bar area. The cable will be used to power the video monitors and the sound system for the speaking program and the hookup for the band, The Touch.

The club had also let them preplace the monitors at that time. There is one on the short wall at the front of the dining room, two on the long wall and one mounted catty-corner at the front of the bar area to serve the tables there.

"Did you have a chance to check out the PowerPoint presentation?" Max asks.

"Yes, looks good."

Max had compiled slides for the event: logos for NCF and sponsors $10,000 and over, plus a mixed bag from Steinkamp's live and silent auction items. None from the "dead wood" committee members even though Max had requested images and copy from them multiple times.

The PowerPoint presentation had been Gupta's idea. Everyone liked it and it was unanimously approved.

"So," Margo had said in summing up, "starting with the cocktail reception, we'll be livestreaming video—"

Max had cut his eyes to her. She shut up in mid-sentence. From the moment Max had met Margo at his interview, he had always thought of her as birdlike because of her diminutive stature. The more he worked with her, the more he came to realize that she was like a bird in another way—tiny brain, big mouth. Whatever popped into her head immediately came flying out of her maw.

We're not streaming anything, Tweetie!

"It's a slide presentation," Gupta interjected.

Thank you, Gupta.

The problem with Margo's misspeaking is that people thought she knew what she was talking about. After she declared how something was going to be or to happen, Max was left with the task of delicately explaining that it just wasn't so. Since Margo always went with the super-duper version, Max's reality was a letdown. It caused people, especially Brandi, to look at him askance as if to say, *How did you fuck that up, Max?* Max knew openly stifling Margo was dangerous but at that point, he had had enough of her bullshit.

∎

"Do you have the videos?" Brian asks.

"Yes. I'll get them to you."

"When does the band get here?"

"They're scheduled for five o'clock."

"Okay. If I have any questions, I'll find you."

∎

Max goes in search of Carolyn. He finds her by the bar unpacking auction items. "Do me a favor?" Carolyn looks up. "Keep an eye out for a manila envelope marked 'Videos' with two CDs inside. When you find it, can you bring it to me?"

"You need it right away?"

"No rush."

"Max." It's Gladys's voice.

Max looks over to the silent auction tables.

"We need the easel for Agnus Aucklander's painting."

"On it."

"And where are the frames for the auction signs? We can't find them."

"Do you have the signs?"

"Yes but the frames weren't in the box with them."

Max thought he had put the frames with the signs. It makes sense. However, by the time he had finished preparing and printing the signs and the bid sheets and cutting up the bedsheets with pinking shears, he didn't feel he could swear to anything he did last night.

"Okay," he calls over to her.

Max walks back into the dining room where most of the staff are.

"Keep an eye out for black cardboard frames for the auction signs. They are in three shrink-wrapped packages," Max announces above the hubbub to everyone and no one.

Max regards the room. All the tables here are set up and the wait staff are finishing placing the white full-length cloths on them. Max is relieved that the room is starting to take shape. One of the staff volunteers comes up to him with the three packages of frames and hands them to him. "Thank you," he says.

Max turns and spots Joseph over in the corner talking to Brian DiPalma.

"Joseph," Max calls to him. "We need the easel over by the silent auction tables."

Joseph returns a thumbs-up.

Max returns to the bar area. He walks up to where Gladys and Mary are standing and puts the frames down on an auction table.

"The easel is on the way. Did you find the boxes and tape that I brought for the pop-ups?" he asks Mary.

"We're not doing pop-ups or the fabric. There just isn't enough time," she responds petulantly.

Max can see that she is upset by this. Max is not. He never understood the importance of the whole department store display obsession by people running silent auctions. If the items are desirable to your audience, they'll go. If not, they won't. Especially considering the stuff they have. A piece of crapola isn't suddenly going to get a lot of bids just because it's sitting on top of a box. Max looks to Gladys. She looks stressed.

This represents a deterioration in her mood from when he first walked in. At that time, she was calm and even chipper. It was as if she were looking at the event to erase everyone's memory of the last humiliating disaster of a Hamptons gala. Now her anxiety is rising. Max can see she's losing her nerve.

"Where do you want this?" A waiter is standing next to Max with a large floor easel.

"How about at the end of the first table? In front. It is lot number one," he proposes to Gladys.

"Yes. I think that would be good."

The waiter sets the easel where Max indicates and turns for everyone's approval.

"Thank you," Mary says.

"When do the other volunteers get here?" Gladys asks.

"Four o'clock. The table setup should be pretty well along by then and you will be able to pull more help back here," Max says. He leaves them to inserting signs into frames.

.

Back in the dining room, the waiters have started putting the bedsheet top clothes on the tables under the watchful eye and supervision of Margo. The brilliant marine pattern of shells and starfish and anemones is in stark contrast to the plain white cloths and plain white walls of the room. Max has to admit, they do dress up the room considerably. Margo looks pleased. Margo looks his way but not at him. She looks through him. Then she returns her attention to the tables. She must know what Brandi did. She must know what he was forced to do. Max wonders how much Margo had to do with it. Had she suggested to Brandi when the bedsheets didn't get cut up to throw it to him at the last minute? Did the two of them plan in advance to wait for the last minute to dump the job in his lap? Two mean schoolgirls playing a prank? Clearly, Margo isn't going to say anything to him about it and he is not going to say anything to her. He also tells himself not to get paranoid. It is over and done with.

3:54 p.m.

Max goes out to the parking lot to get his party clothes out of his car. The second wave of volunteers will arrive any minute and after that he will not get another chance to change. He grabs his garment bag and heads back. Andy Fox is storming toward him coming out of the club.

"One of your people is asking for an electrical hookup on the front deck for computer plug-in for registration. You never asked for this. I can't just pull this kind of thing out of my back pocket! It's Saturday and the club electrician's day off. This is your fault!"

Caterers and theater house mangers. Max has dealt with one or the other all of his professional life. They are the same person. Lying in wait for some obscure patch of their turf to be trespassed on so that they can blow sky-high. It makes them feel in charge in their otherwise lowly positions. Andy had started out snarky. He had only gotten worse, emboldened by Brandi speaking to Max in her increasingly condescending tone. Now standing red-faced in front of Max, he has blossomed into a complete flaming asshole.

∎

Earlier in the week, after Max had counted tables on the floor chart, he realized that, including the staff table, he was short one table. There was no problem adding a table. There was ample room at the back of the dining room to do so. Brandi, for some inexplicable reason, had told him that she did not want to add any tables to the floor plan. However, once the numbers were all in, he needed another table. Max decided that he would just add a table and not mention it to her. She might not even notice. If she did, he would just say that he had forgotten about the staff table when he drew up the original plan. She would have no way of verifying if that was true or not. So, driving home from Islandia that evening, he broke his own cardinal rule about talking on a cell phone in the car and called Andy. He had spoken with Tracey, the manager at the club, earlier in the day and she had kept referring to the dining room as the "ballroom." Max wondered if he had been misspeaking all this time by calling it the dining room.

"Hi, Andy," Max said when Andy picked up. "We need to add one table in the ballroom."

"That's impossible. There's no room!" he crowed over the line, reveling in catching Max in such a stupid error.

"There's plenty of room," Max calmly replied.

"Not unless we reduce your silent auction!"

"Not the *bar*room, the *ball*room," Max said, stressing the first syllables. "You know, the dining room."

"Why didn't you say that?"

"That's what Tracey called it today so I thought that was the correct name."

There was a pause on the line before Andy glumly agreed to add a table without a single word of apology for his overreaction.

Max ended the call, wondering if he treated all of his clients this way.

■

"Don't worry about it, Andy," Max says. "We don't need power on the front deck. I'll handle it." Max is not used to taking this kind of guff from a caterer whose bill he is paying but he has no intention of letting him get his goat. Max brushes past him on his way to the club. Max's lack of reaction only seems to make Andy angrier but all he can do is stand in the parking lot and mutter to himself.

Max enters the small single-occupancy men's room in the club and hangs his garment bag on the hook on the back of the door. When they had been having their conversation about attire for the event, after deciding on "festive," Brandi had added an edict that all men needed to wear ties. Her reasoning was that her husband had been named on a *Vanity Fair* best-dressed list and he was wearing a tie, so that would set the standard. Ties at a Hamptons event? Max can't say that he had never seen a tie in a *Dan's Papers* photo layout but they were in the minority. He had no intention of passing this sartorial stupidity along to any paying guests. Unfortunately, he could not be exempt from Brandi's decree. He had planned to wear a sport jacket but without a tie. As he knots the tie around his neck, sweat begins to drip down from his brow onto it. The bathroom is not air-conditioned and although he has only been in there a few minutes, it has turned into a sauna. He finishes adjusting the tie, throws his work clothes into the garment bag and bolts from the room.

The beach pail centerpieces have appeared on the tables in the dining room. Staff volunteers are inserting pinwheels into blocks of florist's foam at the bottom of each pail. Waiters are busily putting down place settings and crystal. Max walks into the barroom where the scene is duplicated. In the area on the other side of the oval center bar, three six-foot tables with cloths and skirts have now been set up. This is for Steinkamp Promotions' silent auction.

The items in the live auction are the great-deal trips which Brandi is so anxious to be able to offer to her friends. As part of the agreement for doing the live auction, Steinkamp required specific display table footage for a silent auction. Although there was not enough room to accommodate their original request, they finally agreed to three tables. Max looks over to the NCF silent auction. Gladys is no longer there but several volunteers are helping Mary. It appears to be slow going. The easel for the painting remains empty.

"Finding everything?" Max says coming up behind Mary.

Mary turns to face him. "I think so."

"Are we going to make it?"

"Yeah…I just wish it could be more special. I really wanted to do a good job."

"It'll be fine."

When Max was running the women's lunch for the heart organization one of the committee women told him to never to use the word "fine" if you are trying to reassure a women about something. For some reason, they don't consider "fine" fine. Max doesn't care. He had walked into this club today with well over $200,000 paid and pledged. He had already exceeded goal. None of this matters. Everything that happens now is gravy.

"Max."

Max turns to see Carolyn.

"The rest of the volunteers are here. I'm going to start the meeting."

Max follows Carolyn to the lobby. He puts his garment bag down on the registration counter next to his portfolio that he had left there earlier. Some newly arrived staff volunteers are assembled as those who had arrived at 2:00 p.m. drift in from the other room. Max lets Carolyn run the meeting. When she is through, she turns to Max.

"Anything to add?"

"Have fun. It's contagious and we want the guests to catch the bug. As Carolyn said, there's a table in the back of the main dining room for staff. When you are not working, you are welcome to hang out there. Just be cognizant of the times listed on your job descriptions when you need to be in place to do the jobs you're here to do. I have enough to handle without having to go find people when they are not at their posts when needed. Fair enough?"

Murmured agreement.

"One more thing. Who requested electric for computer check-in?"

A Brooklyn woman raises her hand.

"I know we talked about possibly using computers but we've decided against it. Check guests in using the three lists. Carolyn's in charge of check-in. When you have a chance, transfer information about checked-in guests to her list so we have one master. That's it."

The volunteers head off to their designated jobs.

Max picks up his garment bag and portfolio. He heads back out to his car to deposit the bag. When he gets back to the club, Brandi has arrived. She is standing at the front of the dining room, surveying it. She wears a sleeveless metallic dress with clunky, high-heeled sandals to match. Along with her tuned-up, brassy, "summer blonde" mane, she looks like the human personification of a sparkler. A new Barbie Doll—*Sparkler Brandi*.

"Looking good, don't you think?" Max says.

She doesn't respond. She pointedly doesn't say a thing about the top cloths. "Do you have the final floor plan?"

Max opens his portfolio. Yesterday, having already sent the floor plan to Andy, he had created this one by adding the name of the table owner to each table so that anyone, but mostly he himself, could see who was where. For mixed tables, he used the name of the most prominent guest followed by XXX. Max hands a copy of this floor plan to Brandi. She takes it and moves a few feet away, studying it closely. At this point, the tables have all been completely set, including stanchions holding the table numbers. Brandi removes a stanchion with table number from a table at the front of the dining room ringing the dance floor and band area. She walks with it to a table in the barroom, also ringing the dance floor. She places it on this table and picks up the existing stanchion and number.

What the fuck is she doing?

Max sees Gupta in the barroom. She is standing next to her four tables which are placed there, a lioness protecting her cubs. She wears a silk cocktail dress of sari blue which compliments her dark complexion. Unlike Brandi, the only thing flashy about her are her black eyes suspiciously watching her co-chair's every move.

"Gladys!" Brandi calls out.

This halts Gladys in the dining room where she is directing the placement of the fake camp kids' pictures and "Send a Kid to Camp" balloon auction cards on each table. Gladys looks up.

"Get a pen and help me."

Gladys grabs a pen from the ones they're putting on the tables for use in filling out the auction cards and walks to Brandi. Brandi hands her the floor plan.

"So, this is now table eleven, see? Cross out what's there and make that change on the floor plan along with the name on the table." Holding the stanchion from that table, "Now, table twenty-two, where will we put you?"

Leave it to Brandi to take something that is organized and turn it into a confusing mess. She's a bratty little girl acting out at her birthday party just because she can. And she needs a toady to be complicit in her tantrum. She's found it in Gladys. Max has to admit, her instincts are dead-on.

Max walks up to Brandi.

"Brandi, do me two favors. First, only switch numbers on full tables of ten."

"Don't worry. I know what I'm doing."

"And don't touch Gupta's tables."

"Why would I?"

Carolyn glides up and whispers in Max's ear. "Come here."

Max follows Carolyn over to the bar.

"I can't find the videos."

"You're sure?"

"I checked all the boxes before the wait staff collapsed them and took them away."

"Was there anything left in my car?"

"I checked it personally. Nothing in the rear or the front or back seats."

"Fuck!" Max thinks a moment. "Maybe the AV guys found them and grabbed them. Did you check with them?"

"No."

Max goes into the dining room. Good. Brian is behind the AV table in the corner.

"Did you by any chance pick up the CDs for the program?"

"No. I was just going to ask you about them. We need to preload them so we can have a seamless transition from the slides to the videos."

Shit! Shit! Shit! Shit! "Alright. I'll have to get back to you," Max says.

Max wanders away, lost in thought. *I did pack them, right?* He takes a deep breath and holds it for ten seconds. Then he tries to rewind his actions from the night before. Actually from earlier this morning. Try as he might, he can't isolate an image of handling the manila envelope marked "Videos" in black block lettering. He couldn't have forgotten them. They were right on top of his desk.

Max looks up and sees Gladys trailing Brandi through the dining room, taking her table changes. Max has never been a fan of videos. In his experience, that's always when people walk outside to call the babysitter. These videos have been chosen and strategically placed in the evening's lineup to help boost fundraising. The program has been divided into three sections. Program #1 is welcoming remarks by Nick Firestone and Brandi. Program #2 leads off with the Camp Quest video, which immediately precedes remarks by a camp kid from last year and then goes right into the balloon auction in support of the defunct camp. Program #3 commences with the Tranquil Cove video, which sets up the live auction. Max is confident that these fundraising pieces will be successful without the videos—nobody knows to expect them so they won't be missed, right? Who's he kidding? Brandi and Margo and Gladys will miss them and they won't be happy. Max doesn't even want to think about how the rest of his evening is going to go down. He has no choice but to tell Gladys. Much as he doesn't want to, she needs to hear it from him first.

"Gladys," he whispers in her ear. She is standing a few feet from Brandi. Brandi is holding a stanchion with a table number in one hand looking around to see where she can strike next. "I can't find the videos."

Gladys scrunches her eyes closed. Max notices the floor plan in her hand is vibrating. It could be from anger or from loss of composure. Maybe both. This is not the quiet downturn of mood she displayed earlier over the auction sign frames. Gladys is not an events person. She doesn't have the experience to rise above this kind of thing. No, she's deteriorating rapidly. One more snag like this and she could crumble into the sea.

"Both of those videos are online," she says through clenched teeth. "Find a computer and download them."

"Good go!" he wants to say and clap her on the back. *She's finally being useful.* He doesn't do either. *There has to be a computer around here somewhere.*

Max sees Andy standing in front of the band setup with one of the AV guys putting a Lucite podium in place. Max certainly doesn't need any more of his attitude. Then he spies Joseph. Max needs to mention to him about the tables anyhow.

"Sorry about the table situation," Max says, indicating Brandi.

Joseph lets out a warm, good-natured chuckle. "No problem."

Max is relieved to have found a kindred spirit who has, no doubt, dealt with all kinds.

"Can your people help guests find their tables in this car wreck?"

Joseph just nods.

"Also, is there a computer around here I can use?"

Joseph checks his watch. "Greg should be in the office till five thirty."

"Where's that?"

"In the pool house." Joseph points in the direction of the pool, out the front door and to the left.

"Thanks."

Max finds the office on the backside of the pool house behind the showers and lockers. He knocks on the door.

"Yeah?"

Max opens the door. Greg, a young man in his twenties, sits behind a computer with his back to Max.

"Hi, my name's Max. I'm running the party here tonight. I was hoping you'd be able to find a couple of videos for me and download them to a removable drive."

"Where are they?"

"They're National Cancer Foundation videos. I don't know exactly what they're called—"

Greg waves a piece of paper over his shoulder. "Write it down."

Max takes the paper and picks up a pen lying on Greg's desk. He writes, "National Cancer Foundation," then "Camp Quest," then "Tranquil Cove." He hands the paper back to Greg.

Greg takes the paper and begins swiftly punching his keyboard. After about a minute of this, Greg says, "I got three for Camp Quest."

Max steps forward to look at the screen over Greg's shoulder. The names of the videos and their images mean nothing to Max. "Can you click on one?"

Greg clicks on the first one. It starts to play. Kids are swinging from a rope tied to a thick tree limb overhanging water and propelling themselves into it. It doesn't look at all familiar. "No, that's not it. Try the next one." It's a good thing Max watched this video or he wouldn't have a clue what the right one is. It wouldn't matter to anyone but Gladys who picked it out but therein lies the rub. Suddenly, Max flashes on a crystal-clear image of himself watching the videos on the monitor in the conference room in the Suffolk County office. Then, he flashes on what he did next. He's at his desk on his computer, burning copies of the two videos. Then, he flashes on what he did next...

"I've got to check on something, I'll be right back," he says to Greg and he is out the door.

Running across the parking lot, the movie continues to unspool in his head. It had been Wednesday of last week. It was nearly 7:00 p.m. The rest of the office had left for the day. Reviewing and copying the videos was the final thing he did before heading for home. He left the office with them. He opened the back door of his car. He slipped the CDs into the pocket behind the driver's seat. In this business you learned to always have copies of things like videos and scripts and anything whose absence had the potential to fuck you in the ass. Max reaches the car and opens the rear door on the driver's side. Would they be there? Had he remembered this clearly? He slides his hand into the pocket behind the driver's seat. The hard edge of one of the CD cases gently kisses the tips of his fingers. *Yes! Old habits die hard.*

Max returns to the office and thanks Greg for his help but tells him he found the videos. Then, he goes into the club and hands the videos to Brian.

"Cool," Brian says, taking them.

"You're clear about where they come in the program?"

Brian pulls out a copy of Max's minute-by-minute schedule and looks at it. "The camp video comes at the beginning of the second part of the program at the conclusion of dinner. And the Tranquil Cove one opens the third part of the program right after the announcement that the silent auctions are closed."

"Right. The emcee, Nick Firestone, is introducing each video, so you can take your cue from him. If I'm nearby I'll also give you a visual cue. Is the band okay?"

"They're plugged in. We're about to do a sound check."

Gladys approaches Max. She holds out a piece of paper to him. It is the revised floor plan with Brandi's changes which Gladys has dutifully taken. He takes it, resisting the urge to ball it up and throw it in a corner.

"We're all set with the videos," he tells her. "I made copies last week and with everything going on here, it slipped my mind that they were in my car."

Gladys gives him a sideways glance. Her lips don't move but her eyes say, "How could you do this to me?"

She walks away as Carolyn hurries up. "There's still no table for check-in on the front deck," she says.

Max checks his watch: 5:52 p.m. Why does nothing happen without him having to personally chase it down? He sees Joseph talking to Andy over near the dance floor. He walks up to them. Without excusing his interruption he says to Joseph, "We still don't have a registration table on the front deck. Guests could start arriving any time now."

Ignoring Max, Andy gives Joseph a commanding look. "You can take care of that after your staff meeting."

Joseph turns from Andy to Max. "I'm sorry. That is my oversight. I'll do it myself, right away."

"Thank you, Joseph."

Joseph hurries off.

Andy glares at Max.

Max returns the glare. What he sees are Andy's two gray-green, blood-shot eyes looking back at him, olives floating in a couple of Bloody Marys. Max had suspected he was a lush but could he already be drunk? Tippling in the pantry? How else to explain his bizarre behavior?

Max sees Nick Firestone crossing the room toward him. He recognizes him from his picture on the *USA Network-Top Dogs* website. Nick extends his hand as he walks up.

"Max? Nick Firestone."

Max shakes his hand. "Great to finally meet you. Did you get the script?"

Nick holds it up.

"Any questions?" Max asks.

"Seems pretty straightforward."

"I hate to do this to you but I have one addition."

"Shoot."

Max gives Nick a new replacement page with Agnus Aucklander's introduction.

Out of nowhere, Brandi is at Max's side.

"Nick, I'd like to introduce Brandi Napoli, a co-chair of the event." *And the woman who wanted to dump you if we got Joy Behar.*

"Pleasure to meet you," Nick says, taking her hand.

"The pleasure is all mine. I'm a big fan of yours and I am simply over the moon that you agreed to emcee our program."

Resisting the urge to vomit, Max excuses himself to Nick with, "If you have any questions about the addition or need anything from me, I'm around all night."

Max walks into the barroom. Gladys is adjusting Agnus Aucklander's painting on the easel. Max guesses it is about three feet high by four feet long. It is a beachscape. Max is suddenly struck with the shock of recognition. He knows this scene. It was painted on Oak Beach looking toward the Robert Moses Bridge and Causeway leading to Fire Island. One summer, when he was a kid, his family had rented a beach house there. Looking at the painting takes him back. Good times. But he hopes that it is not a harbinger of disaster. Today, Oak Beach is mostly known as the place where dead prostitutes work on their tans. There, along with nearby Gilgo Beach.

Max looks across the central oval bar to the area on the other side set up for Steinkamp Promotions' silent auction. Several young people are busy arranging auction items, signage and bid sheets. Max approaches a young woman.

"Is Jerry Steinkamp here?" he inquires.

"I think he's in the next room."

Max walks to the archway to the lobby and sees Steinkamp animatedly talking to a younger man. Max walks up to him.

"Jerry."

Jerry turns to face him. "Hi, Max."

"Are you finding everything you need?"

"Oh yeah, great. We're pretty self-contained. You know we can check out your silent auction, if you like."

Max has volunteers ready to go as bankers for the auction checkout. However, if Jerry's people can handle it, that is fine with him. It will free up his staff to help with the organization and distribution of auction items once guests have paid. Jerry had made the offer at the meeting at Ross Flanders but Max is very glad that he is reiterating it now.

"That would be a big help," Max says.

Max walks to the other end of the lobby which opens onto the front deck. The registration table is being skirted by a waiter. Joseph is placing chairs behind it. Carolyn stands there with two other volunteers. As the waiter finishes with the table, Carolyn picks up a box off the deck and sets it on top of the table. Her volunteers begin removing the contents: check-in lists, pens, guest table cards, markers, etc. Carolyn turns and sees Max. He gives her a reassuring smile. She reciprocates. *Good. We're ready.* Max sees the first of the evening's guests strolling up the ramp leading from the parking lot to the deck. Max checks his watch: 6:14 p.m. *Early birds. Not a moment too soon.* Nick Firestone comes out and greets the couple, giving the man a hug and kissing the woman on the cheek. *Must be Nick's parents.* They had called in an order three days ago.

Max ducks back inside to double-check the room before the

onslaught. The band is in place. The PowerPoint presentation is running on the monitors scattered throughout both rooms. Mary has two volunteers with her to oversee the silent auction and assist guests with the process. Steinkamp's people are ready by their silent auction tables. Three bartenders are in the well of the oval bar, the late afternoon sun pouring in the windows lighting up the gleaming glassware standing at attention before them. Max savors the moment.

It has been long in coming. Almost exactly a year ago, Max had started at NCF, charged with planning and implementing this event with nary a single volunteer nor lead from the foundation. It had been a challenge. Max likes challenges. He's been good at them. This one, like all the others in his career, he has pulled off. Now he can clearly see the light at the end of the tunnel. It looms large. Mere hours away. Like so many in his profession, his favorite part of an event is when it is over; when he gets to kick the last drunk out the door.

Max walks up to a table. He looks at the top cloth. Despite his best efforts to dismiss it, it fills him with a deep, seething anger. His right eye twitches. He massages its outer socket. There is no excuse for what Brandi did. As long as he works with her, he will never be able to forgive her or trust her. He will always need to be on his guard. In keeping with the sea-themed pattern of the cloths, their jagged edges made by the pinking shears resemble barracuda teeth. Maybe at the end of the evening, they'll all leap off the tables and attack Brandi en masse. *Wouldn't that be fun?*

Max looks at the beach pail centerpiece with its colorful pinwheels jutting up. Resting against the pail is the picture of a young boy. Under his image is the name "Dylan Krazinski." *Good name. Sounds authentic.* Where did Gladys find these kids' pictures? Some child talent agency site? Facebook? Frankly, Max doesn't want to know. Plausible deniability in case it should come out that these are fake Camp Quest kids. Inside the encircling ring of votive lights is a stack of ten cards. "Send a Kid to Camp" they say at the top. Underneath are blank lines for people to write in their names, contact information, donation amount and credit card information.

Max had made a unilateral executive decision to drop the "Adopt a Camp Kid" idea from the women. The whole thing revolted him on many levels. Not least of which is it thoroughly corrupts the word "adopt." The notion that people could buy into that status for a few hundred bucks is obscene. As an adoptive parent he was deeply offended.

6:30 p.m.
FESTIVE IN THE DUNES

Doors open. Max goes out onto the front deck. There is already a short line of guests waiting to check in. Max walks to the far end of the deck. The photographer he hired is taking guests' pictures standing in front of a screen festooned with the NCF logo that has been set up outside the slider leading to the barroom. Max walks through the slider. Bartenders are ready. He walks out onto the back veranda. So far, no guests have migrated this far. The sun is bright and warm but the air is delightfully cool, powered by a steady sea breeze. Max inhales it deeply.

"You're just lucky Claudia Ravel is in Nantucket and couldn't make it tonight."

Max turns to see Margo standing behind him. Max thinks. That name is familiar but he can't, at the moment, place it.

Margo sees Max's confusion. "She's the artist who donated the book and photograph to the auction."

Now Max remembers. *Tomatoes.*

"I nearly fell over when I saw that you had placed the opening bid at a thousand. She's a very prominent local resident. If that ever got back to her, there would be hell to pay and it could damage me, personally."

Claudia had returned her donation form indicating the fair market value as $2,700. When he and Mary were discussing setting opening bids, they questioned that value. The item consisted of a coffee-table book of mostly photographs and a large framed poster-sized photograph of tomatoes displayed at a farm stand. Maybe it could be worth that much. *Considering what a lobster roll goes for in the Hamptons...*

"We wanted to keep the minimum low enough to attract competitive bidding," Max says truthfully.

"You exercised very poor judgement."

"What do you think it should be?"

"Don't trouble yourself. I fixed it. Has the designer Carmen Marc Valvo arrived?"

"You'll have to check at the registration desk."

"I want to make sure he knows that he is seated at my table," she says with a self-satisfied smile, heading toward the front deck.

Ross/Flanders walks up to Max. "Brandi wants to know if *Dan's Papers* is here."

"They haven't checked in with me."

"Did you confirm their attendance?"

"I called them last week. I was told that it was on their photo schedule."

"You don't seem very concerned."

"What do you want me to do? It's Saturday. Their office is closed."

"They're the media sponsor for *Festive in the Dunes*," he reminds Max. "I got them to come to the kickoff event earlier in the week at MacKenzie-Childs," he adds in a superior tone.

"Yes, you did. So why don't you run back and ask Brandi how many events for the same organization she thinks *Dan's Papers* covers in the same issue?"

Ross/Flanders' jaw goes slack.

Max walks back in to the silent auction. He finds Claudia Ravel's item. Margo had slashed through "$1,000" with red ink and written "$1,500" next to it. Often when an item is getting no bids, lowering the opening bid is used to spark interest. But you never raise it. And in blatant red ink? Maybe Margo has some special juju that will cause this reverse psychology to prompt a bidding war. She'd better hope so. Claudia's having to take her tomatoes back would be sour grapes indeed.

7:54 p.m.

The Touch strikes up a lively set. Waiters circulate through the barroom and the back veranda, urging guests to take their seats for dinner. Once the room is mostly down, the bass vocalist with the band does the honors with the Voice of God announcement:

"Ladies and gentlemen, please welcome the star of the hit *USA Network* Hamptons-set comedy series, *Top Dogs*, and your emcee this evening, Nick Firestone!"

Applause accompanies Nick as he crosses to the podium.

"Good evening and welcome to the National Cancer Foundation's *Festive in the Dunes, Inaugural Hamptons Summer Bash*. Our goal for the evening is to have fun, to celebrate hope, and to continue our collective commitment to the fight against cancer.

"Over the past twelve months, the Suffolk County regional office of your National Cancer Foundation has directly helped thousands of your friends, family members, neighbors, co-workers—and maybe even you. Here are just a few of the ways the foundation serves your community."

This section had been the most difficult for Max to write because the work of NCF doesn't directly impact the Hamptons community. However, in light of Margo's dictum that they not appear to be a "carpetbagger organization" swooping in to raise funds from the moneyed South Fork and then swooping back out, Max had to try. In the end he used information that applied generally to New York State, all of Suffolk County, and even Tranquil Cove in the city, despite the fact that their population comes from everywhere. He also added numbers on research grants given to Orient Point Bio-Tech and Deep River Harbor Laboratories. The funding of these research facilities doesn't benefit people living near them but it sounds good.

"It is now my pleasure to introduce to you a co-chair of *Festive in the Dunes*, Brandi Napoli."

Applause as Brandi crosses the dance floor to the podium.

"Thank you, Nick. It is truly wonderful to see so many familiar faces here this evening and equally wonderful to see so many new ones. The success of tonight's event could not have been possible without the very special support of some very special friends. I am speaking of course of this evening's sponsors."

Brandi announces them and then continues. "As we all know, events are about people and we have been fortunate to have wonderful people involved. I would like to thank the very hard work of my co-chair, Gupta Ritter, and the entire *Festive in the Dunes* host committee who contributed so much of themselves to our success."

At the mention of her name, Gupta stands at her table in the barroom and waves at the audience. There is applause. Positioned just inside the dining room, Max can't see around the corner to where Gupta's table is. The low-angled sun is performing a brilliant dying swan outside the windows, backlighting the room. Despite that, what Max can't miss is Brandi's normally tan countenance turning bright red. Once Brandi relinquishes the microphone back to Nick, she strides up to Max. With her index finger she pokes him back into the lobby. Max retreats two steps into the empty space.

"I told you she was not to stand," she hisses at him.

"Maybe you should have told her."

"I told you to tell her."

"Actually, you didn't."

"Did you tell her?" she snaps.

"I had no conversation with her about standing or not standing."

"Then who told her to stand?"

"It's the natural thing to do when you're introduced."

Again, the "emcee face." "No one on the host committee stood."

"No one on the host committee is here."

Nick's voice comes in from the other room. "Now, from what I am told, dinner is about to be served. So please enjoy. And don't forget, the silent auctions are still open. We will be back with you shortly."

Brandi turns on her glittery heel and stomps back into the dining room. The band launches into a set of dulcet dinner music.

Gladys runs through the doorway coming from the barroom. "The lights over the silent auction don't work! Did you know about this?"

"What? No, of course not."

Max and Gladys go into the barroom. The ceiling fixtures over the dinner tables and the bar, including Steinkamp's silent auction are working fine. The back section where their silent auction is situated is rapidly being consumed by gloom as the day's last rays of sun retreat west over the ocean. Mary stands by a table eyeing a set of Global Cutlery looking like she wants to grab the biggest knife and just end it all. Max walks up to her.

"Nobody can see anything," she says despairingly.

"Were they working the other day?" Gladys asks.

"It was daytime. Who could tell?"

"Isn't that your job?"

"I asked Tracey on my first visit. She said the existing lighting covered the entire space. I didn't ask if there were specific fixtures that didn't work."

"Where is Tracey?"

"She's not here. No one from the club is now. Just wait staff."

Max goes up to the bar.

"Do you know anything about the lights back here?" he asks a bartender, pointing to the back of the room.

The man shrugs. "I was just hired to work this event. Sorry."

Max heads off in search of Joseph. He's not in the dining room. Max sees no waiters handy to ask where he is. Max goes straight to the back of the room and through the kitchen door. Startled kitchen workers turn to look at him. He is obviously in the pantry.

"Is Joseph here?" he asks one and all.

The waiters look back at him suspiciously.

I'm not with immigration enforcement, for chrissakes! "I'm running this party. I need to speak to him urgently."

"He's in the kitchen," one waiter finally gives up and disappears through a doorway at the rear. After about two minutes, Joseph appears.

"Yes?"

"The lights in the back of the bar aren't working."

Joseph stares blankly ahead for a moment. "We have nothing to do with that but I'll take a look."

Joseph walks briskly past Max and exits into the dining room.

Max follows Joseph across the floor. The room is in full swing with the din of cutlery clanking, conversation, laughter, and music from the band.

Of course Joseph doesn't know anything about the lights. He doesn't even work here full-time. He only comes in to do special catered events like this. The problem with this place is that you are dealing with two separate entities: the club and the caterer. You have different contacts for each. Different contacts and different bills. The designated caterer for the Southampton Pool and Beach Club, unlike at a hotel, is not the in-house caterer. Their office is in Manhattan. So, when there is a problem with the facility and all the club staff have departed, you're adrift on the ocean without an oar.

They reach the back of the barroom. Joseph looks at the darkened auction display. He goes to a hinged panel set into the wall alongside the sliding glass door to the front deck and pops it open. He studies the schematic on the back of the door for a moment. From it, he is able to locate the switches controlling the overhead lights. The ones marked "rear bar" are all in the off position. Well, that doesn't help. He throws one to the on position. Nothing happens. He throws all of them to the on position. Still nothing. He looks around the room. He is loath to fiddle with the lighting over the tables where guests are eating dinner. He notices that the outdoor veranda lights are on. He finds their switches on the panel. He moves one from the on position to the off position. He looks but can discern no change. He tries another. This time he sees the veranda noticeably dim. He throws them all to the off position. The veranda goes black. Joseph frowns. He pushes all the veranda switches back to the on position and the veranda springs to life. He looks at Max.

"Sorry. It appears this track is not working," he states the obvious. "I'll see if I can find some candles." Joseph goes.

Max turns to Mary. "Take your volunteers and bring the votive lights from the staff table over here. It's in the back of the dining room. Table number five if they haven't removed the stanchions." Mary and her two volunteers head off.

"That's it? Candles?" Gladys says indignantly.

"We'll see if we can find some more." Max is about to suggest that Gladys pull the votives off of her table. It's the last one along the windows, directly opposite the painting propped up on the easel. There is a stout woman sitting at Gladys's table looking at it sadly. *It must be Agnus Aucklander, the artist.* Her poor, brilliant baby relegated to the dark. He doesn't suggest anything to Gladys. He notices a few votive lights scattered around the bar. He goes up to a bartender.

"Do you mind if I take these votive lights? We're trying to get as much as light as possible back there."

Without a glance the bartender says, "Be my guest," handing Max a small tray.

Max collects the glass holders. There are five. He takes them to the auction tables and distributes them as best he can. They don't help much. If they're right next to a bid sheet, they can be used to see it marginally. As for the auction signage, it's hopeless. Items that are actual things need to be held up to catch a glint of light from somewhere to check them out. The painting is doomed. It's a new thing—an auction that's not only silent but blind as well.

8:56 p.m.

Nick Firestone steps to the podium.

"Ladies and gentlemen, forgive me for disturbing your dinner for a moment, if I may. But I have just been hearing about a truly remarkable place which I never knew existed. In its twentieth year, it is one of the very unique programs that the Suffolk County regional office runs. Camp Quest, in Montauk, is a place where kids can be kids while receiving the medical attention they may still need from a professional, caring staff. Please direct your attention now to the video monitors."

The Camp Quest video plays for approximately three minutes. At its conclusion, Nick returns to the podium with two high-school-age young men.

"Ladies and gentlemen, please welcome a member of Camp Quest's class of two thousand twelve, Michael Portman." There is applause. Michael steps up to the podium as Nick steps away.

"On July eleventh, two thousand nine, I was diagnosed with a pediatric brain cancer… medulloblastoma. I went from hospital to hospital. Finally, I was taken into surgery. Then, they gave me a mask. I woke surrounded by my family, only to know that I wouldn't be able to go back to school."

Max stands at the lobby archway just inside the dining room listening to the program. When it was first suggested that they have a camp kid speak, Max was dubious. Inexperienced public speakers can come off as cardboard or worse. This kid seems very relaxed. There is a genuine niceness that comes across as well.

Michael continues. "For the next two months I had radiation therapy and then for ten more months, I had chemotherapy. I went back to school February seventh, two thousand eleven. I thought I was through when I finished chemo but in May of that year the doctors found more. I would need a stem cell transplant. I could only ask God why this was happening to me.

"During this time the National Cancer Foundation has helped my family tremendously. We have had emotional support, financial assistance, and my brother and I got to go to Camp Quest together—"

Michael looks at the young man standing next to him as if he's just now noticing him. "Oops, sorry, bro." He turns back to the audience. "This is my big brother, Kevin. I was supposed to introduce him earlier." Kevin gives a slight wave to the audience. There is a swell of warm laughter. "I'm not used to talking to so many people at once." More laughter.

A finger pokes several times into Max's right shoulder. Max turns his head to the right. It's Brandi.

"Get him off," she whispers.

"Huh?"

"He's bringing everybody down!"

Max looks out across the silent room. No conversations. No clinking of cutlery or glasses. Every glistening eye is trained on the young man at the microphone. Max feels another jab to the shoulder, giving him his marching orders. He could cheerfully throttle her to death here in front of everyone. There isn't a jury in the world who would convict him. He sidles up to the camp nurse counselor who has accompanied Michael to the event.

"Do you know how much longer he'll be?"

"Just another minute or so. I think," she replies. "Sorry, but you can see he's just being carried along by this audience."

Max glances back at Brandi.

"Is there a problem?" the nurse counselor asks.

"No. There's no problem," Max says. He turns back and gives a thumbs-up, a wink, and a smile to Brandi's dumbfounded look.

A hand grips Max's right bicep. It's Gladys. She pulls him to the side.

"Close down the silent auction!"

"Jerry Steinkamp is giving a fifteen-minute warning as soon as he gets to the stage."

"Mary's been telling people all night that the auction is closing at nine o'clock. It's ten after now."

Max is flabbergasted. "Why did she do that? We agreed we'd close it with staggered announcements from the stage."

"People think that they made their final bid right before nine and it's already closed."

"So tell her to pull the bid sheets."

Gladys has released Max's arm but her hand trembles in the space between them. Her low, guttural snarl comes from a place of pure rage. "Close it down, now!"

Max walks around her to the barroom. Michael Portman has just concluded his remarks to sustained applause. Max spies Jerry Steinkamp standing by the front of the stage over by the windows.

"Thank you, Michael. You are an inspiration to us all," Nick says retaking the podium.

Max hurries over to Jerry. "Jerry, as soon as you get to the mike, announce that both silent auctions are closed."

Jerry glances at his watch. "I thought we were going to give staggered five minute warnings counting down from fifteen."

"I would now like to introduce Jerry Steinkamp from Steinkamp Promotions," Nick says over him.

"I can't explain, now. Just do it."

Jerry crosses the dance floor to the podium. "Thank you, Nick. Before we get started with our special balloon auction, I have been asked to make an announcement that the silent auctions are now closed."

Max intercepts Gladys.

"Gladys, I want you to know that this is not on me. I have no control over Mary taking it upon herself to change the plan. I can't be everywhere at once."

"This is not the time to be pointing fingers," Gladys replies.

"You seem ready to point the finger at me."

"We'll talk about this later," Gladys says dismissively, walking back to her table.

"Ladies and gentlemen, I would like to direct your attention to the beach pail centerpieces at each of your tables. Next to each pail is a very special item," Jerry says from the podium.

Max walks back into the lobby. He spots Carolyn standing in the archway leading to the dining room, observing the program. He walks up behind her. "Here it comes," he says to her. She turns to acknowledge him.

"It is a picture of a kid with cancer who has been enrolled in this year's Camp Quest program," Jerry continues. "We are asking your table to send that kid to camp. There is a stack of pledge cards at the base of each pail. It costs two thousand dollars to send a deserving kid like Michael Portman to Camp Quest for two weeks. That's just two hundred from each of you; four hundred per couple. You spend that for gas and tolls going back and forth from the city."

"I can't believe Gladys came up with all these fake kids," Carolyn says.

"Oh, I forgot to tell you," Max says. "That's not all."

Carolyn looks at him in anticipation.

"The camp program has been canceled."

"Since when?"

"Last night when I was at the office getting ready for today, Aggie Potter was also there. She was cleaning out her desk. Apparently they gave her notice earlier in the week."

"That's right, just hold your cards high in the air," Jerry's voice booms from the dining room. "Volunteers are coming around to collect them and tie a pink balloon to the back of your chair celebrating you as a camp sponsor."

"So, we're not only raising money to send fictitious kids to camp, the camp itself no longer exists?" Carolyn says watching the flurry of activity in the dining room.

"What a beautiful scene it is from where I'm standing, all those pink balloons suspended in the air like beacons of hope for these kids," Jerry enthuses.

It dawns on Carolyn. "It's perfect. Given event income is, by definition, unrestricted funds, we can't really be holding an auction to send kids to camp. This money just goes into the general operating fund. If we decide to cancel that program, that's our business. Not that anyone would ask, but we're not accountable to these donors for where their money goes."

"Maybe that's why Gladys didn't hesitate."

Max well understands what Carolyn is saying. He had had a similar experience running the women's lunch at the heart disease organization. The lunch committee insisted that the money raised from the event went to fund a program related to heart disease in women. This would have necessitated creating and maintaining a separate account for the event with regular reporting going directly to the women. If not undoable, at least a logistical nuisance. The organization resisted until the women threatened to pull the plug on the event. A private meeting was arranged between the two lunch co-chairs and the cardiologist chairman of the board. The doctor informed the women that a new call for heart disease in women-related research grants had been added to the organization's existing grants program. In light of the fact that the lunch was bringing in over $500,000 per event, several of the small grants that they gave out to young researchers could be awarded each year. Being board members themselves and having a front-row seat to the inner financial workings of the organization, the two women were not fooled by the charade. However, they accepted it, deeming it the best that they could hope for.

Nearly all funds raised at events under the guise of being earmarked for a certain this or that are simply ploys to get people to open their wallets and plunk down their black American Express cards.

"Do you think anyone at the foundation besides Gladys is aware of this?" Carolyn asks. "Margo?"

"Could be. God knows she'd do anything for a buck. But, you know, it's just now occurring to me that Gladys probably knew about this back when I pitched camp to *Dan's Papers*. It would explain why she didn't seem too excited by the idea."

The balloon auction ends and Nick comes back to the microphone. "WOW! Looking at all those balloons filling the room, knowing what that means, it is truly a beautiful sight."

This is where Nick was supposed to make the second announcement about the silent auction closing before it got changed. Max refers to the copy of the script in his hand. *Oh, shit*! Max wants to crawl under a table, preferably a skirted one. Now comes the part that Gladys had insisted he add. If he gets called out on it, he'll plead that he is just a good German following orders. He reads from the copy of the script in his hand:

> We are pleased to have with us this evening renowned Long Island artist Agnus Aucklander. Agnus, please stand. (AGNUS STANDS.) You couldn't have missed the masterful painting she donated to the silent auction. Thank you Agnus! (APPLAUSE. AGNUS SITS.) Please take this opportunity to place a bid on it. The silent auctions will be closing in ten minutes.

Instead, Nick skips to: "And speaking of beautiful sights, I see dessert coming out. We will be back shortly with our live auction. Enjoy!"

He didn't say it! Max thinks with great relief. *Was it a mistake? Did he miss it?* No, that's not it. He realized that the silent auctions are already closed. Some mistakes have unexpected upsides. *That's thinking on your feet. Good for you, Nick!*

"I'm going to check out the silent auction," Max says to Carolyn and heads that way.

Max sees that several tall tapers in candlesticks have been added to the silent auction tables, creating an eerie funereal quality. Joseph must have found them somewhere. They don't help. "How did we do?" Max says to Mary. He's pissed over what she did to screw up the auction closing but decides not to say anything. Mary hands him a stack of bid sheets. "Did the painting get any bids?" he asks.

"Just my two thousand reserve."

So, the big item that was supposed to bring in as much as ten thousand went for two. Max is aware of a low, angry voice coming from behind him. He turns to see the woman he surmises is Agnus Aucklander standing at Gladys's table speaking to Gladys in a heated manner. Her full face is quite flushed. Her jowls quiver. Then she throws down her napkin and storms toward the exit, followed by her guest.

"She'll probably never speak to me again," Gladys says walking up to Max.

You're telling me this, why? It's your own stupid fault. You wouldn't listen to anyone. Max hadn't directly warned her against having a painting in the auction. He had felt it wiser to just not express any enthusiasm when she brought it up. But Margo and Gupta had both been more candid by saying things like 'art is so subjective,' etc. She should have picked up on that. She didn't. She didn't pick up on anything. She was so wrapped up in her delusion that it was going to be the hit of the night. Gladys Ortiz's brilliant contribution to the success of *Festive in the Dunes*! If she had asked him outright for his opinion, he would have told her that, in his experience, artwork did not go at a general goods and services auction. Especially when the artist is unknown. Gladys had maintained that Agnus was a prominent Long Island artist. Maybe. But that means nothing to these people. Some of them might have Jackson Pollocks hanging on their dining room walls in the city. But an original Agnus Aucklander? Puh-leeze! It might go at an auction held in Smithtown but one in Southampton? No way. His honest opinion wouldn't have made a difference in any event. Gladys didn't trust him. She never had.

"I told you we should have put it in the live auction," Gladys says, scornfully. "Sitting over here in the dark, nobody even noticed it."

Max knew that wasn't true. Most of the bidding had been done during the cocktail reception when there had been plenty of sunlight. No, putting it in the live auction would only have made her friend's humiliation more complete by also making it public.

Max reviews the bid sheets in his hands. Some of the things he thought wouldn't go, did. The "Weight Loss Hypnotism Session" got a surprising number of bids. Well, maybe not so surprising in a beach community. Claudia Ravel's tomatoes didn't get one bid even after Margo slyly increased the opening bid. And Margo's last-minute contribution didn't go—two tickets to *The Book of Mormon*. From Jean Shafiroff to Charlie Marder to the Maidstone golf fiasco to a hit Broadway show, everything this woman touches turns to caca! He hands the bid sheets back to Mary.

"Take these to Steinkamp's redemption table in the lobby."

Nick Firestone is back at the podium. The band plays a fanfare.

"Ladies and gentlemen, may I have your attention, please?"

Commotion in the room continues for another few moments. When the room settles down, Nick continues.

"A crown jewel of the National Cancer Foundation's programs and services, Tranquil Cove is a ninety-five-room residence in the heart of midtown Manhattan which provides free accommodations to cancer patients and their caregivers. Partnering with eight major hospital systems, Tranquil Cove has provided comfort and life-changing services to thousands of patients from twenty-one countries and forty-eight states. More than just a place to stay, over one hundred fifty wellness events and activities are offered annually and add greatly to the quality of life of guests, complementing their outpatient medical treatments. May I please direct your attention once more to the video monitors?"

The Tranquil Cove video plays for approximately four minutes. At the end of it, Nick reintroduces Jerry Steinkamp who launches into the live auction.

"First on the block, we have a six-night Best of Ireland tour with hotel and airfare for two. Suggested retail value: eight thousand five hundred dollars. We will start the bidding at forty-four hundred. Who will give me forty-four?"

Here it is, Brandi's special gift to her friends, Max thinks.

Jerry points to a man for the benefit of his staff spotters. "Thank you, sir. Do I hear forty-five?"

I certainly hope so. At least NCF will make eighty bucks.

"Forty-five," another man calls out.

Jerry points to the bidder. "Thank you. Who will do forty-six?"

And on it goes. After Jerry has whipped through all six live auction items, Max is impressed. He didn't time it but it couldn't have taken more than ten minutes. He didn't jot down any figures but just guesstimating it in his head, he would say that it took in at least $30,000. NCF wouldn't get all of that, but still, not bad for ten minutes' work. From looking at balloons hovering above tables, he surmises another

$20,000 from the camp auction. Nick returns to the microphone.

"Congratulations to all the winners. If you look up at the video monitors, you will see the winners of the silent auctions posted. To redeem your winnings, at your leisure, please visit the redemption area directly across from me through the doors at the end of the bar. And to all of you, thank you again for your tremendous support. After the success of this inaugural event, we will definitely be back next year. We hope you will, too. Good night and be safe."

Good night, indeed! Two of the most beautiful words in the English language. Max checks his watch. The good news is that the program ran over, meaning that it's later than planned. The bad news is there is still one hour and twenty minutes to midnight when he finally gets to blow this dump.

He checks out the operation in the lobby. Steinkamp's people are set up and ready to go. His people, who will be distributing items from their silent auction once they have been paid for, are all in place.

As he heads out of the area, he has to pass close by Margo and Gladys who are standing in the bar area talking. Max does not pause, but he unmistakably hears Margo say to Gladys in her imperious voice, "This is my event, now." Max fervently hopes that Gladys will finally grow a spine and tell the old hag to back off. This is her office's event as surely as any activity within Suffolk County's geographical borders. *Festive in the Dunes* is a success due to the efforts of her staff member in charge. How can she let this useless gasbag just snatch it from her? Doesn't she have any self-respect?

Without warning, Max runs into Gupta.

"Great party," is all he can think of to say. She replies with a blank expression that divulges neither a positive nor a negative response. It is a mask. A mask as murky and impenetrable as the Ganges. She moves on.

Max wants to say more. Although he knows it is ill-advised, he wants to apologize. Not that it would make any difference. He'd never see her again. She is not a fool and unless she's a masochist, she would not be signing up for this event next year. Still, she shouldn't have been subjected to what she'd been through. He feels that they have both been abused by NCF and, in that way, share a bond. It's true, as a fundraising volunteer, she was no house-a-fire and the way she had satisfied her pledge was annoying. By committing to a $10,000 sponsorship and then having part of that pledge fulfilled by ticket purchases from individual guests, it was neither a true sponsorship nor did the revenue hold firm. By the time she told him what she had done, he had had to subtract the individual ticket income from her personal pledge. When dollar figures on a financial report roll backwards, it makes everybody testy. Brandi had done more than she was originally tasked to do, granted. But Gupta did fulfill her commitment, albeit under less than agreeable circumstances. NCF should not have let Brandi say she did not.

■

Carolyn and Max stand by the side of the dance floor. Brandi and Andy Fox dance together. After a moment, Carolyn turns to Max.

"That guy Brandi is dancing with, isn't that—"

"The caterer," Max answers her unfinished question.

"Isn't that—"

"Inappropriate? Uh, yeah."

"She doesn't seem to mind."

"Those two are birds of a feather. She's hiring him to cater her Christmas party."

"That should be a jolly affair."

"If she invites Margo and Gladys, it'll be 'ho, 'ho, 'ho."

Carolyn cracks up. She looks to the dance floor again. "I see what you mean about her being a throwback. I think she's doing the Frug."

Both Max and Carolyn laugh.

11:00 p.m.

The bonfire is lit.

Max stands on the rear veranda looking out over the black ocean. He listens to the crash of the ghostly waves whose curls are highlighted by the light spill from the club. A soft but persistent breeze blows in over the water. Raucous dance music pours out through the open sliding doors behind him. He is exhausted. Weary. Events always take it out of you. But this event has been particularly draining. It wasn't only that he had no help. He had no support. There's a difference. *Festive in the Dunes* had a malice with its own taste and smell. *Fetid in the Dunes is more like it*!

It had started small. A speck. Brandi dissing Gupta in front of everyone at a committee meeting. Max had tried to contain it. He had failed. It grew. It fed on itself, ironically, the way a cancer grows. Thriving on its own poison. Spreading to others. Metastasizing. Soon it was out of control. Max had always believed that respect is a two-way street. What this experience has taught him is that lack of respect is a highly contagious malignancy. Once appeased, it becomes the new norm. Everyone gets to be okay with it.

Whatever the challenges of an event, it was usually this moment that made it bearable. Even energizing. Congratulations for a job well done. These often came from many quarters. It was nice when it came from people who had nothing to do with the event but it really meant something when it came from those who did. People who mattered. Most importantly, from your boss. There had been not so much as a word from anyone. Not Brandi. Not Margo. Most concerning, not Gladys. Kudos from your boss rarely had any real, lasting meaning. You still got dragged into their office two days later to be told all the things you did wrong. But that was why it made this moment so special. It was an acknowledgement of your accomplishment. And it was real because both you and your boss knew that this was something they could never have done. Pulling off a successful fundraising event is no job for a bureaucrat.

Max gazes down on the beach. Gladys and her fiancée Ingrid are among a group dancing and frolicking around the blaze. Gladys breaks into an impromptu boogie which gets everyone clapping her on. Then one of her flip flops catches in the sand. She loses her balance. She topples headlong into the bonfire. She stumbles back out, completely consumed in flames, her pitiful animal shrieks splitting the soft summer night. Ingrid and the others back away from her in silent horror. Burning rapidly, in a moment she is gone in a puff of smoke like a witch in a fairy tale.

The band's music seeps back into Max's consciousness. He looks down on the beach to see Gladys cavorting with the others, as before.

Midnight

The party's finally over. The band is playing its last song which is not the clichéd Donna Summer's "Last Dance" but the Beach Boys' "Help Me Rhonda." Max collects the registration sheets, the bid sheets, and all the financial documents from the silent, balloon and live auction closeouts. He stuffs them in his portfolio and zips it shut, placing it on the counter in the lobby.

"Max, you're going to have to take all of the unclaimed auction items in your car," Gladys informs him. "My jeep's too small. Just bring them into the office." Ingrid joins Gladys by the front door and they head off together.

I guess that was goodnight.

Max grabs a large Wolffer Estate Winery shopping bag from under one of the skirted auction tables where he had preplaced it earlier. He moves down the table, throwing unclaimed items in the bag. Most are certificates which he had created and are of no intrinsic value. They have contact information for redeeming items which he can send to auction winners who did not pick them up. One of the few actual items is Claudia Ravel's "tomatoes" photo and her book. He puts the book in the shopping bag. He'll have to come back for the photograph.

He goes to the lobby. All of his staff volunteers have gone but, as instructed, they have left him a box with clipboards, pens, markers, scissors, staplers, etc. He throws his portfolio in the shopping bag, takes the box under one arm and goes out to his car.

As he is walking back into the club, he is surprised to see Brandi coming down the ramp toward him accompanied by her husband. This could be a good thing. *Festive in the Dunes* is over and in the winner's circle. It wouldn't be the first time Max had used such a moment to smooth over relations with a volunteer which had become a bit rocky. After all, Max could be charming when he wanted to be. Over the years many of his volunteers had told him so.

Max throws his arms open. "I'd say congratulations are in order, Mrs. Napoli."

Brandi shakes a hand in front of her. "I won't kiss you. I'm too sweaty."

She is glistening, illuminated by the floodlights staked in the sand. From after dinner on, she had rarely been off the dance floor. He can't think of a good comeback.

She breezes past him.

Max goes into the club. It is in full breakdown mode. He goes to the table with the photograph. He picks it up. He notices that there are still a lot of their supplies scattered around: frames for signage, tape, string, ribbon, more pens, more markers, another stapler. He knows Gladys would want to get these things back. The frames could be reused. She'd especially want the stapler. As he passes a waiter on his way to the exit, Max says, "You can throw out everything else."

At his car, Max slides the photograph into the rear compartment, standing up with its glass facing the side to protect it.

Who would pay fifteen hundred dollars for this? Margo's fucking tomatoes!

FIFTY-TWO

Margo inhales deeply the perfume emanating from the plump, red tomato which she cradles in her hand. She approves. Into the plastic produce bag it goes, along with her other two choices. Done with her shopping, she wheels her cart to checkout. At this hour, she has the place to herself just the way she likes it. What she is less fond of is the irritating squeaking from the rear right wheel of her cart. The emptiness of the warehouse-like structure amplifies it all the more. *How is it that the cart with the squeaky wheel always manages to find me?*

Margo has her choice of checkout lines and chooses one with a cashier she recognizes.

"Good morning," Margo says, pulling groceries out of her cart and putting them on the conveyor belt. She doesn't know the woman's name.

"Always my first customer," the cashier says.

"I like to beat the crowds."

"You certainly did, coming in midweek. You usually come in on Saturday."

"I took the week off from work," Margo says, emptying her cart.

"I'm sure you deserve it."

Margo thinks that to be a rather cheeky remark but says nothing.

Then, as if Margo had responded, the woman adds, "We all deserve it."

Margo thinks that, somehow, didn't come out the way the woman intended.

"Are these good?" the cashier asks, holding up a package of marinated mini filet mignons. "I've seen them but I haven't tried them."

"My first time, too. I'll let you know." Margo pays, thanks the cashier and says goodbye.

As she is exiting the store, there is a young man standing by the door.

"Help you with your bags, ma'am?"

Margo notices he is wearing a very tattered pair of work gloves, a couple of fingertips poking out. *Maybe if I say yes, he'll be able to afford new ones.*

"Thank you," she says glad to relinquish the cart with the squeaky wheel to him. She heads for her car, the squeaky wheel following her. Halfway there she hits the unlock button on her car's key fob and the rear lights blink once in response. The wheel on the cart still squeaks but not as loudly. Margo turns to see the young man with her cart heading off in the other direction.

"Young man!" she shouts, "My car is over here."

He stops, a puzzled look on his face. Slowly, he says, "Oh…sorry…"

Margo beckons to him with her hand. "Well, come along. I haven't got all day." She watches the young man swing the cart around and head toward her. She's keeping her eye on him now and wondering whether it was a good idea to accept his offer of help. *With so many crazies running around these days, you have to be careful about who you let into your sphere.* Once he reaches her, Margo turns and proceeds to her car. After he has loaded her bags into the back, Margo slips a few bills from her purse and hands them to him.

"Thank you, ma'am," he says, not looking up.

She waits and watches him push the cart with the squeaky wheel back to the store.

Out of her line of vision, inside the store, someone slips a $10 bill into the young man's hand.

Margo turns, pulls open the driver door and climbs up into the SUV. She kicks off her right flip flop and slides it over to the left. It can be dangerous driving with them on. She depresses the brake pedal with her bare foot. She inserts the key into the ignition. She turns it one click. Before she can hit the ignition, a noose is snapped over her head and around her neck. It is jerked painfully tight. Margo attempts to scream but can only gasp. She struggles to reach around her seat with her right hand. She touches a jean leg. The noose is pulled to the right, dragging her by the neck to between the front seats. She is pulled back over the console. She bucks violently, arching her back. Her face brushes back and forth across the roof of the car knocking her Maui Jim sunglasses askew. Her lips smear saliva on the roof's fabric. With her left hand, she futilely claws at the rope around her neck. Then, with both hands, she begins blindly pounding on the horn. The horn responds, sending out her fractured SOS.

Across the lot a woman pulls into a spot. There is a boy in the back seat. He looks to be about five years old.

"What's wrong with that car, Mommy?" the boy says pointing at

Margo's car, the blaring horn shattering the early morning peace.

"Someone probably set off their car alarm by mistake. It'll stop in a minute once they figure it out."

In her car, Margo stops struggling. Her hands fall from the wheel. Her horn goes silent.

"See, I told you it would stop," the woman says, standing at the open rear door of her car. She lifts her son out of his car seat and deposits him on the ground. She closes the rear door and locks the car. She takes her son's hand. "Come on, you help Mommy shop, okay?"

"Okay," he says. "Can I get cookies?"

FIFTY-THREE

SATURDAY, AUGUST 31, 2013

12:14 p.m.

SCHUMACHER RESIDENCE

WESTHAMPTON BEACH, NY

The house is ice-cold. And it stinks. The cold comes from the air conditioning which has been set at fifty degrees. One stink comes from camphor cakes which have been wired to the air duct vents. The other stink is that of a decomposing human body.

"God, it's cold in here," Detective Rooney says. "Can we turn up the thermostat?"

"Not until the crime scene crew is done," says Detective DeMarco. Lab crew officers are busy dusting for prints.

"Come on," DeMarco says and he and Rooney head for the stairs to the cellar, trudging clumsily in protective booties. They both pull on latex gloves as they go. In the cellar, there is blood everywhere. Up the walls. Across the low ceiling. Pooled in the drum of an open clothes dryer. In the middle of it is the star attraction. Margo lies on her side, hands and feet zip tied. The blood beneath her has congealed. Because of it, the detectives can't get too close. Rooney bends forward and peers at Margo's face.

"Her tongue's been cut with pinking shears," she says. "How long do you think she's been dead?"

"Judging from the drying rate of that blood, I'd say a few days. Of course, the cold could have helped that along."

"So before Gladys Ortiz was murdered yesterday?" Rooney says incredulously. "Brandi Napoli's body was placed out on the beach, obviously, to be found as soon as possible. Yesterday, there was no attempt to conceal Gladys Ortiz's body. Why go to the effort to delay discovery here?"

"I don't know."

The detectives go upstairs.

In the kitchen, two paper grocery bags sit on the counter, one wet from thawed frozen food. Rooney looks in that bag. Then she sticks two gloved fingers into it and retrieves the cash register receipt. "Best Market Westhampton Beach, seven thirty-two a.m., eight twenty-eight," she reads. "Three days ago."

"So, she goes to the store early Wednesday morning," DeMarco says. "Then, she is attacked somewhere between there and here."

"Her car's in the garage," Rooney says.

"Carjacked and driven here? Attacked entering or once inside the house? We'll need to come back to canvass the neighborhood to find out if anyone saw or heard anything."

A uniformed officer sticks his head in at the doorway. "The woman from next door who called it in is outside. Do you want to talk to her?"

DeMarco and Rooney come out of the front door of the house. They pull off their gloves and booties and drop them in a container by the door. In the street, a group of neighbors has gathered behind yellow crime scene tape. There is a woman standing at the end of the driveway. She has Margo's Irish Setter on a leash. DeMarco and Rooney approach her.

"Ms. Gravesend?" DeMarco says.

"Is it true? Is Margo—"

"I'm sorry for your loss," DeMarco says. As always in such situations, he chooses to assume a close relationship. "Were you close?"

"We were good neighbors."

"That's Ms. Schumacher's dog, isn't it?"

"That's how I knew something was wrong. I drove out from the city this morning and when I got here, Shamus was curled up in front of my door. The poor thing was half-starved to death."

"I'm surprised another neighbor didn't call in a dog roaming around alone."

"Everyone around here is used to Shamus. Irish Setters are a very skittish breed. He's always getting out."

DeMarco recalls the dog opening a door and bounding from the house when they interviewed Margo after Brandi Napoli's murder.

"But Margo would never neglect him," Ms. Gravesend adds.

"Were you around this past Wednesday?"

"No. I was in the city all week."

"Okay, thanks," DeMarco says.

"If there's anything else, I'm home all day," she says and goes.

"If Max Short murdered Gladys Ortiz yesterday, he did not try to hide the fact that he was driving around the Island in his own car," Rooney says.

"No. As a matter of fact, he seemed to be advertising it."

"But two days earlier, he goes to great lengths to make sure Margo Schumacher's body isn't found for a while. It doesn't fit a pattern."

"Maybe you hit on it. How can a serial killer be a serial killer if he's not a serial killer?"

"Is that what this is?"

"Better fits the definition of a killing spree."

"Do you think there'll be another?"

DeMarco doesn't respond. He looks off into the distance, seemingly lost in thought.

After a moment or two, Rooney breaks into his reverie. "Are you thinking—what? Another Gilgo Beach?"

DeMarco slowly turns in her direction. He throws his hands in the air. "No. My partner did not just say that!"

"I guess my chances of collecting on that Popeye's lunch are looking pretty dim."

"To hell with that," DeMarco says tossing Rooney the car keys. "I'm starving. You drive."

FIFTY-FOUR

"That could use its own diving board." Jeremy is looking at the oversized martini which the waiter has just set in front of Max. Max leans forward and sips down the level of the drink which arrived full to the brim like an infinity pool.

"I'll never know how they do that. Make it from bar to table without spilling a drop," Max says, relishing the icy libation.

"Here comes Gabby," Jeremy says.

Gabby walks up to the table. "Happy birthday, Dad," she says bending over the table and kissing Max on the cheek. "Sorry I'm late. The subways were a mess." She hands Max a wrapped gift whose dimensions scream record album.

"What's this? You weren't supposed to get me anything. Lunch is more than enough."

"It's nothing." Gabby takes a seat on the other side of the table from Jeremy with Max between them on the banquette.

The waiter comes up. "Can I get you a drink?" he says to Gabby.

"Cranberry and club with a lime."

"Are you ready to order?" the waiter says to Max.

"Don't ask me. I'm not paying," Max says with a chuckle.

"Give us a few minutes," Jeremy says.

The waiter goes.

Max rips off the wrapping paper on the gift. "Derek and the Dominos! Cool. Thank you." He reads from the cover, "'Layla and Other Assorted Love Songs.' This is their only studio album."

"Yeah, I know that. Did you know that, Jeremy?"

"Yeah, I think I've heard that before somewhere."

"Okay, go ahead and make fun of your senile old man. Someday you'll be repeating yourselves. Where did you find it?"

"Gabby found it online."

"Thanks, guys. Love my vinyl."

The waiter brings Gabby's drink. She picks it up. "Again, Dad, happy birthday." Max and Jeremy lift their glasses. They all clink.

"How's Mom?" Gabby asks.

"Good. She sends her apologies she couldn't make it. Some all-day meeting."

"Sounds boring," Gabby says. "Are you guys doing anything for your birthday?"

"Dinner tomorrow night. La Panetière."

"Nice," Jeremy and Gabby say in unison.

"How's your rescue dog doing? What's his name?"

"Thor. He's doing…better," Gabby replies. "At first he was pretty fearful of everything. God knows what the monsters who used to own him did to him."

"He's very feisty," Jeremy tells Max. Then, to Gabby, "And very protective of you."

"We'd like to meet him. You should bring him out to the house sometime. And how's school?"

"Good. I'm taking anatomy this semester. It was a breeze until we got to the musculoskeletal system."

"Lots of bones?"

"That's not the half of it. It's the muscles that are making my head explode."

"Just keep reminding yourself, you get through this year and you're done."

"I know. And I've been thinking about what's next."

"What is next?" Jeremy asks.

"I've decided I'm going to go for a veterinary degree."

"Spare us! Our daughter's going to the dogs."

"LOL," Gabby says dourly.

"That's cool," Jeremy says. "Is this to make up for the fact that we weren't allowed to get a dog growing up?"

"Actions have consequences," Gabby says, mock glaring at her father.

Max laughs. "Have you picked a school?"

"Cornell has a good program."

"In Ithaca?"

"Uh-huh. But I haven't made up my mind yet."

"It's got a good reputation," Max says.

"And it's a SUNY like Downstate. I want to continue at a SUNY."

"Tuition is attractive."

"And SUNY students can use any SUNY facility," Gabby adds.

"I didn't know that," Max says.

"Sure. My student ID gets me into any school in the network. I've fallen in love with Stony Brook's medical library."

"You've been out to Stony Brook?"

"A couple of times. This summer."

Max takes a big sip of his martini. "Kind of a ways to go, isn't it?"

"Just under two hours on the train. If I get the first train out of Penn it gives me a few hours to work. Stony Brook is awesome."

"I've never been there," Max says absently. Then, to Jeremy, "How's Sarah?"

"She's great."

"And business?"

"Good. Oh, I want your opinion on something." Jeremy pulls a briefcase up from under the table and sets it on the banquette next to Max. He opens it. "I have a client meeting later. It's with The Food Bank for New York City. They hired us to do the invitations for their gala. I need your honest reaction."

Jeremy carefully lays three sample invitation designs on the table in front of Max. The one on the left and the one on the right Max barely registers. The one in the middle rivets him. A shudder travels up his spine. He blinks a few times rapidly. At the top of the card, in an elaborate scroll, reads: "Your table awaits…" Beneath this is a square of blue-and-white-checked cloth glued to the card. In the center of the cloth is a miniature plastic wine bottle affixed to the card through the cloth. Though not marine in design, the cloth is too familiar. It has haunted his nightmares for the past four months. The cloth has been distinctly edged with pinking shears.

"And if you hate all of them, tell me that, too," Jeremy adds.

There is a lump in Max's throat and he can't speak. He reaches for his drink and takes a sip. He immediately gags on it. He covers his mouth with his free hand so as not to spray the table. Jeremy puts his hand on Max's shoulder.

"Dad, are you alright?"

Max coughs again to clear his throat. "Yes, just a little congestion, that's all." He turns to face Gabby's worried look. "I'm fine." He studies all three sample invitations. "They're all good. I mean, each has its own creative appeal," Max says, striving to sound in control.

Gabby reaches across the table and picks up the center one. "This one is awesome."

"You like that one?" Jeremy says.

"Awesome. Show it last and it'll be first," she gushes. She turns to Max holding the sample out to him. "Dad? Awesome?"

Max stares at the card inches from his face. Its image pulsates. A camera lens being rapidly pulled in and out of focus. Then it settles. Its focus crystal-clear. Max has no choice but to face down his fear. He lets the invitation's tablecloth with its barracuda teeth in. An epiphany is his reward. "Awesome."

"Thanks," Jeremy says.

Max glances down at Jeremy's open briefcase next to him. Coiled up inside is a jump rope. "You jumping rope, now?"

"Oh yeah," Jeremy says. "When I'm out on appointments. If I catch a few minutes in a parking lot or someplace, I fit in a few reps. It's good exercise."

"I bet," Max says. "How long have you been doing it?"

"Picked it up this summer."

Max considers this with a nod of his head. "Excursions to Stony Brook, jumping rope. You two had a busy summer."

Jeremy and Gabby smile at each other across the table. "Taking care of business," Jeremy says, winking at Gabby.

Max smiles at both of his kids. "Shall we order?"

Jeremy raises his hand and signals the waiter.

4:36 p.m.

METRO NORTH TRAIN CAR

Max drops into his seat as the train pulls out of Grand Central Station. He closes his eyes.

My kids are murderers?

Is it possible? He doesn't know how to think about it. All he can do is hope that they were careful. Careful to leave no clues. Careful not to have missed a stray betraying detail. Of course they were careful. They have to have been. He wouldn't be able to deal with the guilt if they were caught. If that were to happen! He'd be furious with them. But he couldn't lash out. That never helps. Lashing out at your children for doing something wrong or stupid only causes self-inflicted pain.

No, they made a good job of it. Better than he could have done. They are smarter and more talented than he is. And it's been, what— over two months since Gladys's murder? The cops haven't come near them. Certainly they would have by now if they had any probable cause. *So stop worrying.*

"Tickets."

The conductor is at the seats behind Max. Max pulls his round-trip ticket from his shirt pocket and holds it out. The conductor comes even with his seat. He takes Max's ticket and punches it before keeping it. "Thank you," he says.

"Thank you," Max replies.

If he had known I'm the father of the "Pinking Shears" murderers, he would have asked me to autograph it.

Ah, yes. Pinking shears. That was a master stroke, kids! Cutting those filthy lying bitches' tongues! Genius. Or, as Margo would say, "it's purrfect!" Max settles into the idea with a slight smile.

Max only wishes he could have been there to see it. The abject terror in their eyes. The struggling. Did they plead for their useless lives? Probably not. Max is positive that their mouths were taped shut. Good. They had to listen for a change. Especially Gladys. Couldn't have that fishwife screaming her fool head off in her office. And then the moment when they find out who their assailants are. Who their father is and why this is happening to them. Why there will be no hope for reprieve. *I'm sure my kids introduced themselves.*

Or, maybe it is better he wasn't there. Maybe it's better—his not having witnessed their murders. If he had, he could have conceivably been moved to have sympathy for them. *Sympathy they don't deserve. Yes, this is cleaner; less ambiguous.*

Were the women's dying images that of Max's face as their lives and all future promise spurted from their ragged necks? Were their dying thoughts, *Shouldn't have been such a bitch*? Not hardly likely. People like that are not sufficiently self-aware, let alone honest with themselves. Still, fun to speculate about.

Then it hits him. Does Patricia know? No, not possible. That's why they revealed it to him today when their mother would not be present. Patricia might not care about the victims but she would care about her children. Too much. This is something Max will be able to handle but not Patricia. She's a better person than him but not as good at compartmentalizing her emotions. It would worry her to death. She can't ever suspect. The kids will know how to play it. It will just be their little secret.

Max had often heard the adage "Take care of your children and they will take care of you." He never in a million years imagined that they would take care of him this way. What had Jeremy said at lunch? *Taking care of business.*

Life is strange.

FIFTY-FIVE

This is always the worst part of Max's day. Patricia has left for work and he is alone. Once the morning is over, things begin to jell. Chores. Things that need to be fixed. In a house, there is always something that needs to be fixed. Moving into the afternoon, he can busy himself thinking about and preparing dinner. If anything needs to be gotten in that regard, it's off to the store. He can settle into the evening in anticipation of Patricia's return. His favorite part of the day. But mornings are tough. The vast empty day stretches out before him daring him to productively fill it up. It's when he feels most useless. Most irrelevant. Most depressed.

It's been four months since the murders. Every day that he has moved away from them has been an improvement. His dreams are no longer populated by Brandi and Margo and Gladys. That happened, to a degree, after the murders and most certainly after his birthday lunch with the kids. Being wise to not only what happened to them but why has been a magic elixir. As long as the bitches of *Festive in the Dunes* lived in his mind, so did his malaise. But knowing they paid the price for their sins has absolved him from their continued torment. He can no longer see their faces clearly. They are like people in a photograph that has sat on a sunny windowsill for too long. And because they had ceased to breath, he can. After not being able to. The parasitic stone that had taken up residence in the center of his chest the day he was fired and which had weighed heavy every day and night thereafter is gone. His kids had dispensed them to hell and he happily slammed the gate behind them. He is free!

A high school teacher who he had greatly admired once said, "Forgive but never forget—people will make a fool of you if you do." He had always believed this to be profound wisdom. No longer. Moving on has nothing to do with forgiveness and everything to do with forgetting. Until you can forget your tormentors, they will not leave you alone. They live inside of you. In your brain. They lurk in the synapse of your every fiber. You must forget them in order to vanquish them and the surest way to forget them is if there's no chance you'll ever bump into them again.

Some people have cancer. Some people are cancer. Malignant, insidious, aggressive. Margo, Gladys, Brandi. Max has had three tumors successfully removed from his life. His kids did that. It is now up to him to keep on top of the self-administered chemotherapy of diligently forgetting. He must prevent the poison of that place, those people from bleeding back into his mind, into his soul. *So the joke's on the National Cancer Foundation. I'm a cancer survivor, too!*

Nevertheless, Max faces the reality of being prematurely and forcibly retired. He's not just unemployed. It's too late for that.

Max sits down with a cup of coffee and the newspaper. A few pages in, he spots a brief item near the bottom. "Pinking Shears Widow Out." It reads:

> Gladys Ortiz, one of the victims of this past summer's "Pinking Shears" killing spree mysteriously changed the beneficiary on her retirement plan with the National Cancer Foundation where she had worked for many years. When her spouse, Ingrid Casales, attempted to collect the benefits, she was informed that she was no longer the beneficiary and had been replaced by the North Shore Animal League. The change had been made by Ms. Ortiz the day she was murdered and one week following her marriage to Ms. Casales. The probate court has decided in favor of the charity, citing that a designated beneficiary prevails in the case of a disputed estate even superseding the provisions of a will.

Max sets the paper down. It starts as a chuckle. It quickly grows to a full-throated laugh. "...The North Shore Animal League..." Max manages to spit out. He convulses into a roar. Max can't remember the last time he laughed so hard. He can't remember the last time he had reason to.

God knows how she did it but this is one hundred percent Gabby! The final fuck you! Gabby and her animals rule!

Once he stops laughing, he feels much better. The day no longer holds the dread it had a few minutes ago. He is one lucky guy. He's healthy. He has a loving family. Patricia has a good job—at least for now. He just needs to stop thinking about the things he *ought* to do and start thinking about the things he *wants* to do.

Maybe he'll paint the garage. Maybe he'll clean out the cellar.

Maybe he'll start that novel which he has always promised himself he'd get around to when he had the time. He has the time.

No, wait. He should call the kids and see what they're up to.

About the Author

Novelist and playwright, TEDD SMITH, pens his second novel with *Fatal in the Dunes: Fundraising in the Hamptons Can Be Murder*. His nearly thirty years' experience as a development professional informs the story's charity event setting. A keen eyewitness to the unfolding scene, dozens of his letters and observations have appeared in the pages of the *New York Times*, the *New York Post* and the *New York Daily News*.

Author's Note

I hope you enjoyed reading *Fatal in the Dunes: Fundraising in the Hamptons Can Be Murder*. If so, please tell your friends about it. In addition, I would be very grateful if you would write a review. I'd love to hear what you think and it makes such a difference in helping other readers to discover it. Your email address will never be shared and you can unsubscribe from my mailing list at any time. Just drop me a line I can use!

Thank you.
Tedd Smith

TEDD.SMITH.DUNES@GMAIL.COM
TEDD-SMITH.COM